Other books by the author:

Zen, Mississippi (novel)
The Salvation of Billy Wayne Carter (novel)

THE FIREBALL BROTHERS

A NOVEL

M. DAVID HORNBUCKLE

Livingston Press

The University of West Alabama

Copyright © 2019 M. David Hornbuckle
All rights reserved, including electronic text
ISBN 13: 978-1-60489-227-7 trade paper
ISBN 13: 978-1-60489-228-4 hardcover
Library of Congress Control Number: 2019930787
ISBN: 1-60489-227-7 trade paper
ISBN: 1-60489-228-5 hardcover
Printed on acid-free paper
Printed in the United States of America by
Publishers Graphics
Hardcover binding by: HF Group
Typesetting and page layout: Sarah Coffey
Proofreading: Brent Stauffer, Jennifer Wolford,
Erin Watt, Ethan Glass, Jayla Gellington,
joe Taylor
Cover art: Pixabay.com
Cover design: Weldon Fultz and Sarah Hansen
Meteor glyph: Erin Watt
Livingstson Press books may be ordered
at normal online outlets, plus
https://livingstonpress.uwa.edu

first edition

6 5 4 3 2 1

ACKNOWLEDGMENTS

Thanks to Jim, Kerry, Danny, Callie, Burgin, and Susan for their feedback on early drafts of this novel. Thanks to Jennifer and Brent for help with proofreading. Thanks to Charlie for his anecdotes and vital information about farming. I'd also like to thank Jennifer and my parents for their indulgent understanding of my writing habit.

I'm much indebted to 1959: *The Year Everything Changed* by Fred Kaplan (Wiley & Sons, 2009) for cultural perspectives on the year in which this story takes place.

I have also relied on weather and farming reports in the *Columbus Commercial Dispatch* from the summer of 1959, courtesy of the microfiche collection at Mississippi University for Women.

Some of the content of Eddie Van Chukker's UFO experience in Korea was based on the information reported on the website of the National Investigations Committee on Aerial Phenomena, attributed to John Timmerman.

Information in the text about the Sylacauga meteorite that struck Ann Elizabeth Hodges in 1954 is based on interviews with Billy Field from Tuscaloosa, AL, an eye witness of the historical event, who has spent many years researching and writing about it.

Lyrics attributed to Sun Ra in Chapter 11 are paraphrased from *Space Is the Place: The Lives and Times of Sun Ra* by John F. Szwed (De Capo Press 1998). The words are actually from an interview where Sun Ra discussed an experience of a "trip to Saturn" that occurred around 1936. He often spoke extemporaneously along similar lines during performances while on Earth.

"Space is the place" —Sun Ra

THE FIREBALL BROTHERS

ONE

He saw her reaching for the switch, hoped she wouldn't turn on the light while he had his shirt off, but it was too late. She had seen it. To her credit, she pretended not to at first, but the curious bend of a brow, however brief, gave her away. It wasn't that he thought people in their sixties shouldn't see each other naked. It was just that until that point, he had been so pinkly elated about how the date was going—how the entire relationship was going—the scar had barely entered his mind.

At their initial meeting, they'd had coffee at a shop that sold powders and tinctures he thought only existed in the witches' chant from *Macbeth*, and she'd read Tarot cards for him. These last two weeks, they'd had dinner together three times, and now here they were, feeling half or maybe even a quarter their own age, taking their clothes off in Esther Ruth's enormous house in the venerable neighborhood called Redmont Park, where she told him, "the Birmingham steel barons built their mansions on the ridge to look down on their refineries and the rough-shamble towns of their workers."

She really talked that way, and she seemed to know a lot about Birmingham. The way she told it, Esther Ruth's family history seemed to be the city's history. Back at the coffee shop, she'd said her grandfather "owned saloons back in the early wild days, back when they called it *Dirty Birmingham* and *murder capital of the world*." Her father had continued the family business on the sly through three decades of Prohibition. She asked Robert if he knew why they called Birmingham "the Magic City." He did not.

"Well, technically," she said, shuffling her tarot deck like a seasoned blackjack dealer, "it has to do with how quickly the city grew once they ran the railroads through here after the Civil War, but that's the boring version. I take it quite literally. There's magic in these little mountains, in this red clay, in the blood and sweat of the people who built it and damn near destroyed it, in the long-fought battles over human dignity and civil rights, and in the music. Especially in the music." They quickly discovered they shared

1

a love of music, of jazz in particular, and especially that frenetically paced, often cacophonous jazz from the decades of their youth—Bird, Miles, Coltrane, and Sun Ra, the prophetic space jazz progenitor who had his roots here in Birmingham, though he claimed to be from Saturn. In addition to jazz, Esther Ruth adored opera, while Robert's passion was folk, bluegrass, old time, and classic country.

Over dinner earlier that night, Robert told her that though he had done a good bit of traveling when he was younger, he'd done little in his life other than farm work. His family had gone through some lean times where they relied on catching squirrels or rabbits so they'd have something to eat. He and his brother had learned to get a squirrel out of a hollow tree by getting a long sapling and pushing it up into the hollow. They'd swirl that sapling around and when they pulled it out, if it had hair on the end, they'd know something was in there. Then they just kept doing that until the squirrel appeared.

"We always had dogs, for hunting. Pop loved the dogs. We'd starve before the dogs would. Of course," he added, back-pedaling a little, "we always had the land, so we were never as poor as some folks." In the '70s, he'd migrated their main crops over from corn and cotton to soybeans. That had been a lot more profitable for them. He had married but never had kids. Edwina passed away ten years ago. Now, with her gone and his parents gone, and no kids of his own, he had nobody to leave the farm to, so he sold it and downsized into a small apartment in town, just down the mountain from her on Highland Avenue. So far he hadn't met many people.

"You'll fit right in before you know it," she said.

She'd been a painter and a poet; she'd never married and had always been independent. He thought she was a treasure of contradictions and eccentric charms. She never learned to drive, had grown up with chauffeurs, but now she rode the bus by choice. She was a vegetarian, and yet she'd worn a fox stole when they went to dinner earlier that night at a white table cloth restaurant downtown. Now, in the dark of her bedroom, she smelled like butterscotch, and it made him hungry for her.

During dessert, she had asked him if he ever experienced anything unusual, and he asked her what she meant. "I've always been sensitive to things," she said. "Spirits and such. I talk to ghosts frequently. One in particular. Her name is Kate. She gives

2

me advice. And you know what?"

"What's that?"

"She likes you. She says you're very charming. And she likes that you let me talk a lot. And she likes the way you say your name when you call, like: 'this is Robert Mackintosh,' sort of formal but still friendly."

Robert liked hearing all this. It was true that he never had been much of a talker. He reached across the table and took her hand. The hand-holding had led to a kiss on the way out the door. And then she'd said, "I'm not tired at all, pumpkin. Why don't you come over to my house for a drink?"

He supposed that was how things worked. It had been a long time since he'd been in that situation. He supposed he'd never really been in that situation. But he agreed. Her house was indeed a mansion on the hill, a stone castle with a panoramic view of the city. It had been in her family for generations.

After the scar was exposed, however briefly, Robert covered his eyes, pretending the mild lamplight was too bright. Then he switched it off again and lay beside her on the bed, wanting to touch her, not touching her yet, staring at the blackness above. He was about to turn seventy, and he hadn't been with a woman since Edwina passed. He and Edwina had never been as close as a husband and wife should be. He knew that if he was going to make any inroads with Esther Ruth, he was going to have to tell her what was on his mind and without her asking.

"You asked me earlier if I'd ever experienced anything *unusual*. Well..." he said, "I mentioned earlier that I had a brother."

TWO

On a pale Tuesday afternoon in early June of 1959, fifteen-year-old Robert Mackintosh had just jackknifed off a high rock into the green pond about a mile from his family's farmhouse. This was in rural Alabama, close enough to the Mississippi line that you could walk there. For much of the country, it had been a summer of reds and a summer of blues and a summer of blacks. The communist threat hung in the air like acrid rain. A young man born in Tupelo had shaken his hips and reduced every female Robert knew to shrieks and quivers. In Montgomery and in Birmingham, Negroes were gathering in churches and making plans under a backdrop of jubilant gospel music. It was as if they were living in the stitch between two fabrics of time.

But in this little bucolic edge of Alabama, it had been a summer mainly of rain and bugs and pulling the weeds that threatened the cotton. That's what Robert and his brother Wally, two years his junior, had been doing all the hot morning before going to cool off in the lake down the road and leaping off the rock into the water. Naked as Adonis and glowing in the sizzling sun, Robert dolphined up, arched his chest and shoulders, farmboy white to where his shirt sleeves stopped when rolled up. The pink and purple pompoms of the hydrangeas shook in the breeze to cheer him. Wally, also jaybird naked, cannonballed in behind him, emerged, and paddled toward him, spitting and coughing. Tiny fish, none worth catching, skittered away from the splash.

"I can smell something, Bubba. Like sulfur," Wally said. Robert smelled it too, like the devil was about to materialize before them. At the same time, there was a scent of blood in the water, like the fish had all been turned inside out.

A whistling approached from above, but Robert saw nothing but glare. He felt Wally's left hand, soft and cold, ease up under his arm and land on his chest, and he felt the younger brother's left shoulder pressed against his back. Wally's grip was tighter than Robert would have expected.

4

That's when the fireball fell out of the sky, churning and burning its path from above the tree line. Its crimson tail licked the wispy clouds. Whether it was a meteor or a satellite or the smoldering remains of a failed alien visitor, the images in the flames did not tell. Both boys screamed when they saw the streaming projectile splash down at the opposite end of the pond, maybe fifty yards away. The brown-green pond water heated up faster than when a kettle is poured into the bath. Robert started swimming, despite a growing dull pain in his chest and a weight on his back.

"Swim, Wally!" He couldn't stop to find out why Wally was still just holding on to him. Between strokes, he thought he heard Wally say he was stuck, but he didn't know what the boy could be stuck to since they were somehow still moving. When they finally climbed out over the reeds and crabgrass at the nearest edge, Robert glanced down and saw what Wally meant. A thin jelly-ish white seam had formed around his brother's hand. Wally's left hand, forearm, and shoulder were stuck to Robert in an embrace from behind, just as they were positioned when Wally swam up on him in the water. As much as they tugged at it, they could make no progress. Robert was stuck in his brother's grip, and there seemed to be nothing they could do about it.

They lay there in a pile on the edge of the pond for some time, bare to the sun and exhausted from struggling. It seemed that even the mosquitos sensed something wrong and were leaving the boys alone. It smelled like Wally might have peed. A couple of lizards scurried away into the scruffy nandina and young oak that lined the perimeter, dotted with bright orange day-lilies that had just come into bloom that week. Robert had to tell Wally to quit trying to pull away. Every time Wally tugged, it felt like he was going to yank the skin right off of Robert's chest. They needed to rest and think.

Wally's full name was Walter Scott Mackintosh, after the Scottish author—Mama was obsessed with all things Scottish—and as far as most people were concerned, Wally was unlikely to live up to any of his names. He was gangly and buck-toothed and had fiery red hair like Mama's that sprouted into shocking curls. Robert (whose middle name was Burns, also after the writer), was a hard worker and reasonably smart, though not so brainy that he stood out. He'd always figured on taking over the farm from Pop, so he wasn't too concerned about having a brilliant mind for school subjects. Recently, he overheard Edwina Hunter tell another girl he was the handsomest boy in Pickens County; she compared him to Paul Newman, whose visage adorned the poster for that *Cat on a Hot Tin Roof* movie they showed at the Princess Theater in Columbus all last spring.

He wondered if anyone else saw the fireball, if his parents had seen it, or the few neighbors. It might have been seen as far away as Columbus or even Tuscaloosa. He pictured his father—Dewey Mackintosh, Pop—wiry and goat-bearded, tinkering with the antique musical instruments he collected and sometimes repaired for extra money, nipping at a bottle of moonshine he'd procured from Eddie Van Chukker—sometimes to the point that he would pass out in the barn and not be seen until morning. Chances were he was oblivious to this invasion from the sky. Their nervous, bookish mother, Lucretia, was probably reading. After she dropped out of college to marry Pop, she never did give up her impractical interest in literature. Mama took Benzedrine for her asthma, which kept her up at night, nights she'd often spend with her nose in a book. Surely, even if the fireball itself hadn't warranted a search party, someone would come looking for the boys if they weren't home for dinner. His mind quickly jumped into the deeper dread of what they would do when and if they *did* get home. This year, he was going to move up to first string on the football team. That was right out. Just yesterday, he'd cleared a respectable section of brush that had been encroaching on the turnrows and set out the wood to dry for the winter. The only thing Wally was particularly good at was playing the fiddle, and he couldn't do that with one arm. How would they do anything at all?

As if he could hear these questions in Robert's head, Wally began crying, a screaming panicked cry like the bellow of a wild animal with a paw caught in a trap. Robert didn't know what he could say or do to calm his brother, so he just let Wally go on and on. Honestly, he felt like screaming too, but he didn't see much point in the both of them blubbering. The sun had already dried a thick layer of pond muck on their skinny legs. They lay there in that absurd clinch, the ricochet of both their hearts creating an audible buzz to match the mosquitos.

Robert said after a couple of minutes, "A'ight, we got to try and move. I'm gonna stand up. Move with me and not against me." But it took another several, more than a few, minutes before Wally was ready to cooperate. As much as Robert pushed, Wally was just a dead weight trapping him on the ground. Standing required coordinating. "On the count of three," Robert said, "get up on one knee. Come on now." He counted off, but he found he was trying to lead with his left knee, and Wally was using his right, causing the both of them to tumble straight back down again.

"Bubba?"

"What's that, Wally?"

"This is really bad."

His younger brother's propensity for stating the obvious was not making this predicament any easier to take.

"Pretty fucking bad, I'd say."

This set Wally blubbering again, and Robert again waited it out, putting his own panic out of his mind by closing his eyes and staring into some internal blank space where he could still see that fireball screaming across the sky, coming right at them as if they had targets painted on their backs. Opening his eyes again, all Robert could focus on was Wally's left hand, gripping his chest, and that milky seam that looked tender like new baby skin but felt as rigid as leather. The weight of it was like a yoke around his neck.

He noticed then that Wally's noise had died down, and they started over. It took Robert pushing with both arms and Wally simultaneously pushing up with his one good arm, to get up on their knees. From there, Robert had to swing one leg out and provide the leverage for the both of them to stand completely. Robert was relieved at least that Wally's legs could reach the ground on their own. He'd had an image in his head of having to drag Wally all the way home on his back. He was strong, but not *that* strong, and he was already worn down as a piece of gum on the bottom of a shoe.

After an extended side venture to collect the pile of clothes, which they didn't even attempt to put on, they began to inch their way toward home. Walking was impossibly awkward at first. Within a few steps, they developed a crude technique and a rhythm, a sort of lumbering waltz. They counted to three together, and Robert led off with a step. Then Wally followed in a side step shuffle. Their muddy feet were toughened from going barefoot often, but the newly discomfited way their weight now shifted when they moved seemed to make the gravel from the road dig in deeper and harder. They could keep it up for about ten or fifteen yards at a time before they had to stop, rest, start over. It made Robert think about football—ten yards, first down, time out. Robert imagined they looked like a hunchbacked octopus coming up the road.

Rows of pine and sycamore and dogwood loomed above on either side of them, the woods and pond all owned by old Jimbo Bobo. Beyond that was Eddie's peach orchard, and past that were the fields where the Mackintoshes grew corn and cotton mostly, but also beets, sweet potatoes, and tomatoes. Many times, Robert had worked beside Pop and other men in the field. Robert had been out there when one older man would start to sing "Hey… Oh…" and then another on the other side of the field would answer back in a deep baritone voice, "Hey…Hey…Oh…" It would go back and forth like that for a while, and it would gather speed, and then others would join in, layers of voices harmonizing. The singing filled Robert with the sensation that he and his fellow workers were all as much products of the earth as the cotton they were harvesting. The work songs filled the sky and connected the sky to the earth. On those hot days, the music was the glue that held the universe together.

There would be no singing in the fields this year. Several weeks of heavy rain during April and May meant there would be a spotty cotton crop for their family and many others in the area. And much of what they'd managed to save had suffered from high insect infestations during the hot, wet summer because they'd been too late in spraying for boll weevils. The cotton now was low and shrinking. The corn was not faring much better and withered like a defeated army on a bronze battlefield.

Beyond the shy purple of the cotton fields and wasting corn, there was the fenced yard and small barn where their mother kept chickens and sometimes a couple of hogs or cattle. They'd butchered their only cow to get through the winter before, and the few lean chickens had supplied them with scant eggs through the first part of summer. No animals were kept on their property now other than the dogs, who stayed in a pen just outside the house, and the occasional feral cat.

They lived in a pinewood house their grandfather had built after the first war, which had gone to seed during the depression, but their father had been fixing it up gradually, and he had already replaced the rotten floorboards and the windows before marrying Mama. Then in '42 he had gone off to the Philippines where he served as an army mechanic, not then knowing that Mama was pregnant with Robert. Over the next couple of years, using army money he had saved up, Pop added insulation to the walls, plumbing, and electricity. During that time, Wally was born, and that same week Pop found an old fiddle that had belonged to his own grandfather—Robert's great grandfather.

When Pop found his grandfather's fiddle, back before the boys were born, it had been in rough condition. He thought he would fix it up and sell it, but he didn't know where to begin. At an auction, he bought a couple of other fiddles. He studied how they were put together and used the hopeless ones for spare parts. Over the years, he became so proud of his work, he couldn't bring himself to sell the items. Instead, he bought other instruments and learned how to repair those too. Eventually, a little side business arose, doing repairs for some people in the area, but it was never more than a hobby, and he continued collecting.

Pop had also enrolled the boys in music lessons, hoping to put some of these items to better use. Their teacher was a lady named Rhenetta Tate who had lived in Nashville for many years, played onstage at the Opry, and then had retired to the small town where she'd grown up, a few miles north of the Mackintosh farm. She'd arrived wearing a white cowboy suit full on with studs and spangles, a lean six feet tall, with long white hair that spilled out the back of her Stetson like an icy waterfall. She came by every Wednesday night, dressed exactly like that. Wally had a good ear, it turned out. Robert lacked the proficiency and the interest that Wally had, but he continued on for a year or so. When they didn't have as good a crop the following harvest, Robert stopped his lessons. Wally did odd jobs in his spare time for some of the neighbors so he could afford to continue on. Rhenetta kept coming every week, even when Wally couldn't pay, up until she died a couple of years ago.

It had now been thirty minutes of trudging gradually down the road, and they were only halfway home. A peach ice cream of a sunset spread across the horizon, and the grinning countenance of a rust-red '49 Ford pickup truck approached, grumbling loud across the gravel. Their father had gone out looking for them, finally. His silver beard twinkled in the headlights when he came to check on them, as did the handle of the Colt Python strapped to his hip. He must have thought they'd been attacked.

"Where's your damn clothes? What the hell you boys gotten into now?"

"Pop..." Robert interjected. Pop must have noticed something was off kilter but hadn't quite processed it yet. The look on his face softened, and his voice lowered to almost a mumble. The warm scent of shine wafted by as he exhaled deeply, seeming to release all the air his lungs could hold in one heave.

"You hurt? What the blue hell happened to you?"

Robert felt ashamed at his nakedness and of the attending absurdity. He showed the pile of clothes and tried to explain, though his voice would not rise above a hoarse whisper, and the events in his mind were so jumbled, he could barely organize them into words.

"Swimming...Not hurt...Stuck...Can't get him off me."

Wally squalled again.

Being a man who respected action more than words, Pop didn't ask any more questions, just helped them into the truck bed and carried them the rest of the way. Robert felt every gully and trench in that weather-beaten path as a sharp pain through his lower back and chest. Wally cried out the entire trip. Both boys struggled and moaned the whole way home.

The dogs yipped at them when the truck growled up the dirt driveway. Pop rattled the fence to shut them up before opening the hatch on the truck bed and helping the boys down. The house's doors and windows were open to counter the heat from the wood-burning stove, where cornbread was cooking in a cast iron skillet. Butter beans bubbled from another pan. The boys stood naked, with patches of dirt, coal dust, and wood shavings from the truck bed spotting their bare flesh. When they stumbled into the house, for now unable to recreate the system of walking they had worked out on the dirt road, Mama became apoplectic.

"Stars, what is all that racket? Where have y'all been, and what in the world have y'all gotten into?"

Her auburn hair was up in curlers already, and she was wearing her housecoat, a homemade yellow thing with blue butterflies on it that engulfed her pale body like a fever. Wally started bawling again. Robert was already getting tired of this. Mama finally saw that they were stuck, and if she'd had any color in her skin to lose, she'd have blanched. In tears that matched Wally's, she rushed to them. She smothered the both of them with kisses and coaxed them out of the blazing hot kitchen into the living room, where she covered their nakedness with a blanket.

"Tell me everything," she said.

Before Robert could open his mouth, Wally started in saying, "We was swimming down at the pond..."

"Were. You *were* swimming," Mama corrected out of habit. "I'm sorry. Go on."

"We were swimming..." Wally explained everything just like it happened. *Sulfur in the air...blood in the water...a white light...*

By the end of it, Wally's voice had lifted itself out of the hopelessness of before and bounced along as if this had all been some lark they'd ventured on to fill the emptiness of a summer afternoon. He could change gears so easily. Robert just half-listened, stared at the bits of gravel and mud on his bare feet. Since neither Robert nor Wally understood much of what had occurred, it didn't take long to tell her what they knew.

In turn, their mother told them that Martha Jean Van Chukker had seen a flash in the sky, thought it was lightning. Martha Jean's husband Eddie then came home talking about a UFO or some such. Before long, every phone in the county was ringing with gossip, and Mama had started to wonder where her boys were, had a very uneasy feeling, and sent Pop out to fetch them.

Now, Pop was already on the phone with the family physician, Dr. Stanhope. Stanhope lived across the state line in Columbus, Mississippi—about a half hour's drive away—and he wasn't going to be able to come out until the next morning. The common joke about his name was that you *hope* he can *stan'* up straight when you go see him. Stanhope was willing to make the drive for house calls, though, and he'd take a home cooked meal from Mama, or sometimes a bag of cornmeal, as payment. When they couldn't manage that, sometimes Mama or Pop went to his house in Columbus to do small chores for him. Mama would clean house, or Pop would fix something that was broken.

To get into the bed that night, Robert had to partly bend Wally over his back, like a wrestler flipping his opponent onto the mat, and then he'd plant his hands and use the momentum of the not-quite-dead springs to vault himself into the middle of the mattress. From there, he could roll back until Wally settled into position. Mama pulled the sheets up over them. They'd slept in the same bed their whole lives, though they usually rolled into the opposite edges immediately, unless it was the dead of winter. Spooned by Wally, Robert was not exactly comforted. Since he was the older one, the tougher one, he felt like he should be the one on the outside, the protective outer shell. He soon drifted into semi-consciousness, but the smell of sulfur and the feeling of being trapped underneath Wally made his sleep uneasy through the night. When he dreamed, briefly, between bouts of waking panic, it was of suffocating pythons and tree roots entangling him in their gnarly snares and pulling him down into the center of the earth.

THREE

Munford Coldwater packed his pipe with Yorkshire tobacco and leaned back to light it with a green-tipped match. A note on his desk from Gil instructed him to drive down to a rural area outside Columbus, about 70 miles south, and check out a lead. Something had fallen out of the sky. They didn't know what it was, or they weren't saying. Looking at the map, it appeared the location was only a few miles from his relatives' place in Aliceville, Alabama. Two framed photographs sat on his desk: one of his cat Captain Fancypants and one of himself at a much younger age, maybe twelve, with those same Aliceville relatives—his grandmother Audra May, his aunt Edna, and his great uncle Zeke. The photograph had been taken during a vacation to Gulf Shores, and young Munford Coldwater was holding a bonefish that was nearly as long as he was, with some assistance from Zeke whose Coke-bottle glasses lent him an air of shock or surprise, which had become more exaggerated in recent years. They had all aged—evolved seemed like a more appropriate word—since that day on the coast. Munford could see his features now molding themselves into Zeke's, minus the spectacles—especially the wide jawline that crept up toward the eyes and squared off his face. Edna had not adjusted well to being an old maid in her dotage. She had put on so much weight that she looked like a giant bullfrog, and she drank like one too, however it is that a bullfrog drinks. Audra May was now wheelchaired and emaciated, but in the picture she was on her feet and fit. It had been Audra May that had helped him pull in that monster fish, which they never did eat. He didn't remember what happened to the fish.

Coldwater wadded the note and wandered circuitously on an Odysseyan journey toward the editor's desk, puffing thoughtfully at the pipe as he crossed the room.

"Gil," he said. "Why don't we just let the Columbus paper handle this? You want me to drive an hour and a half for something that might not even pan out to be a story?"

"It's already a story." Without looking up, Gil scratched at a patch on his scalp that lay fallow among weedy gray. "Those ignoramuses...or is it ignorami, ignoratti...those dumbasses in Columbus wouldn't know a story if it walked up and shot the governor. There's already a team there from the Air Force. At least try to find out what they're looking for in that pond."

"How about ignorazzi?"

"Like it. Do you have to smoke that thing in here? I go home every day smelling like a Christmas ham."

"What's wrong with Christmas ham? Where's your love for baby Jesus? Anyway, it's too hot to smoke outside. But I'll take your suggestion under consideration."

Something fell out of the sky. Could have been a meteorite. Or a satellite. A Russian satellite—that'd be a story. He drove his Eldorado south on Highway 45 with the window down, letting the wind ripple at his shirt sleeves. He'd driven this road so many times, he could do it with his eyes shut. The trip was pretty uneventful, but he did like long drives sometimes. It gave him time to think over stories he was working on or whatever else happened to occupy his mind. He'd been at the *Tupelo Daily Journal* now for a couple of years—it would be three years in fact come September.

Since so much of his work involved traveling, it had been important to have a reliable car, and driving the Eldorado made him feel good, like he was going places in more ways than one. In truth, he could probably successfully lobby for a job at a larger city paper in Jackson or Birmingham, maybe even Atlanta. But Tupelo gave him a lot of flexibility; they didn't much care what he wrote about, as long as it filled up space between the advertisements. It also gave him a degree of anonymity, since the reach of the *Tupelo Daily Journal* didn't stretch that far. In addition to newspaper work, he also had some private clients that paid him to investigate small, sensitive matters. Though he had not done very much of that work lately, it had helped him save up money for the car. Sometimes those clients found him, or he found them, in the course of doing reporting work, and he could get paid twice for the same job. It wasn't strictly ethical, but nobody had complained about it.

Before following up on this alleged lead, he would pay a visit to his relatives in Aliceville. They'd raised him after his mother and father died, back during the Depression. They lived in a big old house on what had been a plantation at one time. When he pulled up to the house, all three were on the porch, Zeke and Edna hunched on either side of Audra May's wheelchair both looking through binoculars, which they put down when they saw his car coming down the road. Audra May had the enormous *Encyclopedia of Southeastern Ornithology* spanned over the arms of her wheelchair. Munford recognized it immediately, for she was rarely without it.

"You scared them off," Edna said flatly, feigning annoyance, when he emerged from his vehicle. Despite her cigarette-harshened voice and red face, Munford knew she was just messing with him.

"Who?"

"A whole family of black-bellied whistling ducks," she said.

Audra May banged her fist on the book. "I tell you, they were *white-faced* whistling ducks."

"Either way," Zeke piped in. "They shouldn't be here in the summertime. They shouldn't ever be this far north, especially in the summer."

"White face or black belly, y'all are a bunch of whistling ducks yourselves. You got any tea for a hard-working newspaper man?"

The old people all laughed and ushered him inside. He sat on the sofa while Edna got him some tea. The house always smelled like cigarette smoke and lavender. Audra May pulled her wheel chair up to beside him. "What brings you out this way?"

"Well, I was going to go out and look into whatever it was that fell out of the sky earlier this afternoon. Hear anything about it?"

Zeke said, "We were outside looking at some hummingbirds. Saw the whole thing through the binoculars."

"That right?"

Zeke was getting old. Munford looked for the similarities he'd noticed in the photograph that morning, knowing he was looking into his own future of sunken eyes and hunched shoulders, that old man paunch. Edna set his glass atop a coaster on the side table next to the sofa.

"Sure he did," she said in her usual non-committal tone. Munford wasn't sure if she meant to cast doubt on it or if she was simply agreeing. When Munford lifted the glass to take a sip, he was startled for a moment by the image of a train on the coaster. Above the train, it said, "Visit Gatlinburg," and the train was already marred by a series of water rings, as if it were passing through a series of ghostly hoops along the mountain ridge. His parents had died in a train wreck when he was a baby. As he stared at the image on the coaster, the bloody arms and legs of his parents and their fellow travelers began to appear in place of the rings. He quickly put the glass back down, letting the syrupy sweetness of the tea linger on his tongue as a distraction while he wiped his eyes.

"When did y'all go to Gatlinburg?"

"End of last summer," Audra May said. "I forget why you didn't go. But Zeke, tell him what you saw through the binoculars."

"In Gatlinburg?"

"No, you silly goat. The fireball. Tell him what you saw this afternoon when the fireball came down."

Edna said, "I'ma call Charlie and report those whistling ducks," and she disappeared into the back of the house.

Audra May called after her. "Make sure you tell him they were *white-faced* whistling ducks!"

Munford tried to get them back on track. "What about the fireball?"

"Yep, I saw that fireball," Zeke said.

"He saw a face in it," Audra May finally said.

"A face?"

"Yessir. A face. Eyes, nose, and a mouth. Looked a bit like Myrna Loy."

"Myrna Loy," Munford said. "The movie star."

"That's right. Looked just like she did in *The Thin Man*."

Munford prodded, but Zeke had nothing else useful to add to the tale. When Munford left, it was still early in the afternoon, and the wind was still. Since he wasn't able to get much more information out of them about the fireball, he wanted to talk to the Mackintosh boys before dinner time. The distinct waa-hooo of the black-bellied whistling tree duck cooed through the air. Must be lost, Munford thought. Those ducks aren't supposed to be this far north in the summer.

FOUR

Robert woke, not with the sulfuric odor of the fireball haunting him, but a sour stench that was nearly as bad. Moreover, his backside felt wet. "What the hell, Wally?"

"I'm sorry, Bubba. I couldn't wake you up."

This was all so humiliating, Robert thought, like being an infant again all of a sudden. They didn't even know how to bathe properly anymore. Mama had to come and help get them cleaned up and put clothes on them. Luckily, it was hot enough they could go shirtless, since no regular shirt would fit them in their current condition.

Around noon, Dr. Stanhope stumbled in already smelling of gin and garlic. The dogs always seemed to rattle him even though they were safely fenced in to the side of the house. A quick sip of something from his breast pocket settled him. As he examined the boys, Robert observed his brother straining his neck away from the doctor's squirrel breath. Stanhope told him to stop fidgeting. Mama went out to the barn to retrieve Pop.

Once everybody was in the room together, Stanhope addressed the family. "Mr. and Mrs. Mackintosh. Robert. Walter," he said, as if he were making a formal speech at an awards ceremony, "This is quite serious. This situation is far beyond my expertise. I suggest you take these boys to the university hospital up in Birmingham." And then he sat down at the dining table and said, "So, what's for lunch?"

"Now wait just a minute, you pussy-lipped snapping turtle," Pop said. "You can't just look at this for two seconds and ask what's for lunch. What the hell are we supposed to do with these boys?"

It was more words than Robert had heard Pop say in one stretch for as long as he could remember. The doctor took another quick swig from his flask.

Mama said, "You keep that in your shirt... The children." Robert rolled his eyes.

"Pardon me, Lucretia." Stanhope suppressed a belch with a

fist on his chest. "Folks, I am not just being politely self-deprecating when I say I am a *country doctor*…"

Pop said, "We don't need none of your candy-ass fancy language, Stanhope. Just say what you mean."

"I was getting to that, Dewey, if you'd just bear with me. Now, I was saying…I can help if you are pregnant or broke-legged. I can even help if your cow is pregnant or broke-legged. But this . . . I have never seen anything remotely like this in any textbook. No textbook in the *world* could have prepared me for this." His arms stretched out to demonstrate the bigness of the world, and he stood there, posed, for several seconds before anyone else spoke. The Mackintoshes were surrounding him, the boys facing him directly and the parents on each side.

Pop said, "We need these boys to hold up their end of the work around here."

"I know it, Dewey. I grew up on a family farm myself, down in the Delta. You know we had it hard, harder than you even some years." Robert looked at Stanhope's hands, as pale and fluffy as bolls of cotton. Stanhope continued. "Like I said, y'all should go up to the medical college in Birmingham. They have all the newest equipment there, and they'd be interested in this just from the standpoint of research."

"Birmingham?" Wally said. It was a good three- or maybe four-hour drive, depending on weather and traffic. Neither Robert nor Wally had never been that far from home before.

The doctor shrugged. Robert sat quietly fuming, wanting to jump up and wring the doctor's neck, or maybe just grab the flask out of his pocket and have a good swallow of whatever anesthetic was in it. Instead, Wally's weight anchored him firmly in his place. Pop slinked closer to Stanhope so their faces were inches away. Robert thought Pop might actually hit him. "Don't bullshit me. What can they do that you can't do?" Pop asked.

"I…I really couldn't say, Dewey. Lucretia, how's the asthma?"

"I could use another prescription as long as you're here," she said.

Mama conceded to make a sandwich for the doctor since he'd driven all the way out there and she was making some for the boys anyway. Robert and Wally, meanwhile, struggled with how to sit and stand. They learned that by placing two stools catty-cornered to each other, they could both sit in relative comfort, though facing perpendicular directions. One of them could sit at the dinner table, but the other would have to hold the plate in his lap. Robert volunteered for that position since he didn't much feel like looking at anybody else at the moment.

Wally said, "How are we going to go to the toilet?" It was true that they'd already managed to urinate simply by taking turns, but they'd yet to face that other challenge.

Mama said, "We'll discuss that with your father when we're not eating lunch."

The dogs started barking again outside just as they were finishing their meal. Stanhope said to nobody in particular, "Dang those hounds. How can you stand it?" A minute later, the doorbell rang. When Mama answered, a short, stocky man in a white lab coat, with short-cropped chestnut hair and spectacles asked after the boys, said a neighbor indicated they "may have been near the location where the incident occurred."

"A neighbor?"

"Fellow named Eddie Van Chukker. Been all over us since we got here. We had to run him off."

Mama muttered something unintelligible as she waved the gentleman inside.

More men in white lab coats followed close behind, a half dozen of them carrying Geiger counters and talking all at once in rapid bursts of scientific jargon. The men were like a pack of mosquitos, poking them with needles, taking measurements with bleeping devices, shining lights into their eyes. The men all wore facemasks and thick plastic gloves and goggles like they expected the boys' bodies to glow as bright as the fireball itself and potentially blind them all. They took blood samples, skin samples, urine samples. Their living room looked like the basement laboratory of a crackpot scientist with all the machines, metal boxes, wires, and tubes strewn about. Robert wondered if the floor and foundation were strong enough to hold all these men, all this equipment.

Stanhope hovered around, leaning in on the conversations and asking questions. It seemed they were planning to fence in the pond and bring in some heavy dredging machinery. The doctor became somewhat giddy. "So y'all are probably studying the chemical qualities of the water and such, trying to figure out what in the blue hell it was that fell out the sky? Am I right?"

"That's right," the man in charge said. His name, it turned out, was Colonel Whitehouse. It seemed they were guessing that the fireball was a meteorite, but it was only a guess. Whitehouse said that a few years ago, in '54, a meteorite had hit a lady in Sylacauga, just a couple of hundred miles east of here.

"What happened?" Robert said.

"It was about the size of a grapefruit," Whitehouse said. "Fell through the roof of her house and hit her in the leg, I believe."

Mama said, "Oh yes. I remember reading about that. Don't you remember it, Dewey?" Pop didn't answer.

"But what happened to *her*?" Robert said, imagining that she became fused to the sofa or perhaps started hearing Russian radio through the silver fillings in her teeth. "After?"

Whitehouse fingered his chin.

Stanhope chimed in from the periphery and said, "If I remember correctly, Mrs. Hodges suffered for several weeks from a severe contusion."

Robert was relieved at this, but he could feel Wally's hand vibrating. Robert tugged at the hand, forgetting for a moment that he couldn't budge it. "Settle down," he said. "That just means she got a bruise."

"Mrs. Hodges is as active as ever now. As for what happened at the pond," Whitehouse continued, "it could have been something like that. But that doesn't explain what happened to you. Then again, it could have been part of a Russian satellite. It might have been something that fell out of an airplane."

Wally offered that it might have been the devil, which took Robert a little by surprise. They hadn't been raised to believe in such things, but you heard all kinds of religious talk at school and around town. He'd always assumed that was just a story people told to scare children into behaving, though he knew some adults who took the devil as a literal embodiment of evil. He remembered smelling that sulfur and had to admit the devil was the first thing that had popped into his own mind. Whitehouse pretended to give this hypothesis brief consideration. The voices of Whitehouse's men were muffled behind surgical masks. They asked a lot of questions:

"Are you citizens of the United States of America?"

"Have you ever travelled outside the United States of America?"

20

"Have you ever heard of Karl Marx?"

"Do you speak any Russian?"

"Have you had any contact with anyone from Russia, China, or Cuba?"

"Have you heard of the Rosenbergs?"

The examination lasted up to and beyond supper time. Mama offered to fry enough chicken for everybody, but she was fidgeting when she said it. Robert knew there wasn't enough food for that. It was their last one, and its life would have been spared if it had been any good for laying. The rest of the summer would be pole beans and potatoes, some grits and cornbread maybe, unless Pop killed a rabbit or a deer. They weren't above roasting a possum now and then. Whitehouse politely refused anyway on behalf of his men. Robert said he wasn't hungry. Stanhope said he'd take a piece of dark meat.

Convinced the boys were not radioactive, and most likely not Communist spies, the men in white lab coats finally left with as little fanfare as they had entered. Stanhope followed them out, with the chicken leg still in hand. Whitehouse's prognosis for the boys was the same as that of Dr. Stanhope; they ought to get up to the hospital in Birmingham for more tests. He was curious about the case himself, but this wasn't his area of expertise. His mission was to gather information about the object in the pond. He mentioned that he might have further questions for them, and he said they would be setting up a temporary station by the pond to monitor the situation for a few weeks.

Pop had slipped out earlier and spent the afternoon building an angled seat in the bed of the pick-up truck to accommodate the boys. They decided that they would undergo the three-hour drive to Birmingham first thing in the morning. Preparing for bedtime, Robert put toothpaste on Wally's toothbrush, and they took turns at the sink. They had been accustomed to bending down to the faucet to rinse and spit, but they found this was no longer an option and had to use a glass. This seemed to Robert a more civilized practice than the old way, and he was glad, momentarily, that all this had led to at least one positive discovery.

In the morning, Mama presented them with a custom shirt she

had made out of sack cloth with two neck holes and three sleeves. She had obviously been up all night, which wasn't unusual for her, but Robert could always tell when she was on the verge of crashing. Her eyes were red and her shoulders twitched. When she finally slept, she'd be out for two or three days.

Though the shirt fit perfectly, Robert was not pleased. "Damn it all," he said under his breath, but Mama heard him.

"Robert Burns Mackintosh. What are you cussing at?"

"I don't know, Mama. I'm glad to have the shirt and the car seat. But . . ."

"What?"

"I don't like the fuss."

"Listen, son." She gripped his cheeks and looked him dead on. For a moment, some clarity came back into her face. "We don't know what's going to happen. But, we all hope and pray that these things will soon become hilarious souvenirs from a very strange and frustrating week. Just wait. You'll be telling this story to your grandkids, and you can show them this shirt, and they will gaze upon it with wonder."

Mama had a way with words when she set her mind to it, but Robert did not find these thoughts as comforting as they were intended to be. Wally's hand vibrated on his chest. Mama's gaunt complexion returned, and she looked as if she might faint.

Pop finished feeding the dogs, and the three males departed. Robert hoped Mama would get some rest, but he doubted that she would. As they pulled out of the driveway, Wally waved to her with his good arm. She waved back faintly and turned away.

In the truck on the way over, Wally said, "Do you think there's such a thing as space aliens?"

"It's *aliens*, no t at the end," Robert replied, feeling Mama's voice inhabiting his body. "Anyway, I don't know enough about it to say. Could be. It's a big universe."

"So, everything that's outside of the earth is in space, right?"

"Sure." Robert wasn't sure what he was getting at.

"So are space and heaven the same thing?"

"Some people say *the heavens* to mean *space*, but they aren't really the same thing."

"So then does God live in space?"

"There ain't no God, and there ain't no heaven. There's only space." He sounded more irritated than he intended, but it shut

Wally up for a while. Although the seat Pop built for them was certainly more comfortable than lying flat on the truck bed, it was still rough. They arrived in Birmingham with several splinters from the wood and covered in dust that got kicked up whenever they hit a bump in the road.

The hospital was a new-looking building, taller than anything Robert had seen up until now. Everything was a stark, sterile white. When they entered the emergency room, they were greeted by an apple-faced student nurse in a blue and white striped uniform with a white bib and a cap that sat improbably on the back of her head. She seemed to be expecting them and, after filling out some paperwork, took them to an examination room that smelled like chemicals and flowers. There was only one chair in the corner, so the boys remained standing, letting their father sit. The doctor that greeted them was young and tall with a shock of black hair, and he spoke with some sort of northern accent. His name was Dr. Weisman.

"Siamese twins, eh?" He said this with a chuckle. Robert, Wally, and Pop stared back at him. "Well, anyway, let's take a look. Tell me what's going on."

Wally seemed to enjoy telling the story, so Robert let him. It went exactly the same way as when he told it to their mother the day before: *Sulfur in the air...blood in the water...a white light... men in white lab coats...*

The doctor listened attentively, occasionally looking at Robert and Pop for confirmation that Wally was telling the truth. It occurred to Robert that he could spend the rest of his life trying to understand everything that happened in that one moment, looking at it from every angle, and he would never be able to grasp it because the moment itself is changed every time you look back at it. Afterward, the doctor said that even though they didn't know what exactly had caused the fusion in the first place, he hoped it would just be a matter of cutting through the skin that adjoined them, but he needed to run some tests and consult with some of his colleagues before he could be sure. When they had a better idea of what the treatment would be, they'd bring in the appropriate specialists.

When the doctor left, Robert began to feel more hopeful than he had been since the whole ordeal started. But he could tell by the way Wally tugged at the seam that he was starting to get agitated, like the doctor had put some obscure insult upon them. It felt like Wally was trying to bow up his chest, which caused Robert's to bow up as well, and he felt Wally's hand stretching with his skin. Wally said, "Why'd that doctor call us Siamese twins? We ain't twins."

Robert tried to explain, "It's after these two brothers from Thailand who were born joined together. I read about them in one of Mama's magazines. Damn, Wally, stop squirming."

"Son," Pop interjected from his chair in the corner, "watch your fucking mouth."

Robert started looking around the room. There was a poster on the wall of a skeleton with muscles, lines pointing to unreadable words in small italic type. He looked closely at the heart and chest on the model illustration, and for a moment thought a small ember glowed there. Beside the poster was a counter that held golf magazines and a box of latex gloves. Several cabinets painted crimson red were closed and did not invite inquiry. Tired of standing, Robert leaned up against the examination table. This seemed to take some weight off Wally's feet also, doubling Robert's relief.

"Siamese." Wally thought for a minute. "Siamese. Does Siamese mean joined together?"

Robert said, "No, you dummy."

"Robert—"

"Sorry, Pop... Look, Wally. Back in that time, Thailand used to be called Siam. That's where the word Siamese comes from. People from Siam are called Siamese."

"Why'd they change it to Thailand?"

Robert looked at his father for an answer. He shrugged. "I don't know."

"I don't understand. Why did he call *us* Siamese? We ain't from Thailand."

"Settle down, Wally," their father said. "He didn't mean nothing by it."

The nurse came back to retrieve them, took them up an elevator and into another exam room. For the entire day, they were corralled from room to room, floor to floor, getting prodded and photographed and measured, just like the team of scientists had done at their house the previous day. Wally told their story to at least a dozen doctors and nurses, who took x-rays and blood tests and urine tests. The x-ray machine was as big as a horse's stall and looked like a gymnasium of metal plates, wires, and tubes. The boys were made to stand in the most uncomfortable positions imaginable, trying to expose as much of the seam as they could to the plating. Before they were halfway done, Robert was pining for their bed, uncomfortable as it was with the two of them crammed into it.

Finally, they were taken back down to the exam room. The doctor came back pale and befuddled. "I'm afraid I have disappointing news. The tests showed that the fusion is more than just skin deep. There are some abnormalities that I can't really explain."

Their normally quiet father said in a slow, almost threatening tone, "What kind of abnormalities?"

"Well," the doctor said, "let's start at the beginning. At first, we were looking at this case essentially the same way they would treat a case where two siblings were conjoined at birth. Siamese twins."

Wally shuddered, and it reverberated through Robert's torso. The two of them both had their elbows propped up on the exam table for support, their heads hanging with fatigue.

The doctor continued, "What makes most of those cases complicated, however, is that sometimes the siblings share organs, or they are joined at especially volatile areas like the spine or the skull. Currently, there's no safe procedure for separation in those cases. Now, I thought your case was simpler than that. Even though we don't know exactly what caused the fusion, it didn't appear on the surface that any vital organs would be involved." The doctor looked at the three of them as if to ensure they were following his story so far. Then he continued. "I was surprised to learn, after a little research, that even simple cases where twins are joined at the shoulder create complications that make separation dangerous. This wasn't something that came up much in medical school. It can be done in theory, but it's actually never been done successfully. However, we have some of the best surgeons in the world here, and we would have been willing to give it a shot."

"*Would* have," Pop said.

Robert saw that his father now refused to look the doctor in the eye, was just staring at the wall as if he couldn't hear this conversation at all. Robert said, "So you can't do anything? Why the hell not?"

The doctor said, "There is something else that we, quite honestly, don't understand. Underneath the area where you are joined, the x-rays show something. Here, I'll show you." He took two large pieces of film from a folder and placed them on a lightboard. "You see this?"

It didn't look like anything to Robert except a bunch of white light, and he said as much.

"Exactly," the doctor said to him. "That's where your heart is supposed to be. There's something there preventing us from seeing it."

The three Mackintosh men all stared back at him. When a moment had passed in silence, Pop stood and examined the inverted silver and black image on the light screen. "What do you think it is? I mean, any guesses?"

"We don't have a clue. I thought it was a problem with the machine, but we tested it, did another x-ray. It came out just the same. We could open you up, but without knowing what we're dealing with, frankly, it's too risky. There are major arteries in that area, and if we can't see them…Well, the chances of survival, especially for you, Robert, are not very good."

Robert considered what the light could be—something alien, some Russian weapon previously unknown. Ultimately, he thought, it didn't matter. This was no way to live. "We should do it anyway. I'll take my chances."

"Conjoined siblings are often able to settle into a surprisingly good quality of life. Things might change in the future. But I'm afraid that's the current state of things."

The news coming out of the doctor's mouth seemed to strike him just as heavily as it did Robert and his family, as if he was surprised to hear himself say it out loud. Robert wondered if that feeling of his chest tightening was actually Wally, increasing his grip. Or maybe it was that fireball from the sky, now inside him, growing ever hotter. Maybe, even, he was starting to glow.

FIVE

"That's what it comes down to," Stanhope said to a figure in the shadow of a French doorway, whose wrought iron grates bloomed with wisteria and jasmine, poorly masking the odor of the jimson weed growing along the road. Montalto stepped into the light briefly and brushed a gray wisp of hair out from in front of his spectacles. Thick frames, thick lenses, made his eyes seem like they were bulging out of two small television sets.

"Have a safe trip back, Henry," Montalto said, baritone and aristocratic, that old patrician New Orleans intonation that Stanhope associated with the halcyon days of medical school at Tulane. They exchanged the handshake of their old fraternity. Stanhope began to leave but turned back again.

"You're sure about the amount?"

"That's just an estimate, now. I have to examine them before I can say for sure."

Stanhope nodded and backed away from the stoop, got into his chartreuse Nash Rambler, and sat without turning on the ignition. This weekend trip to New Orleans had been for two purposes: to consult his old schoolmate about the case of the Mackintosh brothers and to visit Nell. He had noticed the liquor store next door to the schoolmate's practice, and thought of a third purpose. It would do as well as any other, he thought, and so he got back out of the car and walked inside.

A bell rang, and the iron grate on the door clanged. A local station played an old song by that famous gravel-voiced singer with the big cheeks. *Stardust.* Stanhope did not know much about music, but that particular singer's voice was distinctive, inimitable. A bit sentimental, but the melody was comforting, like Nell on the sofa on a full-mooned winter night, like being wrapped up in a bear skin rug. Inimitable wasn't quite the right word. If one were to manipulate, squeeze the vocal chords in just the right way. Distinctive but not inimitable.

He perused the racks of bottles of clear and golden brown liquors with their old-fashioned labels, the nineteenth-century lettering serving as a kind of provenance to the liquor's origin. Each was a pristine artisanal masterwork in its own way. The bourbon selection was not impressive, all told, but he would take what he could get since real Kentucky bourbon was still illegal in Mississippi with its never-ending prohibition. There were bigger stores with better selections across town, but he was here now. Lower shelf included something called Old Billy Goat, made him laugh out loud, cartoonish satyr screaming out on the label. Stuff will feck you up good, probably eight percent formaldehyde. Tempted to buy it just for the label. Probably would be a good life with goats. Find a place to retire with Nell up in the hills, raise goats, plant some corn, and make your own whiskey in a still. But no, Old Fitzgerald it is. Reputable. Bottled in bond. Barrel dates stamped on; 1953-1959.

"Having a party," he said, carefully placing four bottles of Old Fitzgerald on the counter, going back for two more.

The coffee-faced clerk, in a starched white button-down shirt and crimson vest, counted the change. His fingers were laced with gold rings that matched the buttons on his vest, and he spoke without looking up. "Not my business."

"Damn right it's not."

The radio in the background had now changed to some other song. Stanhope could see himself becoming infatuated with this kind of music. Made his feet move. Perhaps it lacked sophistication; he wouldn't know. Tin ear, he would even say. But this music had rhythm, and rhythm was something you could feel, not something you had to hear or analyze in any particular way. Something he could feel in his groin.

"But I see you got Miss'ippi plates on that Rambler," the clerk said.

"That ain't your business neither," Stanhope said.

"Just be careful of them troopers if you going back to Miss'ippi with them bottles," the clerk said. "Miss'ippi still a dry state."

"I'm aware of that. Point taken."

The sunwarmed handle on the car door burned his white hands, causing him to jump back and nearly drop the package, so he used his handkerchief as a barrier to the heat. After rolling down his windows, he gently nested the six bottles behind his seat and covered them with a blanket. Then he turned on his radio, trying to find the station that had been playing in the liquor store.

Static. Static. Clarinets and trombones. Good enough. He started down the road toward downtown.

As he drove, he thought about his schoolmate Montalto. He and Stanhope still marched in the parades with some of their old krewe every February. Started as a mystic society in Mobile before the Civil War. The sons of the originals—his friend's father had been one of them—started the Louisiana krewe before he was born. It was Montalto who had sent him the mysterious invitation all those years ago. Now he claimed to be able to do what so many qualified people had said was impossible.

Even if Montalto was up to the task, unlikely the Mackintoshes would ever be able to raise the money, but perhaps it would give them some hope. Stanhope had delivered both of those boys and even some of their livestock. Even a couple of goats over the years. They'd been among his first patients when he first came back from medical school and set up shop in Columbus. Could never pay outright. Lucretia had washed his laundry and cleaned his bathrooms in exchange for a prescription. Sometimes he had even thrown clean clothes into the pile just so she would have something to do. She was a good woman, too good probably for that Dewey. She wasn't the prettiest of women, with her eczema made worse by lack of sleep, but she had a body some men would go for, plump in the right spots, maternal. Too proud to ever think about using that to pay her debts, not that he would ever ask that of her. Though there was a time or two when she had that look of desperation. Nell too had that look when he first met her. Perhaps, he thought, it was his impossible love for Nell that kept him from lusting after Lucretia, kept away the temptation to put on that final bit of pressure when it looked like she might break, the way some men would, a lot of men. He wasn't like other men because he did have love, however impossible it was, however maddening and miserable and torturous. As for Lucretia, she could scrub floors, repair clothes. He always found something for her to do.

He stopped at Johnny's to get a couple of po' boys. The sun had begun to set and cast an orange glow over the river. A putrid green Negro with delirium tremens on the sidewalk outside the shop asked if he could spare a dime. Stanhope gave him a dollar. The sickly fluorescent light inside the sandwich shop cast an unfortunate pallor on the patrons; at least he hoped it was the lighting and not the oysters. No R in July, so no oysters. Better stick to shrimp. Maybe crawfish.

The Mackintoshes were a proud clan. Yes, a clan. Mackintosh was a Scottish name, was it not? That made them a clan, he figured. Like a group of geese are called a gaggle, crows are called a murder, and butterflies are a congress. All made up by a nun in the fifteenth century. A clan of Mackintoshes. Where are the rest of them then, he wondered, maybe on some highland tor squeezing the bladder of a bagpipe, driving the cats and sheep into a frenzy. They have goats too in Scotland. A trip of goats, says the nun. Goats and golf. Undulating fields of green.

Anyway, Stanhope thought, if Nicholas Montalto could help them, then maybe he could help me also. That's why he'd tell them. And because he had been a farm boy too, or at least a planter's son. They had called it a farm, their five hundred acres on the Delta, which had become two hundred after the war. They had some years better than others. First Reconstruction, then floods, and then the war. But his folks had still been able to send him to school in Oxford and then medical school at Tulane.

He continued down St. Claude Avenue, through the Bywater and into a neighborhood of tiny houses that felt cramped together between the canal and the river. Louis Armstrong. That was the singer's name. Now the radio was playing something slow and sweet, a female singer, a voice he also thought he recognized as famous but could not identify. *I hate to see that evening sun go down.* The tune made him melancholy. After he stopped the car and killed the engine he sat still for a few moments, steeping in the sadness of it. *I hate to see that evening sun go down.*

Stanhope passed under what seemed like a jungle of clothes lines, to a tiny red house with a tiny front porch. It could have been a doll's house almost, if the doll were poor and desolate, and the house had been through both flood and fire. The musty odor of damp wood mingled with the greasy fried fish smell emanating from the paper sack he carried. He crept onto the front porch, ducking to avoid a low railing, and walked in the front door, which was open.

"It's me," he said. He took a seat in at the kitchen table, which had once been art deco in chrome and red that matched the red of the house exterior. The vinyl on the chairs was torn and peeling, and the red finish on the table was cracked all over.

Nell's sultry voice, almost a whisper, returned his greeting.

"How long you staying?"

"Just the night. I brought dinner." He placed the bag of sandwiches on the table.

She poured a glass of whiskey and set it in front of him. Her gingham dress matched the table that matched the house, and she wore a matching handkerchief on her head. She was caramel skinned, with shaving cuts all along her arms and neck.

"Shrimp for you. Crawfish for me," he said. He took a big sip of whiskey from his glass. "What brand is this?"

She put the bottle on the table. Old Grandad was the name on the label.

"It's not bad," he said. "I've been to see my old schoolmate, Nicholas. The one I wrote to you about. Who might help the Mackintosh boys."

"I remember him," she said. She was flat-voiced, weary-faced. Her expression had not changed since he arrived. It was as worn down as the worn-down doll's house in which she lived with her worn-down doll's house furniture. "I remember you telling me."

"Nell," he said. Their bond was one he had never been able to describe. He had never even said anything about it to Nicholas, about where she had come from, her absolute and unquestioning dedication, or her extraordinarily hirsute nature. It had been one of those rare cool and sleepy nights in the Quarter when nobody seemed to be around, after New Year's but before Mardi Gras, and he was wandering as young men are prone to do.

"Nell, if it works, if he can help those boys, maybe he can help you too."

"Don't need help."

He had nearly tripped over her as he turned down Pirate's Alley, making his way for the trolley at Toulouse. At first, he'd thought she was a dog lying in the alleyway, a German Shepherd maybe. She was covered head to toe with shiny black hair. Then she made a sound that was more human than canine, and it sounded like the word "sorry." So then he knelt down and saw the muddy brown eyes set into an oval face that was all woman. He'd asked if she was alright and helped her to stand up. Her hands were woman's hands, though rough and patched with fur, and they were warm like mittens on his soft white doctor hands. That night, he moved her into his little apartment and took care of her. To the detriment of his other medical studies, he ploughed through textbooks ancient and modern, looking for answers. Eventually, he determined it was a kind of lycanthropia. Her condition changed with the moon, though, like the moon, it never completely waned.

"But Nell, do you really want to always be this way?"

"It's not that I don't appreciate everything you've done for me, Henry, everything you continue to do," she said. "But I'm happy the way things are. I don't want to change."

"You don't want to change anything? Anything?"

She turned her back to him, hiding her face. "Well…you know. I won't even say it."

"Nell, you know that's impossible."

She had stayed there in his apartment until he was done with medical school, loyal and affectionate as a golden retriever. But there was also the affection of a lover. The first time they made love, he had been working, poring over his medical books on the leather sofa, and she was curled up around his legs as she had been many times. Resting his eyes from the text, he looked at her, and she gazed back at him. The powerful urge seemed to overtake them both at once. He grew erect, and she noticed. The relationship grew after that into this impossible love, not just because the world would find her monstrous, but also because she was a Negro. He didn't know which secret tortured him more.

Coming back to the table, she touched his soft, pale hands. After his residency, he went back up to the Delta, where his people were from, then later to Columbus to start his own practice. Seventeen years he had kept her in this little Bywater shack, visiting a couple of times a month, giving her enough money to get by, finding her waiting for him every time, never straying. In all that time, she had been loyal to him, even if she didn't jump his bones as soon as he walked in the door anymore, even if her eyes were tired and her deep black hair had lost a bit of its luster. Maybe it was time to give her something more. Stanhope cocked back the glass and swallowed his whiskey, then poured himself another glass. The evening sun tucked itself coyly behind the horizon in a burst of yellow flame. He thought of the song of that gravel-voiced singer. "Well," he said, "I suppose anything is possible."

Back when he was at Tulane, there was an old absinthe house

in the Quarter where the medical students used to convene called Zelenko's. Of course, actual absinthe had been outlawed since 1912, but Zelenko still had a few cases that he pulled out on special occasions. This was back in '29, so the general prohibition was still in effect, though you wouldn't know it in New Orleans. Federal agents made a show of raiding some of the more high profile bars like Arnaud's and Commander's Palace. And they shut down the Dixie Brewery too. At Zelenko's, drinking went on quietly and without disruption, as long as Zelenko knew you.

When you walked into the place, you would make a hand signal—1, 2, 3, or 4 fingers—to signal the strength of the drink you wanted, and he would relay the signal to the runner who would come back from a stash next door with the appropriate amount of whiskey. The house specialty was called an Inoculation. Ingredients: one pony glass of the smokiest Scotch whisky they could get, a half pony of Zelenko's homemade coffee liqueur, and a healthy dash of Tobasco sauce. The sweetened coffee provided a jolt to counteract the alcohol. The smokiness of the whisky blended surprisingly well with the coffee. The hot sauce, though, was the *piece de resistance*. It was just enough to give the whole thing a spicy kick that made you feel invincible.

On those late Inoculation-infused nights, the students would talk, fantasize about obscure or unusual surgeries. Island of Dr. Moreau-type stuff. Frankenstein. With heads full of rum and scotch, they would theorize about the logistics of those literary horrors. It was in those discussions that Nicholas started speculating on the types of procedures that eventually got him in trouble. But Stanhope had never talked about Nell at those meetings. In fact, he was especially careful to remain silent when the alcohol had loosened the tongues of everyone else in the room.

"This is your house? It looks like a ball gown." Nell stared up in wonder at its baby-blue Victorian arches and gables, the white lacy lattice that skirted the bottom. "Three stories?" She punched him lightly on the shoulder and threw her arms around his neck.

He had timed the trip so they would arrive after dark. "I know, I know," he said, not quite sure what he was agreeing with. "It's only two stories really. That window at the top is from the attic, which is just for storage." Her excitement made him look at the house with fresh eyes. It was true that it was a nice house, and he had kept it nice. In gray dusk, it had the appearance of a stately lady.

Inside, she continued gaping as if at a museum, though the rooms were sparse. He did not keep many possessions other than books, medical supplies, and a few pieces of old furniture his family had sent him. Lucretia Mackintosh had chided him about his Spartan decorating on many occasions. "It just isn't right for a doctor to live like this," she said. "You should at least put something on the walls, and get something for people to sit on other than these dusty old chairs. What if you have company?"

But he never did have company if he could avoid it. He spent most of his waking hours either at the hospital, on house calls, on a golf course, or in New Orleans and only came to this house to sleep. Most likely he would not even have bought such a house in the first place except for the fact that Lucretia was right about a doctor needing to keep up a certain image in the community. It was a good bet that there wasn't any food in the kitchen either, just a mess of empty bottles, cans, and food wrappers. He would take care of that tomorrow. Things would be different now with Nell here.

"Remember what we talked about. Discretion! I can't have people seeing you going in and out." He heard the panic in his voice and took a sip from his flask.

"I know, I know," Nell squeaked, bunching her fists up under her chin and quietly stamping in a girlish dance. "I can't wait to see the rest of the place!" She ran into the kitchen and then up the stairs.

Stanhope sat on his old sofa and drank his whiskey, soaking in the quiet of the evening. He hated to see that evening sun go down.

"I'm going to take a bath," Nell called from the top of the stairs. "Come join me. I'll wash your back."

SIX

Each task of every day exercised their collective ingenuity. While Pop and the boys were away at the Birmingham hospital, Mama had chased off several reporters from area newspapers, some from as far away as Memphis. Over the following week, she made more shirts. She had books delivered from the library in town and read to the boys, just like when they were babies. In addition, she ordered many books on science and medicine, hoping to learn something about her sons' condition, but she found nothing helpful. Every day she seemed to Robert weaker from not sleeping.

Pop spent his mornings trying to rid the cotton fields of grass and weevils so they'd have some kind of crop in the fall. In the afternoons, he was making furniture that better accommodated the boys, fine tuning the heights and angles of seats to increase their comfort. As often as he could, Pop went hunting early in the morning and came home with a rabbit, possum, or raccoon in a bloody sack, the hounds slobbering in a pack behind him, awaiting their share of the bounty. On Saturday nights, they listened to the Grand Ole Opry show on an old Philco radio that Pop had found and fixed up. Wally always caterwauled along with every song right in Robert's ear. The music made Robert melancholy, even the peppy dance tunes, but he tried to remain stoic and said nothing about it.

Newspaper men continued to drop by from time to time, but the family usually sent them away without comment. The exception was one afternoon when they first got back from Birmingham, when Robert and Wally told their story to a bevy of reporters who showed up during lunch. When they all left, one remained—a crusty vulture from Tupelo named Munford Coldwater. Even though it was one of the hottest days in July, he wore a brown suit that was maybe a size too large for him, like he expected to grow into it. He was not a young man; his stubble was peppered with gray patches. But he was scrawny and sinewy as a dressed fawn. Coldwater sat at their kitchen table scribbling notes in his black and white composition notebook, more of a schoolboy's notebook than a reporter's. Robert almost didn't notice him there, until the man said, "Tell me what it was like for you before."

"Before what?" Robert said.

"Before this happened. What were your days like? Did you two get along?"

Nobody else had asked them that. They only asked what happened at the pond and at the hospital and how they've been coping since. Before Robert could think of anything, Wally said, "Sure. We got along."

Robert figured it was truthful enough. They didn't fight. Mostly, as he remembered it, they didn't have all that much to do with each other, that day in the pond being a rare exception. "We had our own lives," he said.

"So," Coldwater chuckled, "This event has, quite literally, brought about some fraternal bonding... I'm sorry. I couldn't help myself. What were your lives like? What did you do with yourselves?"

"Well...We worked on the farm, went to school, did things normal people do. Wally was a musician. He played the fiddle."

Coldwater smiled and nodded his head.

Wally added, "Robert liked this girl named Edwina—"

"That does not go in the paper," Robert said. Munford nodded.

"And he was real good at sports, especially football."

Robert wouldn't have said it was something he was good at, but it was something he enjoyed doing when he was able to. It was true that he had a pretty good arm for throwing, but it wasn't something he was passionate about, the way Wally seemed about music. What was he passionate about? He supposed it all came back to working with his hands. In the fields, he always felt engaged and satisfied.

He said, "Work. Work is what I liked doing. Here on the farm."

Coldwater looked up from his notepad and looked Robert in the eye. "Work? You're fifteen! You should be having fun. Chasing pussy. Playing football." Robert shrugged and matched the reporter's stare. He wouldn't lose the staring game. Throwing a football seemed like a rather foolish endeavor in the context of all that had happened to them.

"Well," Coldwater said without breaking his gaze. "Do you miss it? That life?"

Of course they did, Robert thought, wondering if maybe the reporter was trying to make them both cry. Tears dammed up behind his eyes, but he stubbornly pushed them back. It was a ridiculously obvious question. After a moment, with his voice tightly holding back the flood, he said, "We try not to dwell on it. Get on out of here."

The boys couldn't do the same chores they'd always done, but they managed to help their mother with a few things like washing dishes and folding laundry. For the first few days after returning from the hospital, these chores were enough to keep them relatively distracted from the new reality to which they were trying to get accustomed, but at night when Robert tried to sleep, thoughts about it swirled around his head. Now thoughts about their conversation with Munford Coldwater were added into the mix, and it overwhelmed him some nights.

It was a couple of days later that the boys were helping to clean up some detritus around the old barn, which was also Pop's workshop. Here, there were a couple of fiddles, an accordion, a tenor banjo, two ukuleles, a trumpet, a rusted out sousaphone, a few drums and other miscellaneous percussion instruments, as well as discarded bottles and jars that had once held Pop's moonshine. The disemboweled guts of a piano leaned against a wall near a work bench and a collection of tools.

As they picked up stray shine bottles from around the barn and stacked them neatly in a corner, a tool caught Robert's eye—a violin knife used for carving precision designs in the wood. He examined the beveled edge and sharp tip.

Robert asked Wally, "What about what that reporter asked. Do you ever wish you could still play?"

"I reckon. I hadn't thought about it much."

"Sure you have. And maybe you'll be able to," he said. Robert set the knife down on a bale of hay and removed his part of their shirt. When Wally asked why, he said he was hot, even though it was a relatively mild morning, low eighties and clear skied. He examined the seam, no different than it had been on any other day since the incident—pink and leathery, tender to the touch. As he ran his finger lightly along it, he could feel the tickle. Wally laughed and said "Stop it." He was oddly surprised that Wally could feel that too. It was part of both of them he guessed—unclear where one of them ended and the other now began.

He lifted the knife and touched the point of the blade to a spot at the top of his chest. With a little bit of pressure, the knife dug in, and the pain shot through the both of them like a kick from a horse. Wally shouted and writhed around until the knife fluttered out of Robert's hand and into the piano board causing a loud dissonant chord to reverberate through the barn. The boys ended up on the ground just like they had when they first crawled out of the pond, legless primordial beasts.

No blood issued from the wound. When Robert looked down, he saw only a bright silver light peeking out. In a moment, the light was reduced to a pinhole, and then it was gone. The cut had disappeared along with it, sealed up just as before. Robert thought he smelled bacon frying, and he noticed that it didn't even hurt any more. Wally was still bawling though.

"Do you still feel it?"

Through wet sniffles, he said, "Why'd you do that?"

"You know why I did it. Does it still hurt?"

"No—no, I guess not."

A warm sensation began filling Robert's chest, and he felt light-headed but relaxed. What had happened over the last few minutes was already a fuzzy memory, and they continued on with their chores.

When they came back inside for lunch, Martha Jean Van Chukker, their nearest neighbor, sat at the kitchen table, wearing jeans and what was probably one of her husband's work shirts, smoking a cigarette. She and Eddie had been married for five years or so and hadn't yet had children. When they saw her across the room from where they had entered the back door, Robert could feel Wally getting an erection.

"Tamp that down," Robert whispered.

"I can't help it. Look at her."

Robert *was* looking at her. He could picture actual bees buzzing around inside her blonde beehive, running scheming ideas from one end of her honeycomb brain to the other. She was a young woman, in her early twenties, and sort of pretty, but not effortlessly so. Robert had never seen anyone wearing so much make-up outside of the movies, and in the movies it somehow didn't seem to have the same effect of making a person seem *less* real. Though she was friends with Mama, she had always insisted the boys address her informally as Martha Jean. She wasn't old enough, she had said, for teenage boys to be calling her Ma'am. And Mrs. Van Chukker, she said, was what her mother-in-law was called.

As the boys approached, Mama called out to them, "Martha Jean brought a pie. Isn't that nice?"

There was a sharpness in her voice that Robert found surprising. She and Martha Jean always acted like they liked each other, despite some past misunderstandings. Robert was thinking of the time a couple of years back when Eddie was away serving in Korea. Martha Jean used to constantly ask Pop to come over and do things for her. Mama had gotten irritated for a while, but all had been forgiven and forgotten when Eddie came back from the war. Maybe Mama was just irritable from lack of sleep. Martha Jean didn't seem to notice it.

She turned around to face the boys, "Well bless your hearts! I saw Dr. Stanhope at church, and I thought I knew what to expect, but...never mind about the pie. Tell me what in the Lord's name happened?"

"Martha Jean," Mama said. "Don't start in about it."

Sulfur in the air...blood in the water...a white light...white lab coats...Birmingham...reporters...

The hand on Robert's chest, Wally's hand, felt heavier, just from thinking about it. He was sore and fatigued.

"I'm sorry—I don't mean to...anyway. You know Eddie has been down there at the pond every day since it happened. He thinks they're hiding secret alien corpses or something. I tell you, I'm tired of hearing about it myself. He's obsessed."

Wally said, "Mama, can I have a piece of the pie?"

"Well," Martha Jean said. "All I can say is that if this happened to someone in *my* church, they wouldn't be keeping it quiet. And everybody would be chipping in to do something about it."

Robert said, "Ain't nothing to be done."

"*There is* nothing to be done," Mama corrected.

"Nonsense. Now remind me, Lucretia. I don't recall where

y'all go. Where is your spiritual community, if you don't mind me asking? I don't think I even know your denomination."

Wally said with a mouthful of pie, "Spiritual what? What's our domination?"

Robert hit him on the leg to shut him up. He was thinking about those workers in the field during harvest. Hey-oh. Hey-oh. The call and response in the rhythm of work. The Mackintoshes didn't go to church; work was their only religion as far as he knew. On those days when the singing started, the cotton fields were Robert's cathedral. He could almost hear the echoes of those voices still lingering, whispering their work songs through the trees.

He was shocked out of his internal reverie when he heard his mother blurt out, "We are Episcopalian."

This was news to Robert. Wally said, "Why do you keep hitting me?"

"Episcopalian! Do Episcopalians even go to church? Do they even believe in God?"

"Thank you for the pie, Martha Jean," Mrs. Mackintosh said. "I think you should be on your way."

"Alright now, but I'll tell you what. You tell those…Episcopalians…to put their heads together and help out their people."

SEVEN

Early one morning, while Robert was still drowsing and the dark of the horizon had just a hint of red-orange glow, Wally said, "I dreamed I was climbing a mountain, and when I got to the top I kept climbing. I was climbing the air, higher and higher, and then I was in the clouds, in heaven actually, and heaven was made of pillows, and it tasted like butterscotch."

Robert realized then that in his dreams, he was still attached to Wally, or attached to something. Sometimes it was the bed or the ground. He was planted in the earth like one of Pop's seeds. Even in sleep he couldn't escape it. His dream life was basically the same as his real life—repetitive, frustrating, heavy. There was never any climbing, floating, or flying. No freedom, and no rest. Before all this, Robert hadn't spent a lot of time talking to his brother. Used to be, when Wally started talking nonsense or being annoying, Robert would walk away. Now he was frequently impatient, said things he later regretted. So he tried to compose himself and indulge his brother.

"Butterscotch, huh?" He kind of liked the idea of a heaven that tasted like butterscotch.

"I've been thinking," Wally said. "Maybe if we go down there, back to the pond, it will undo what it did."

Robert sighed. Doing anything at all felt like so much work. But when he considered this idea a moment, he was almost surprised he hadn't thought of it himself. Sort of like when people have amnesia or are hypnotized. He'd seen it in the movies a few times. Maybe, in fact, they were hypnotized and this was all a wretched illusion.

"What if that just makes it worse?" He could imagine coming out of the pond with more of Wally's parts stuck to him, parts of himself stuck to other parts of himself. He could easily imagine not coming out at all. "Besides," he said, "Colonel Whitehouse fenced it off. They're still trying to find whatever the blue hell it was that fell in there."

He heard that irritable harshness creeping up in his voice.

41

That impatience wasn't the real Robert Mackintosh, but he'd noticed over the past few days that it was getting worse. He'd been trying to get away from it, if only for his own physical comfort. Wally's hand always felt heavier on Robert's chest after one of these exchanges. So he backtracked and said, "I guess it couldn't hurt to call that Whitehouse and see what he says about it."

Robert dialed the operator, who turned out to be Edwina Hunter, the girl from his school who had called him handsome earlier in the year. She recognized his voice. Hers sounded like fresh-baked brownies. "I heard you and your brother had some kind of, um, accident? Down at Jimbo Bobo's pond?" she said.

"Guess everybody's heard about it by now. Been all over the papers." He was irritated again, and didn't like starting off that way, with Edwina especially. After a breath, he said, "Listen, Edwina. I'm trying to contact somebody there at the pond, a Colonel Whitehouse. He's trying to help figure out what happened. Is there a number you can connect me to?"

"I'm sorry, Robert," she said. "I don't think so. I could connect you to Jimbo."

A pause hung on the line for a couple of minutes before Edwina came back and said there was no answer. Robert hung up the phone. "Well, Wally, I guess we'd better just go on down in person."

It was the first time they had been on that road since it happened. They had their shoes now, so the gravel road didn't fight them so much. Already walking was a lot easier than it had been on that first day. Nothing much seemed different at first, but soon they noticed smoke in the distance. Rounding the corner past the crossroads where their own property stopped, they started to hear the sounds of the dredging machines. They were making good time. Soon, they were near the end of the Van Chukker's orchard where early peaches were already littering the ground. Wally made Robert stop and find a couple that weren't too bruised.

In twenty minutes, they were in sight of the long aluminum gate at the entrance to the dirt path that led down to the pond. A guard in military uniform, Air Force, stood at the gate with a rifle across his chest. He was probably only a year or two older than Robert, a baby-faced boy with freckles.

A few yards away, Eddie Van Chukker marched back and forth in front of the gate. He looked ruffled and unshaven, and he held a wooden sign on which was scrawled in red paint, "End the Conspiracy. Remember Chorwon." When he saw the boys coming, he started yelling, pointing at the clear gray sky, "I saw it in Korea. The iron triangle. This is the same thing. Chorwon!"

The guard was ignoring Eddie. Though he was a little curious, Robert decided to focus on the task they had come to perform. The young soldier's eyes barely shifted when Robert addressed him.

"We want to see Colonel Whitehouse."

"This is a restricted area under quarantine by the U.S. Government. No civilians allowed."

"They are hiding something in there, boys. I saw it before." Eddie was still pointing upwards, where there was nothing but the sun and a few wisps of clouds. Down the path, just as Stanhope had said, a ten foot tall fence had been erected around the perimeter of the pond, topped with rings of barbed wire. On the other side, cranes and drills roared and spouted steam. Two trailers occupied a clearing on the far edge of the pond.

"Colonel Whitehouse sent for us." Robert said. Wally, with a mouthful of peach meat, started saying that they had tried to call, but Robert interrupted, "No need to go into all that shit, Wally. Hush up. Whitehouse wanted to see us, the Mackintosh brothers."

"Just a minute." The soldier spoke a few gruff noises into a two-way radio. A garbled response came through a few seconds later. "Wait right here," he said. "The colonel will be right out."

The boys looked out over the pond. It didn't have the same earthy smell as before. There was almost no smell at all, and the wildlife seemed to have disappeared. In a few moments, they saw Whitehouse coming up the path, no longer in a white lab coat but instead wearing a blue uniform. Eddie began yelling, but the colonel ignored him. He had a grim look on his face, but he smiled when he recognized his visitors. "Boys! Come on back to my office."

The young guard unlocked the gate. Eddie called out, "Don't believe anything he says, boys. They are hiding aliens in there. Chorwon!" Then he made a run for it, trying to enter the gates, but the guard clotheslined him with the broad side of his gun, dragged him back outside the gate, and laid him up against a tree before locking up again.

Whitehouse said Eddie would be alright and hurried the boys down the path. His office was one of the trailers on the edge of

43

the pond. Inside, there was only a desk, a chair, and some filing cabinets. In a corner, there was a coffee percolator, a disheveled stack of paper cups, and a box of powdered creamer. The wall held a map of the world, dotted with thumbtacks. There wasn't really any place where the boys could sit, so they stood. Out of politeness, perhaps, Whitehouse remained standing also. "What can I do for you?"

Robert started to answer, but then his own questions took precedence. "What are you doing out here exactly?"

The colonel laughed. "I work for the National Aeronautics and Space Administration. Do you know what that is?" The boys both shook their heads no. He explained that in essence, they were a branch of the government concerned about what the Communist Russians were doing in space, and his job was to make sure that whatever the commies were up to there, the Americans could get to it first. "So if that thing that fell in the pond was man-made," he said, making a molding or sculpting gesture with his hands. "I want to know everything I can about it. And if it wasn't, we still want to know, for the sake of science. Do you have any information on your end?"

He gazed at them seriously, waiting for an answer. The boys stared back at him. It seemed like they'd been doing a lot of staring at people since this all started.

The top of the colonel's desk was covered with papers. One of those coffee cups stood half full, with a two big clumps of the powdered creamer clinging together on the surface. A legal pad and pen sat on top, which displayed a doodle the colonel must have been working on when the boys showed up. It appeared to be a caricature of Eddie wrestling with some sort of tentacled multi-eyed space beast.

"No sir," Robert said after a moment. He told the colonel about the brainstorm he and Wally had earlier in the morning.

"I suppose there's a small chance there could be something to that. But I can't let you get anywhere near that water right now. We're still testing it for safety. I haven't even dipped my hands in it." Robert took a breath, bowed his head. Wally was surprisingly silent also. "For what it's worth, I think it was most likely the impact that caused your, uh, situation to happen. I don't think going back in the water again will make things any better or any worse. And it's definitely not going to help me fight any commies

44

in space."

"I understand," Robert said.

"I don't," Wally said. Robert poked him in the ribs. Wally pulled back, which Robert felt with a sharp pain. As they stepped down the couple of wooden steps that led from the trailer door, Robert felt Wally steering him off the path, more forcibly than he really thought possible. Next thing he knew, they were tumbling down the slip and into the murky water's edge. He knew what Wally was trying to do, and stopped resisting until he found himself wet, covered in weeds and mud—otherwise, as the colonel predicted, no better or worse off than before.

"Private Townsend," the colonel said, shaking his head. "Get these boys out of the muck, put them in a jeep, and take them home."

When the private dropped the boys off, they saw Stanhope's white Cadillac parked in the drive. They found Stanhope himself at the door, looking ridiculous in a wool checkered hat of yellow and black with matching socks that were also tasseled, navy wool pants, a wine colored V-neck sweater, and orange golf cleats. The outfit hung loose on him like it was afraid of his skin. He had just put something away in his leather satchel and was reaching out to ring the doorbell.

"Oh, morning, boys. I was just passing through on my way to the club up in Aberdeen," he announced. Then he asked to speak to Mr. Mackintosh. "Why are y'all sopping wet?"

Wally said, "Never mind that. What's that on your neck?" It looked like a rash or a series of scratches that ran from the side of his neck down to his shoulders.

"Nothing," he said. "A mild allergic reaction."

"Maybe it's that dog you've been around," Robert said. "There's fur all over your tweeds."

"Yes, that's probably what it was. Another patient I saw on the way here. House covered in dog fur."

The boys invited him to sit down in the kitchen as they lumbered away to retrieve Pop from the barn. Mama was at the kitchen sink shelling peas. She looked a lot better than she had in recent days, but she seemed almost hypnotized by her task and said nothing to Stanhope when he came in.

When the boys returned with Pop, the doctor was staring at her from across the table, while she kept shelling in silence. He stood at seeing Pop and said, "Morning, Dewey." He told them that he had a colleague down near New Orleans, a Dr. Montalto, who might be up to the task of separating the boys using some experimental techniques, assuming he wouldn't have to cut through any vital organs. "There's no guarantee that he'll do it, but I can at least get you a consultation with him."

"Of course," Pop said. "Thank you, doc. We appreciate it."

Robert said, "You shitting us?" He didn't want to get his hopes up, but he couldn't help feeling excited.

"He'll see you. If he agrees to operate, it's going to be expensive. You'll need maybe a couple thousand, but that's just an estimate based on what I was able to tell him."

Mama gasped at the figure. Pop showed no reaction.

"Dollars?" Wally said.

"But let's not worry about that just yet. Y'all need to get yourselves down to Louisiana. Did y'all already have breakfast?"

"We did," Robert lied.

He seemed disappointed, kicked his toe at the ground. "Well, I'll let you go. I have a tee time of 7:30 anyway; can't be late. I'll talk to y'all later. Good luck."

Later that night, they all sat down at the kitchen table. Pop had a grave look on his face. "Well, we could sell the farm," he said.

At that suggestion, Mama seemed to wake from the dreamy daze she'd been in all morning. "No! It's everything we have. What would we live off?"

"We could just sell off some of the land. Keep the house. Go work for somebody else."

Robert thought about it. Without a farm to work on, what sort of life would they have? He knew they were fortunate that they even had a farm to sell. He'd seen tenant farmers coming into town to gin their cotton, dressed in their ill-fitting dirty clothes, their one pair of shoes razored at the toe to ease the pressure of their corns. Even if he had a few sackcloth shirts himself, he knew there were a lot of others worse off. But still…where would they even go?

"There has to be another way to get the money," he said.

"I'll write to my family," Mama said. "Surely they couldn't deny us in this situation. In the meantime, I could sell some clothes." Her parents had written her off when she married Pop. She hadn't heard from them in years. Almost under her breath, she added, "You could sell your collection."

Pop jumped up. "I ain't selling that. We can sell the land, sell your clothes, but I ain't selling the instruments...Stop looking at me like that, woman." She was glaring, but Robert wasn't sure if it was because of the collection or because he'd said *ain't* twice.

Pop shuffled across the living room and out the kitchen door. Robert and Wally got up to follow. Mama stayed seated, and the boys left her there pulling at fistfuls of her hair. They found Pop in the barn tuning a fiddle.

"These instruments are all older than the two of y'all," he said. "I've probably spent more time nurturing these hunks of wood and metal than I have you."

Robert couldn't disagree, though he was surprised to hear his father speaking so wistfully. He waited for Wally to respond first. Wally cared about these objects almost as much as Pop did. When he didn't say anything, Robert said, "Do you think you can get enough for them? I mean, if you decided to sell them."

"Could raise a few hundred at best," he said. "It wouldn't be enough. You took a few fiddle lessons when you were little. Remember anything?"

"I don't know." Pop handed it over, and the bow shook and rattled with uncertainty in Robert's hand. His fingertips lumbered over the strings like the spindly legs of a drunken giraffe. The hairs of the bow grazed and squeaked at a string. He tried to imagine Miss Rhenetta Tate telling him what to do, standing behind him in her spangles, with her silver waterfall hair. Wally's voice came in her stead.

"You're holding the bow wrong," he said. With his good hand, Wally showed Robert where to put his fingers around the handle of the bow, which is called the frog. "Don't hold it too tight. Don't draw the whole flatness of the bow against the strings. You'll get a better tone if you just use about three-fourths."

After a long minute, and a few more tips from Wally, Robert made a couple of clean notes in a row. A few tries later, he managed to eke out a melody that someone very patient and imaginative could possibly have recognized as "Dixie."

A wide-eyed look came over their father's face. "You sit here and play that over and over until you can do it cold." Their father put a drum with a kick pedal in front of Wally. "Keep coaching him, Wally. Keep time with that, and make sure your brother stays on it. You won't be going back to school in September."

"And?" Robert said.

"You boys are gonna work. You worry about that fiddle. I'll work out the other details." Wally kicked at the drum pedal, but Robert just stared at Pop, his eyelids bearing the weight of his doubt about this plan. He hadn't played in a couple of years, and he'd never been very good. Wally was the one with that kind of talent. Admittedly, he hadn't quite figured how school would work logistically, and thinking about it made his brain hurt. So he gave in and tried once again at squeaking out a melody. Pop clapped his hands in time with Wally's beat, grinning and nodding his head.

EIGHT

On a stony gray Sunday afternoon, Munford Coldwater sat looking out the window of the room he rented from the obtrusive widow Mrs. Howard Jordan in South Green Street in Tupelo. The overfed orange tabby named Captain Fancypants stood on his lap, sniffing at the wisps of pipe smoke as they drifted from the corners of Coldwater's mouth and out into the air. Mrs. Jordan's house had loose floorboards, bad pipes, and bugs, but she allowed cats, and it was convenient to the courthouse and the offices of the *Tupelo Daily Journal*. The cockroaches, at least, served the purpose of keeping the Captain entertained when Coldwater wasn't around. His room held only his small, creaky bed, a desk for his typewriter, a rolling chair he'd smuggled out of his office building, a stumpy dresser, and a bookshelf containing mainly journalism textbooks and some pulp detective novels he'd accumulated in his college days. He also had a second-hand phonograph on a table just big enough to hold it and a dozen records stored in a milk crate underneath, mostly classical. The Captain had a small covered litter box that was kept in the corner opposite the bed. Mrs. Jordan had wanted to put some of her needlework on the walls "to give it some color," but he preferred the room bare.

Sometimes, while smoking his pipe, he wished he had something well-made to sip on, some Scotch or fine brandy. He'd developed a taste for well-made liquors in college, but it wasn't easy to get such things in this dry state, unless you were rich, in which case you could get anything you wanted, unless you wanted something like equal rights for black folks or sex education in the schools. While he puffed at the pipe and scratched the Captain on the head, Munford meditated on this and on other things, like that fireball that fell from the sky and the ordeal of the Mackintosh brothers. Like Munford's parents, they too were just in the wrong place at the wrong time, he supposed. He'd interviewed all the neighbors and also that Colonel Whitehouse (who wouldn't tell him anything). There probably wasn't any story there anymore, and yet he couldn't get it out of his mind.

There was a knock, Mrs. Jordan asking him if he was going to take lunch. He opened the door just a crack so he could be heard, and she edged her way into the room. The landlady was a reedy woman with thinning gray hair and chronic rosacea, causing her to resemble a moldy dried cranberry. Coldwater's aunt Edna had had the same skin condition and was close to the same age, which was another thing that made Mrs. Jordan somewhat endearing to him.

"No ma'am. I believe I'll go out today," he said, moving out of her way. Her eyes scanned the room as if looking for a secret stash somewhere. He wasn't sure what she could be looking for or where she might think it is. There were few places to hide anything in the room. He supposed she thought he had a bottle of whiskey hidden somewhere because she thought writers were supposed to like drinking whiskey. She over-romanticized his profession, which tended to work out well for him when rent day came around and he needed a little extra time.

"I haven't heard your typewriter today, Mr. Coldwater. You haven't got the writer's block have you?"

"No, ma'am," he said. "I've just been doing some research and thinking things over with the Captain here. He's my editorial assistant. Besides, it's my day off."

"So it is. So it is. The days all run together for me since Mr. Jordan passed on. Working on any interesting stories?"

"Nothing I can really talk about." He winked at her. "I think I will head on down to the diner and see what they have on special today. You have a good evening, Mrs. Jordan."

He sat the Captain down on the bed and excused himself.

Wanda June's Diner was run by Wanda June Stavros, who greeted him at the counter with a cup of black coffee. She was portly and pink in her kitchen apron, quite the opposite of Mrs. Jordan. An old-timer Munford had never seen before sat a couple of seats down from him, a man of his father's generation, he guessed. The man wore blue denim bib overalls and was pushing around some bits of omelet on his plate.

He looked over at Coldwater and said, "Ever in the service?"

Munford was not ever affiliated with that overly revered organization known as the U.S. military. He looked forward to a day when men were not defined by which war they had been in because maybe by then there won't be any more wars. Hell, he thought, half of the people he knew were still obsessed with a war their grandfathers or great-grandfathers fought, or maybe nobody they knew had even fought in it, but they still thought that war had taken something away from them. On top of that, it had only been a few years since half of Munford's friends had been sent off to Korea, and he'd already been hearing rumors about an operation to stop the spread of communism in some former French colony in Southeast Asia.

"Had some health problems," he replied, a bit too gruffly perhaps. It was a disease called college education. He'd been too young for World War II, but he turned 22 in 1950, the year they started calling people up for Korea. He'd managed to stay in school in Hattiesburg for another couple of years getting a Masters degree in Journalism while interning at the local paper. By then it was the summer of '53, and there was an armistice.

Wanda June said, "What'll you have?" A sweat mustache glistened and highlighted the little bit of dark black stubble she hadn't waxed off yet.

"Look healthy enough to me," the old man said.

"I'll have the special."

"One burger with pimiento cheese coming up."

The grill cook, a scrawny teenager Munford didn't know by name, took a frozen patty out of the bin with a pair of tongs and tossed it onto the sizzling grill. Munford started looking around the counter for some bits of the paper. He'd already read it at the office, of course, but he only wanted a distraction from the old timer. The old man kept staring at him, expecting some sort of response to his implied criticism.

"You know what's wrong with your generation? No initiative."

"Here we go," Coldwater mumbled to himself.

"My daddy," the old man started with a rumble, "was no good. We had a small farm in Blount County, and my daddy did some different jobs from mining coal to mending fences. He got fired a lot because he'd get so drunk that he couldn't work. My brother and I would have to go out and find anything we could to feed the family. There'd been one time we decided we'd take a truck full of coal that Daddy had parked out back and sell it. We didn't know where he had gotten that coal. He might have stolen it, for all we knew. We couldn't do much with it in the rural area where we

51

lived, but we figured if we could get it to Birmingham, we could sell the whole truck load by peddling it in the streets. I was eleven then, and my brother was nine. I could barely reach the pedals on the truck, but I got it going and somehow got to the city. And I tell you what, we had a field day. We sold the coal in buckets to whoever we could find, and had money sticking out of all our pockets by the end of the day. Now that's initiative."

Coldwater's burger arrived on a yellow plate. The old man continued.

"We headed back home, and coming down a big hill, we got stopped by a highway patrolman. We climbed down from the truck all covered in coal dust. The patrolman asked 'Where's your father?' I said, 'He's at home in the bed drunk.' 'Well, who's driving the truck?' the patrolman asked. I said, 'I am, sir. Me and my little brother took it to Birmingham to sell coal so we could get some food for our family.' The patrolman couldn't believe it and didn't know what to do with us. Finally, he let us go with a warning not to do it again. We climbed back in the dump truck and drove on, but stopped on the way home to get groceries for our mama."

Coldwater realized he hadn't touched his hamburger, so he asked Wanda June for a to-go bag. Having packed his lunch into a paper sack, he decided to go into the office for a little bit. Yes, it was his day off, but he had a telephone call to make, and he didn't want to make it from Mrs. Jordan's house where she'd be prying into everything that he said.

As he walked, he began thinking again about the old-timer at the diner, about war and invasions, compromised spaces. He had been to Chicago and to New York, and one thing that stood out to him about the South is that people here were used to having their space. Even in the larger cities, like Birmingham, if you accidentally came within five feet of a person, you were expected to say, "Sorry, pardon me." Even in New Orleans this happened, though not so much in the tourist areas.

Out in the country, though, like where his relatives lived, there was plenty of room for a person to stretch out. Ironically, that's just what his relatives didn't do. They were always on top of each other. And those Mackintosh boys too, though they couldn't help it. He thought about how those boys got around in that awkward embrace. If one were to make up a story about two people conjoined like that, the author would have an easier time if he connected them at the hip or the shoulder—easier to move them around that way, to imagine how they would move, sit, sleep, and shit. Those boys were twisted up in such a discomfit, the complications were just about too much for the mind to process when you were no longer looking at them. When you stopped looking, you almost couldn't think about them properly or see them in your mind's eye. He almost wished he had someone to role play it with him so he could describe the boys better to his readers. It occurred to him that Mrs. Jordan would be all too willing if he were to ask, but he was not going to go near that can of worms.

To get to his office, he had to cross the railroad tracks. Hadn't thought of that before renting the flat from Mrs. Jordan. Always stopped there and looked both ways several times, even if there was no signal. If there was a signal, he'd just turn back and go the other way, try to cross again in a little while. It was another twenty minutes before the next train was due to come through—of course, he had the schedule memorized. But one never knew. It was that thing they used to say about Mussolini. He liked Ike as much as the next guy—well, that wasn't true; he was a yellow dog Democrat since birth. But Ike, with all his problems, wasn't fascist enough to make the trains run on time. Nor was J. P. Coleman or even J. P. Morgan for that matter.

After crossing safely, he entered the offices of the *Tupelo Daily Journal*. It was quiet—only a few copyeditors and type-setters around finishing up tomorrow's edition. He dropped his sack lunch on the corner of the desk and then rooted around in the top drawer until he found what he was looking for—a phone number for Gustie Glassworthy, an old flame of his who was now a librarian in Birmingham. She was a whiz at getting any sort of public documents—birth and death certificates, marriage licenses, construction permits, and newspaper clippings from anywhere in the world.

He had a list of the major characters he knew about so far: Dewey and Lucretia Mackintosh, Dr. Henry Stanhope, Colonel Blake Whitehouse. Might should check on Eddie Van Chukker while he's at it, and that Jimbo Bobo who owns the pond, supposedly.

"Hi dollface, it's Munford Coldwater."

There was silence on the other end of the line for a moment. Somehow, he thought he could hear her pulling her neckline down, or up.

"You calling to make a date? It's been a while."

"I'd love to see you anytime, Miss Glassworthy, but I got a lot of business to take care of here in Mississippi."

"Well, maybe I can come see you then?"

"Got a nosy landlady," he said. "We'll never pull it off."

"You never seem to have any problem pulling it off."

As much as he'd love to sit and bandy flirtatious one-liners across the state line, he really did have to get on with things, so he came right out and told her he needed a favor, maybe several favors. He listed off the names and any other relevant information he had. "And one more thing, before I forget," he said. "See if you can find out what happened at a place called Chorwon during the Korean War."

"That's quite a laundry list. Will that be all, Mr. Coldwater?"

"That'll cover us for now."

"Well, please do let me know when we can get uncovered."

"I'll do that, Glassworthy. Have a good night."

He hung up the phone and leaned back, then realized he'd forgotten his pipe. He'd have to cross the tracks again and go all the way back home before he could finish up his relaxing Sunday off.

NINE

Robert and Wally had been practicing for a few days, but Robert was still having trouble getting his fingers to cooperate with the strings of the fiddle. It also didn't take long to exhaust the few melodies he remembered how to play—a couple of simple reels and a half dozen old folk songs. Wally was trying to teach him some others, some more contemporary things they would hear on the radio like Hank Snow, Johnny Horton, and Marty Robbins because he wanted to sing some songs younger people would know. He also wanted to incorporate some older tunes by Bob Wills and Hank Williams. Wally would have liked to have even done some rock and roll too, but Robert said that was just a noisy trend that wouldn't last. "Besides," he said, "who ever heard of playing rock and roll on a damn fiddle and kick drum?"

They struggled through the songs at about half tempo, the only way Robert could keep up. Wally hummed into his ear with the names of notes. While Robert struggled to make the right sounds materialize, he could feel the hand on his chest, Wally's fingering hand, itching to form into the correct positions, unable to curve. If Robert paid close attention, he could even sense which finger Wally wanted to use on the fingerboard, and this helped him sometimes find the spot.

Working on music brought out an uncharacteristically serious side to Wally. He pitched a fit after Robert messed up "Old Joe Clark" for the fourth time in a row. "Dang it, Bubba," he said. "It's so easy. It's all first position!"

"Settle down, Wally. I'll get the hang of it if you just give me some damn space." That word, *space*, came out of his mouth before he realized what he was saying. Of course, there was never any space. Even the inner space of his mind was overcrowded with fear, exhaustion, and confusion. The space inside his body was filled with the weight of something alien. Whatever extraterrestrial parasite had invaded them kept them both on edge, but Wally was better than Robert was at hiding it. They were both always tired and had to learn quickly to be on guard against lashing out because there was no escaping each other.

They tried the song again. Wally's singing voice was high but had a reedy timbre, and he could yodel just like Jimmy Rogers. When Wally was singing, Robert was supposed to just chop out the chords using double-stops, kind of like if he was playing rhythm guitar. In between the verses, he played the melody. Every sour note made Wally cringe, and Robert fell even farther away from the sweet spot on the string.

"This whole idea is fool ridiculous," he said. "We'll never be able to pull it off. There must be other ways to raise money."

Wally said, "Let's take a break for lunch and then try it again from the top."

He'd naturally assumed the authoritative role of bandleader, but it surprised Robert to hear him speak with such confidence. When they were walking back to the house from the barn, they noticed Munford Coldwater, the reporter from Tupelo, creeping around the front door, peeking in the corner of a window.

Robert yelled to him from across the yard, "Hey you there, Coldwater. What do you want?"

Coldwater's pants were coated in the red dust that his car had kicked up. He looked surprised at first, but he shifted into a smile. "Howdy, boys. You're just who I was hoping to talk with today."

Robert mumbled that the feeling was not mutual. Coldwater waved away the cloud of dirt that still hung in the air between them.

"My name is—"

"I know who you are," Robert said as they got closer to him, refusing to shake the outstretched hand. "It's a name that's easy to remember." Coldwater wasn't particularly any worse than any of the rest of them. Robert just didn't trust him. It was also so annoying telling them all the same things over and over, seeing it in print in so many permutations.

"Look, son," Munford put a hand on Robert's shoulder, the shoulder that was now attached to Wally's shoulder. It was the first time someone had touched it so casually, and it startled him a little. "...er, sons. You've got me all wrong. I'm not just snooping around. I have some relatives who live nearby...in Aliceville. So I was in the neighborhood, and I just thought I'd see how y'all are doing. As a concerned neighbor. See...no notepad."

Robert said, "Well, sir, as you can see, the situation has not improved. Thanks for checking."

"We're going to have surgery as soon as we get the money," Wally volunteered. Robert shook his head.

"Is that right? I was under the impression that the best doctors in Birmingham were unable to do anything for you."

Robert sighed. He couldn't see the harm in telling him about the surgeon in New Orleans. The reporter exhaled a breath of patience.

"Montalto?" Coldwater said. "Don't think I've heard of him."

Wally answered, "Dr. Stanhope recommended him."

Coldwater put his fist to his mouth, stifling a chuckle. "A'ight. If Stanhope's word is good enough for you, I don't suppose I ought to try and talk you out of it. How much money…no, it's none of my business I guess. Never mind. I reckon I'll go down and see if they've found anything in that pond yet. Some joker has been calling me claiming they're hiding aliens down there. I'll be seeing you boys around."

Coldwater climbed into his car, a brown Cadillac Eldorado with huge tailfins, which looked to Robert like a cross between a space ship and a turd. Just before he drove away, he stood up behind the door and said, "I sure would be curious to find out what Montalto's angle is. He's sure to have one." A huge wake of dust cropped up when he roared off down the driveway. Robert covered his mouth and turned his face away.

"Sure is a fancy car for a newspaper reporter," Wally said.

"It's just a matter of priorities, what people choose to spend their money on," Robert said as the air cleared again. "He probably lives in a snake pit and eats bugs."

Later that afternoon, Martha Jean arrived dressed for church in a navy dress and flowery hat, carrying a paper bag full of money. When Robert opened the door, she burst into the kitchen before he had a chance to not invite her. "Praise Jesus, boys. I have very good news. At church this morning, Dr. Stanhope made a stirring speech about your predicament, and look! We took up a collection! Look at all this money!"

Wally said, "You sure look pretty today, Martha Jean. Like a movie star." Wally's crotch was crawling up Robert's back again, just like the last time Martha Jean had been over. Robert decided not to say anything.

Mama came in from the living room to see what all the fuss was about. When she saw the sack of cash, she squealed, ran up and hugged Martha Jean around the neck. "I haven't counted it. I have no idea how much it is," she told them.

They called in Pop, who was confused at first. Nobody ever called him in when Martha Jean was over. He usually just stayed in the fields or in his workshop. For her part, Martha Jean smiled and relaxed her shoulders when she saw him enter. "Dewey," she said. "So nice to see you. You look…fit."

Mama looked down and smoothed invisible wrinkles on her gingham dress. Pop swallowed but didn't return Martha Jean's salutation. To the ceiling he said, "How's Eddie?"

"Augh," she said. "They finally arrested him for harassing those folks down at the pond. But they let him out with a warning after keeping him overnight in the county jail. He needs to get over this whole alien conspiracy nonsense. Boys, you were there. Hasn't the sheriff talked to y'all about being a witness?"

Robert didn't know Eddie had been arrested. "No, ma'am. I mean no, Miss Martha Jean. Nobody told us he was arrested. We only saw him rush the gate and then the guard knocked him down."

Mama interceded. "You were there? What were y'all doing at the pond anyway?"

"Never mind all that," Pop said. "We'll sort it out on our own time. Martha Jean, what's the occasion of your visit?"

"Well, first off, I wanted to make sure y'all could come to our Fourth of July party. Maybe it will take y'all's minds off things. Secondly, there's this."

She showed him what she had brought and then poured the bills and coins out on the kitchen table. Each person started smoothing, stacking, and counting. They soon saw there was nothing larger than a five, and few of those. Many of the one-dollar bills had been crumpled to take up a deceptively large amount of space in the bag. "Lord be," Martha Jean said.

"Hey Bubba, can we sit down on that end?" He asked why, but Wally didn't have to answer. After they moved, he soon saw that Wally had a better angle of Martha Jean's red lips pulsing in and out as she counted to herself. While Robert helped count,

Wally kept craning his neck so he could watch Martha Jean.

"I'll put some tea on," Mama said after counting up the thirty dollars and change that was in front of her. Robert handed over his bundle, which had totaled almost forty. He already knew this money could probably get them to New Orleans but wouldn't go far once they were there.

In the end, Martha Jean totaled up each stack and said with satisfaction, "Bless it. You got two hundred eleven dollars and twenty five cents... Why isn't anyone smiling?"

Wally woke Robert up in the middle of the night. "Bubba, I want some water."

"Water? I'm exhausted, Wally. Go to sleep."

Robert had not been sleeping though. He'd been lying in bed thinking about all the ways in which the hand, Wally's hand, manifested its weight on him. Those past couple of weeks, it was frequently on his mind. In the best times, it was a benign embrace, and Robert could almost forget it until Wally opened his mouth, and so these moments tended to be when Wally was sleeping, when Robert wished he too could sleep, was trying to sleep, or was just waking up. Other times, it was like a small animal, a squirrel or chipmunk maybe, sitting on his chest making rabid agitated noises. Sometimes it was a load, like firewood, so heavy he couldn't see over it, and he always felt like they both might be on the verge of tumbling over, spilling over each other like cats wrestling.

When they were walking, sometimes Wally would get distracted and forget for a moment that they were attached, and he'd try to wander off toward something that had caught his eye, and then sometimes they *would* trip each other up and fall over, scrambling confused in the dirt until Robert could get Wally to stop and regain his composure so they could coordinate standing up again.

"C'mon, Bubba. I really want a glass of water. I can't sleep."

"Okay, okay. I know if you can't sleep, I'll never get to sleep either."

In the living room, Mama and Pop were sitting on the sofa, asleep on each other's shoulders. It made Robert smile to see Mama sleeping. White noise hissed from the Philco in the corner.

The latest issue of *Life* magazine was spread out on the coffee table in front of them, Zsa Zsa Gabor "and her famous ghost" on the cover. Robert didn't remember ever seeing his parents like this before. Pop was not a man who showed affection easily. All the work they were doing to keep the family going must have completely worn them down, and Robert felt a wave of guilt about this, though he knew it was nothing he could help.

The improbable love story of his parents passed through his head like a whisper. Mama had told it to the boys many times.

She had been an idealistic, bullheaded, and rebellious student at the women's college over in Columbus. Pop had inherited land and knew how to work it. One day, Mama was sitting out on the quad reading a book, Pop walked by wearing blue jeans, a cowboy hat, and no shirt. He told her he'd be back in an hour and take her to lunch, and then he went home, showered and changed his clothes. When he came back, in the same old pickup that he still drove, she was waiting on him. So he took her to a diner downtown and that was that. Her family lived down on the coast, near Mobile, and her parents thought she could have married a hundred men more refined than that brash, overconfident, bad-mannered, foul-mouthed dirt farmer Dewey Mackintosh from Nowhere, Alabama. She didn't listen, and the two eloped to Pensacola. Mama's family completely disowned her, cut off contact. Even after Uncle Sam sent Pop away to the Philippines for two years, she had nobody.

The improbable part was that they still claimed to love each other, at least according to Mama. Perhaps they did. Robert wasn't sure if he believed in such things. Maybe he loved Edwina. He supposed it didn't much matter anymore if he did, though, since he'd never have her now, not like this. There would be no sitting next to her in a movie theater or driving her through the countryside. If she tried to put her arms around him, she would end up holding his little brother, the worst possible chaperone. He couldn't help but be in the way at all times.

Wally was about to say something; Robert could tell by the way he drew in his breath, so he pre-emptively turned his head and shushed him. He whispered, "Go slow. Try to get to the kitchen without waking them."

They brushed by a lamp that sat on an end table near the doorway, and Wally caught it as it teetered next to his hip. Their parents didn't stir. Once they were past that end table, all that separated the kitchen from the living room where Mama and Pop were sleeping was a stretch of beige carpeting that the Mackintoshes had bought from Sears during one of their more prosperous years after the war.

Finally at the sink, Robert reached for a glass from the shelf, but Wally pulled all of a sudden and the glass slipped out of his fingers. It cracked on the linoleum counter, and the dogs outside started in. Mama sat up with a startled gasp in the other room.

"Sorry, Mama. We'll clean it up. Go on back to sleep," Robert said. Then to Wally, "What the hell did you do that for?"

"I got scared by something, but I guess it was just my reflection in the window."

Robert looked to the window and saw nothing but stars.

TEN

When Coldwater got back to his office, it was after six, and the night shift was bustling to get out the evening's edition. He rang up Glassworthy again.

"I have another name for you."

"Why, Mr. Coldwater, what's wrong with my current name?"

"You know what I mean, Miss Glassworthy. Let's skip the antics."

"Why, Mr. Coldwater, you are in such a rush. Hello, Miss Glassworthy. How's your day going?"

She went on like that for another couple of minutes until he finally interrupted her to apologize for his abruptness and remind her of the reason he called. It was the quack in New Orleans, Montalto. Glassworthy said she would add it to the list and hoped to get back to him the next day.

One by one, the lamplights scattered throughout the office were extinguished, finally leaving Munford alone in the gold-white glow of his own cantilevered desk lamp, the round brass canopy of which resembled the flying saucers that had populated so many tabloid front pages in recent years, especially since Mr. Welles' radio prank and more so still since Sputnik. What was it about that glowing disk shape that made it such a ready symbol of the unknown? He began doodling circles on a legal pad. Circles within circles. He lit his pipe, sat back, and gazed at the diffuse particles of dust dancing in the beam of light, like spermatozoa under a microscope, doing the boogie-woogie of destiny. Circles within circles.

As if entranced, he started jotting his thoughts down on the page. The paper would never let him get away with using the word *spermatozoa*. Too racy for Tupelo. Embers in the pipe burned red and popped as he drew air in and then blew a cloud of smoke through the dusty lamplight. It was possible he would never know what happened to those boys out there at Bobo Pond.

Munford paced the dark room, continuing to talk to himself, filling the room with the pungent smoke from his pipe. He picked up a paper from a stack by the door, tomorrow's early edition, and returned to his desk to thumb through it until he quietly nodded off to sleep in his office chair somewhere around 4 a.m.

ELEVEN

Their first performance was to be in Columbus, Mississippi, a trial run close to home, only about a ten-mile trip. Mama didn't come. It was the day before Independence Day, a Friday, and if it went well, they'd maybe try playing at the Van Chukkers' party on Saturday. Pop had explained to the boys that they'd only take day trips at first, but there were plenty of towns within a three- or four-hour drive, including Meridian, Philadelphia, Birmingham, Tuscaloosa, and Tupelo. And there were lots of smaller towns in between where they might be able to perform in the square, if they timed it right. Later, they could probably make it to Jackson, Biloxi, Oxford, Memphis, maybe even Nashville or Atlanta without too much trouble, and if they could convince someone to put them up for the night, they could extend their reach farther. Pop had already made improvements to the boys' seat in the back of the truck in anticipation of future travels. He'd sanded it down and added cushions. The final extravagance was a camper top Pop acquired from a junkyard, which he affixed to the truck to keep them out of the weather, with windows on the sides and back so they could see out.

Driving into Columbus along Highway 82, the clock tower at the women's college greeted them from behind the wrought iron gates. This was where Mama had gone to school briefly before marrying Pop. Robert tried not to think about the two thousand girls just a couple of years older than him who inhabited those dormitories. A gaggle of students in their social club uniforms had formed on the lawn of the school. They frequently came into Columbus to get supplies or groceries, and on a previous trip, Mama had tried to explain the idea of the social clubs to Robert.

Each social club, she said, had a theme: the Highlanders wore plaid skirts and sashes, the Jesters wore harlequin suits, and so forth. Unsurprisingly, the Highlanders was the group Mama joined before she dropped out. There were others called Lockhearts, Revelers, Troubadours, and the self-consciously mysterious Blacklist. Robert had seen them all before at one time or another. Even though she participated, Mama had thought it was silly. They all looked to Robert like they belonged in a circus. Then again, he supposed he and Wally looked like they belonged in a circus these days too.

The girls were standing in homogenous groups singing songs at each other. Between the girls' costumes, their high pitched singing voices, the uncannily green lawn, and the spooky old brick school buildings, the ritual had an eerie resonance. Each club had specific songs they would sing, and they would compete. Sometimes they would sing all at once, each trying to be louder and drown out the other. At other times, there were songs that one club would sing in response to songs from another club. Robert didn't really understand the point, but the girls seemed to have a good time.

It was nearing lunch time, and Robert was concerned that some of those girls would find their way downtown, a few blocks west of the campus, where they were planning to set up shop for the afternoon.

"I hope all those girls aren't coming downtown for lunch," Robert said.

"I sure hope they do," Pop said. "Those are our customers."

Downtown Columbus had two main drags, Main Street and South 5th Street. Pop decided it would be in their best interest to perform as near as possible to the corner where the two streets met. He wore what he considered to be his nicest and least farmer-like outfit, a clean white shirt and string tie with brown denim pants and a white felt cowboy hat. For security, Pop kept his Colt Python pistol holstered to his hip and one of his old shotguns locked up inside the truck.

They parked in front of the Princess Theater, a movie house that had been around since the 1920s. Robert saw Pop taking a long swig from a jar that had been hidden under his seat as they set up and tuned. A few people were going in for the matinee.

Most of the people going into the theater appeared to be girls from the college with their buzz cut dates from the Air Force base ten miles to the north. Robert wondered if the soldiers guarding the pond were from there, if word had been passed around the base about what happened at the pond, if everybody who would come back out of the theater in two hours and see them would know that these were the boys that got stuck together by the fireball from the sky.

Pop helped the boys disembark from the truck bed and brought them their instruments. Wally had his kick drum and a tambourine. Robert tuned up the fiddle, glistening white from rosin dust he'd kicked up through many hours of rehearsal over the past month. Already, a few people were starting to gather around. Pop placed a coffee can in front of them with a taped on sign that said "TIPS" and turned to greet the small crowd.

"Howdy folks," he said a little too quietly for anybody to hear really. "Please, er, gather 'round. These boys want to share some tunes with you." He stammered as people continued walking by, many of them probably having heard about the boys already and deliberately trying not to stare at them.

Without waiting for the crowd, Wally counted off and then launched into "Billy in the Low Ground," banging away at his kick drum and keeping a rhythmic chord on a harmonica. Robert froze up. His bow was in position, but he couldn't move. He put Wally's words out of his mind. It wasn't that. He was simply paralyzed. Eight measures went by with the steady beat. Several young couples were watching, edging closer, growing in layers.

Sixteen measures passed.

Beyond their meager and expectant audience, Edwina Hunter was holding hands with a long-faced boy Robert didn't recognize. She was wearing a pink dress with polka dots. Her date almost dragged her away, but she stopped him, her head at a curious angle, her mouth open. Robert wished he was the one holding her hand. He wanted to run and grab her away from the boy, but he couldn't move. There was an enormous bloodsucker on his back playing a kick drum.

Thirty two measures. A couple of people walked away.

Pop turned to Robert and said, "You can do this, son." He pivoted back to face the crowd and tipped his hat toward them. "Just getting warmed up, folks. Come on up."

Edwina waved and mouthed, "Hi, Robert."

Robert took a deep breath and on the next count of eight, he squeaked through the melody. He was a little behind the beat and played a lot of wrong notes, but he got through it. On the reprise, playing the same melody again, he got it a little closer. Edwina tried to dance a little with her date, but he stood rigid, uninterested, impatient. Sweat dripped off Robert's forehead and made puddles along the line of his shoulder piece. After the first song was done to smattering applause, a few people put coins in the bucket and moved on. Pop thanked each of them, shook all their hands, a weak grin plastered on his face. Some others donated but stayed for an encore, which Robert was not sure he'd be able to pull off. His entire body was drenched and trembling.

The boys waited a couple of minutes while Robert tried to pull himself together. Another couple gave up and walked away. Edwina and her date were still there, a little closer now, though her facial expression had not particularly changed. Robert wanted to ask her what she was gaping at. He was still the same person she'd compared to Paul Newman just a few months ago. Just now Paul Newman was stuck to Howdy Doody.

Wally suggested in a stage whisper that they do something where he sings, like maybe "Hey Good Looking," a song everybody knew. Robert would have to play the double-stops, which were harder on his awkward fingers, but he'd only have to play three of them and get them in the right order. Plus the tempo wasn't as fast as on the reels. So he nodded, positioned his fingers on the D and F#, and waited for Wally's count.

The performance was not too bad. Wally's voice was crisp and clear. Robert was late on a couple of changes, but it didn't seem like anyone noticed. It was easy enough that he got his confidence up a little bit. A few people clapped and sang along, and another four or five people joined the onlookers. Edwina twirled and laughed, her arms in the air, while her date looked on with his arms crossed. Her dancing introduced a ripple in space between her body and Robert's, like a stone cast into water. It emanated from her, growing in wavelength as it moved outward, hitting Robert with a splash and a jolt, just as the tune reached its denouement.

They were encouraged to play a third song. Wally called for "Old Joe Clark," and Robert went along. However, every time the refrain came around where he was supposed to play the melody, the song fell apart a little bit. Wally kept it going by humming and keeping the drumbeat. At one point, he even tried singing the names of the notes Robert was supposed to play, like he had done in rehearsal, but it all was going by too fast—too fast to keep up with but also terrifyingly slow. Every note Robert did play sounded wrong to him and seemed to drag on and on. Before the song was half over, he looked up and saw that Edwina had left.

At the end, his heart was kicking him in the chin. The white light in his chest flared up as much as the July sun above. A few people were still standing there, but Wally told them they were going to take a break. The last of them finally left after a couple of minutes. Robert once thought he saw Munford Coldwater lurking around down the block but decided it was an illusion. When the last coin clinked into the bucket, Robert told Pop that he didn't think he could get through another one. Not today.

Pop said, "Alright, son. Alright. You did good. We'll get there." He was clutching the tips can against his chest.

The money stayed in the coffee can until they got home and counted it, about twenty-five dollars. Pop got the old bass drum from the barn where he was keeping the money from the Baptists. "We gonna fill that up by the time we get to Nawlins," he said.

Robert refused to go to the party and try another performance. He didn't even want to get out of bed. Mama and Pop were both looming, trying to coax him out. He had embarrassed himself in front of Edwina Hunter, and he wasn't quite sure how life would go on after that. Her dancing, he knew, could be interpreted as a compliment by someone else, but he had seen that vacant stare. He knew she was just making fun. Her dancing was ironic, blasé. She was not moved by his performance but just bored and trying to entertain her horse-faced date.

"Pop said if it went well, we'd try it again today. It didn't go well."

Wally, slightly muffled by a pillow, said, "Aw, you were just nervous."

"We made good money for a day's work," Pop said. "At this rate, we could have the money in a few months, but we got to keep at 'er."

"I need a day to recover. I can't face that again right away." He wasn't sure he would get over it that quickly, but he knew Pop wouldn't be patient with him much longer than that.

"There were some rough spots," Wally said. "I guess we should take a day to run through those before we go out again." Robert was grateful Wally knew better than to push him too quickly. He'd seen what happened, had probably felt it himself through the electrical impulse of whatever it was that connected the two of them.

Mama said, "Well y'all don't have to play if you don't want to, but you can still go with me over to the party."

The Van Chukkers' annual Fourth of July party was their little community's social event of the year, if there could be such a thing. Eddie's cousin the bootlegger did so much business that day, he paid off the sheriff to turn a blind eye.

"Mama, I don't want to see nobody."

"ANYbody. Well, you've got until late afternoon to think about it. But Eddie is roasting a whole hog, and I made a peach cobbler with some of Martha Jean's peaches."

Wally perked up at the name, not to mention the spread that would be available at the party. "Come on, Bubba. We should go. A whole hog!"

Robert relented, and they arrived at the Van Chukkers' house in the early afternoon. The wide yard in front of their home place was already abuzz with people. Martha Jean had apparently invited everybody in her church, every neighbor within ten miles, and half of the town of Columbus. Two picnic tables, joined end to end, held casserole dishes, trays full of fried chicken and fish, roasted or grilled vegetables, pies, and cakes. Eddie Van Chukker tended a large wooden box twenty yards or so back, which must have held the hog. Hickory chips burned in a steel barrel next to the box. While Robert was looking around to see if there was anyone he recognized, particularly anybody he might want to avoid, Wally started pulling him toward the food tables.

Wally handed him a plate, upon which he began stacking edibles. "You want anything?" he said.

"Nah. I'm not hungry."

"I'll get some extra in case you change your mind. Plenty to go 'round."

Robert was still looking everywhere for signs of Edwina and for hiding places if he should happen to see her. He noted Martha Jean, wearing a red, white, and blue dress, talking to some other made-up ladies. Doctor Stanhope was sitting under a tree with a chicken leg. Mama and Pop were merging into the crowd. Robert wished he could merge in as well, to disappear into anonymity. A few other people from around the county were there. He was glad that Edwina Hunter wasn't one of them.

Eddie was holding court to a group of five or six that had gathered around the smoker. "I'm telling you, I saw the same thing in Korea back in '51, outside Chorwon in the Iron Triangle."

As they lingered around near the picnic tables, a few people said awkward hellos; a couple said they were praying for the family. Most people ignored them, though Robert couldn't shake the feeling of being stared at from distant eyes. He watched as jugs of shine and bonded whiskey were passed discretely between small groups.

"We were encamped on the side of a mountain above a village that we had cleared out earlier and were now bombarding with aerial artillery. To our right, we saw a large object, glowing orange like a jack-o-lantern, wafting down. It went down all the way to the village and it sat unharmed right in the middle of artillery explosions. Stayed there about an hour, and then it started coming back up the mountain toward us, now turning from orange to blue green. A brilliant, pulsating light."

Stanhope was among those talking and passing around a bottle. Someone asked the doctor if he'd ever been married, and he said, "No, no I wasn't." He was toeing the ground and rubbing his neck, and though he had no way of knowing the specifics, Robert knew there was some tragic love story in Stanhope's past. His parents too struck him as tragic, though they put a good face on it. Because of their rebellious love, the family was cut off from Mama's relatives who otherwise might be able to help them out of this mess they were in. Pop had no living relatives. And his parents' relationship anyway was little more than a charade. Everybody knew something had gone on between Pop and Martha Jean a few years ago. Even Eddie knew, but everyone pretended it wasn't so.

Mama now was deep in conversation with none other than Munford Coldwater, who looked ridiculous in a green checked short-sleeve shirt. It was no wonder he always wore that ill-fitting suit; he was even worse off in casual wear. She was surely leaning in that close to him because the noise of the party made it hard to hear. Papa was all the way on the other side of the yard with some other farmers, probably talking seed and fertilizer.

"I hope I never fall in love," Robert said. Wally had a mouthful of biscuit and didn't say anything for a few seconds.

"Why do you say that? Because you're stuck on me?"

Wally's tone was hard to read. Robert wasn't sure if he was being facetious or if he was actually insulted. He decided he didn't care and answered lugubriously. "It always ends terribly," was all he could get out.

"Is this because of that girl in Columbus? Damn, Bubba. She's just a girl."

She wasn't the only girl in the world, not the first he had liked nor the first that had liked him. But she wasn't just a girl. She was supposed to have been his summer romance. It was as if it had been written in the pages of one of those books Mama always read and re-read. It was fate, and you can't change fate.

The hog was unboxed, and Eddie stood over it, wearing an apron, passing out chunks of flesh to anyone who lined up, still talking to anyone who would listen. "We fired on it with armor-piercing bullets. You could hear the metallic pang when the bullets bounced off. It was descending down on us, and it had a sound like diesel locomotives revving up. Next thing we knew, it was attacking us, emitting a ray in pulses. Kind of like a search light. You'd only see it when it came at you, and then you would feel this burning, tingling sensation all through your body."

Robert was feeling a little better by then and took a slab of shoulder. It was the first meat he'd eaten in days, and it tasted like a dream. The protein gave him a burst of energy that he hadn't felt since before the fireball.

As it got dark, someone started a small bonfire. A couple of people brought out banjos and guitars and started singing. Wally's hand on Robert's chest was itching to play also. When a jug ended up in Robert's hands, he took a big swig. Wally said, "Bubba!"

"Hush up," Robert said. The shine tasted sour and burned as it went down. He took another swallow, and felt his head swim a little. He began to relax, and the music sounded better. Whenever the jug came back around, he took a sip and passed it on, enjoying the music and the heat of the fire. However, after a while and a few more swigs of shine, his stomach started to turn.

"Uh oh. Wally, we've got to get to a bathroom quick." This was going to be a problem, as they had not yet tried this except at home. The easiest way was when Wally was going and Robert could sit on his lap. When Robert had to go, it was more difficult. They'd pulled the toilet away from the wall so Wally could squat down behind it.

Instead of taking the risk of finding adequate quarters inside the house, they stuffed a few paper napkins in their pockets, crossed a barren field and went a little ways into the woods. As soon as they were out of sight of the party, Robert dropped his trousers. Wally barely had time to get out of the way.

When they came out of the woods, they passed Eddie and Pop in the field and stopped to watch what they were doing. They'd filled an iron cauldron with fireworks—mostly bottle rockets but also some Roman candles and other sundry homemade explosives. They stacked the fireworks well above the rim of the cauldron, until there was a tower of them nearly four feet tall. It looked like something from a cartoon, but it also looked dangerous. And it was. Pop poured kerosene down a funnel in the middle of the tower, and then he set the whole thing on top of a tree stump. Eddie took a shovel full of burning coals from the fire, dumped the coals down the funnel Pop had made, and then ran. They both told Robert and Wally to run too.

They ran, but with difficulty, and they tripped over themselves and tumbled away from the blast of light. For a quarter hour or more, the explosion of light flowed like a white river into the night sky, accompanied by an orchestra of whistles and booms. Watching the lights shoot up into the sky and then descend on the horizon was to Robert like a thousand little fireballs coming after him again, and he had to turn his face away. When the memories of the pond faded away into the noise, his chest warmed under the gun powder smell as papery debris rained down over them. When the last rocket shot away, the tree trunk that the cauldron sat on was red with flames that seemed to originate deep underground.

TWELVE

While the sun sank behind the peach orchard, Eddie watched from his front porch, thinking the sun resembled a giant peach itself, a peach god. A peach he had picked that very morning sat submerged in the Mason jar of shine he held in his lap. Martha Jean was in the back hanging linens, and the pot roast would be ready in about an hour. It was a perfect moment in a perfect day. He looked forward to after dinner when he would write more letters about the secret space alien project going on down at Jimbo Bobo's pond. Bobo was a senile old goat, a recluse. But Eddie knew what he saw that afternoon when the fireball fell out of the sky. He'd seen things like that before, and he was the only one around there that knew the truth, or would admit to it anyway. People acted like they were humoring him, listening to his spaceman stories.

Yes, he knew they were making fun the second he turned his back. Not even Martha Jean believed him. They would find out in time what the truth was.

When he saw that fireball, it took him back there, to Korea—the lights and sulphuric odor, the sickness of the sound. That "police action," that forgotten war. When they used to say the South would rise again, they didn't think it would be South Korea we would be defending—and doing that right alongside both Yankees and Negroes, Brits, Aussies, even Ethiopians. "But we did it," he heard himself say out loud. Pushed them back to the 38th parallel. He was in what the newspapers called the "Iron Triangle," near Chorwon. He regretted that he'd started thinking about it again because then the terror of it all came roaring back to him relentlessly. The mountains were before them, scarred and scabbed purple. From their trenches, they surgically attacked the communist disease with artillery, after first warning the villagers in the valley to evacuate. The mountains were like those he'd seen as a child in north Georgia and western North Carolina, worn down to round nubs by the centuries. Like the Appalachians, the mountains were called hills, and like those Appalachian hills, they were confounded by spirits, which Eddie believed had come from far across the universe. Those spirits had been hiding in those hills since before the dawn of man.

People he grew up with in the hills had seen things like that, experienced things like that. There were alleged abductions and saucer sightings, so he knew those stories. But it wasn't until Korea when he saw for himself. And then he saw it again. And felt it. Still had a bad leg from that night in Chorwon. A piece of that bright light had struck him and stayed in him, though doctors continued to claim there was nothing there, nothing wrong with that leg. No shrapnel, no nerve damage. But the light was there, and he could feel it burning. He knew also, though no doctor would admit it, that was the reason why he and Martha Jean had never been able to have children.

It was on his way back home from the orchard that he saw the fireball, a bright orange sphere of light that seemed to set the clouds on fire. He had run limping into the house and told Martha Jean about it, but even she didn't understand him or believe him when she did come to understand what he meant. Martha Jean then had called the Mackintoshes next door and other people they knew, and others had seen it. Then they found out what had happened to the Mackintosh boys. "Do you believe me now?" he had said to her. She believed it was something, but not what he said it was. For Martha Jean, this all had to do with God and the Devil or some such. He had never seen God or the Devil, but he had seen the lights.

From here out, letter writing would be his main form of protest. Getting himself arrested, it seemed, had gotten him only a concussion from the rifle butt and bruises on his wrists from the handcuffs. And he was writing to everyone, from President Eisenhower on down. *Dear so and so*, he would start off. *A man in your position will obviously be aware…* or *Because events regarding national security should naturally be brought to your attention.* He would hold off until at least the third paragraph before mentioning aliens, extraterrestrials, flying saucers, or anything of that ilk. After all, he was no crackpot. He had to establish his credibility, and he did so by recognizing that he understood men with important jobs do not want their time wasted with cracked theories. His concerns were all well-documented, and he kept copies of all his letters in a safe deposit box. *The most recent event that has caught my attention is practically in my own back yard*, he would say. He would not say outright what they were covering up there at the pond, but he would give enough hints to let them know that he knew what they were up to. He was going to start reaching out to the press soon too. He had left several messages for that reporter who had been coming around. It was only a matter of time. Writing, keeping it all on paper—that was the way to go.

He hadn't slept too well in the county jail either—yet another thing that reminded him of Korea. It was perhaps lucky, he supposed, that Colonel Whitehouse had put him in the hands of the sheriff instead of shipping him off to some secret military prison overseas. Such places existed. And the sheriff had been kind enough to let him out in time for his annual Fourth of July party because it was something the entire community looked forward to all year. Whitehouse probably hadn't liked that, but he'd given up his jurisdiction on the matter.

After setting down his shine, he pulled tobacco from his bib and rolled a cigarette. And those boys next door, he thought...He looked over at their dry, brown front lawn across the property line and thought, Mackintosh can't even grow grass this year. No wonder the cotton was so low. No telling how those boys would end up, but it didn't look good for them. They carried something with them, something from the fireball crash, a light, like what he had in his leg, and that's what fused them together. There was something there worth looking into more, if only he had an idea of how to go about it. Maybe if he could get that reporter on his side...

Eddie would never wish any harm to Dewey Mackintosh or his boys. That confusion, that unpleasantness that he heard about when he got back from the war, was just people talking. His father had bought the orchard from Dewey's father back during the Depression. Dewey was like an older brother to him. Eddie was grateful Dewey helped look after Martha Jean while he was away. Dewey's wife had dismissed the rumors, and so had he.

The cigarette burned down to a nub, and he discarded it into an old coffee can, resumed sipping his peach-infused shine. Two jeeps roared up the road kicking up dirt and turned into his driveway. Colonel Whitehouse sat regally in the back seat of one, accompanied by a uniformed guard with an M-60. The other car held two more guards with M-60s and a driver who probably only had a sidearm. Eddie put his shine on the ground between his legs

75

and picked up his shotgun.

"Relax, Eddie. I just want to talk to you."

"You always bring three apes with M-60s to tea time?"

"Only a precaution. I had a feeling you wouldn't be happy to see me." Whitehouse was still in the jeep, but he jumped out then and signaled to his men to stay. "How was your party on Saturday? I heard your hog was well received."

"Who did you know there?" Eddie said, feeling himself panic a little. He didn't appreciate being spied on, but he knew it was inevitable as long as Whitehouse and his people were still around.

Whitehouse smiled. "It's the event of the season. I couldn't go anywhere without someone talking about it."

"People talk too much," Eddie said.

"All the same, we'd appreciate it if you would come with us."

"Come with you?" Whitehouse was reaching out his hand, as if to shake. As he was being led away, Eddie thought he saw Martha Jean peeking through the curtains.

THIRTEEN

Pop planned their route to the coast with a large Cities Service road map of the southeast spread out over the kitchen table. Robert was mesmerized by the simple beauty of the map itself, all the blue and red lines that led from one little white circle to another. There was a kind of magic in having this view of the world that he had never noticed before. He looked for their little white circle in Pickens County. He saw Gordo, Reform, Ethelsville, Aliceville, even Macedonia. The little road off Highway 82, a mile from the state line, was not on the map. Their farm, the Van Chukkers' orchard, and Jimbo Bobo's pond circled by Whitehouse's trailers and equipment did not even exist according to the cartographers of Cities Service.

The plan that Pop laid out was to make their way down to the coast, playing music on the way to raise money. When they got to Mobile, they would try to talk to Mama's family. From there, they would travel to New Orleans to see this Dr. Montalto. Whatever they did after that would depend on what the doctor said and how much money they still needed. Instead of taking the most direct route south, Pop decided they'd go through Tuscaloosa, Birmingham, and Montgomery to hit all the major cities on the way to Mobile, to maximize their profit. Martha Jean would take care of the dogs while they were gone.

The Mackintoshes easily found the downtown area in Tuscaloosa. The main street was flanked with huge department stores on each side, F. W. Woolworth's on one and S. H. Kress on the other. They parked at the end of a long block near the courthouse and the Bama Theater, and the boys prepared themselves on the corner. Robert thought about the previous experience in Columbus; at least here he wouldn't be likely to run into anyone he knew. It was a warm, clear day, and a lot of people were out—college students and business people alike.

While they played, Mama sat in the truck either sewing or reading a book. The performance was better than their first, if only because Robert didn't freeze up. There was still quite a bit of fumbling. They stopped after an hour because they'd exhausted their bodies as well as their repertoire. Wally's singing voice was straining, and Robert's arms weighed as much as steers. They rested for half an hour and then played a little more, but that was all they could do. Fifty dollars and some change came out of the coffee can and into Pop's shirt pocket.

Robert had been to Tuscaloosa the year before with classmates from his school for a visit to the Natural History Museum on the campus of the University of Alabama. The expanses of flat green grass and stately old buildings had impressed Robert. Perhaps, if he and Wally ever got out of this mess, he would come here to study land management or something similar that would help him contribute to the family business.

The main room of the museum had been a large vestibule presided over by the bones of what looked like an enormous swimming lizard, about fifty feet long. "That's just what it was," a museum guide said. "Millions of years ago, Alabama was covered in water, and these creatures ruled the area. It's called a Basilosaurus or king lizard."

Robert imagined it in Bobo's pond, this ancient monster floating within inches of their feet while they innocently splashed about. He didn't like thinking about it. It was bad enough to think about water moccasins, much less that giant beast.

As they counted their money and prepared to drive on to Birmingham, Mama said, "I was thinking while I was sitting here listening to you play. Do you know that old song 'Stars Fell on Alabama'? Y'all should learn that one." She sang a few lines, and the boys agreed it would be a fitting tune.

The only time any of them had been to Birmingham was on that visit to the hospital about a month before. Pop had rigged the canopy on the back of the truck so the boys could sit up and see out from their specially made seat. They could see only what they had just left behind and not where they were headed, but both boys sat quietly captivated by the scenery unfolding behind them. On the way out of Tuscaloosa in the late morning, they passed the Moonwinx Motel with the giant neon moon on its sign that actually winked. Even though it wasn't the first time they had driven this route, the sites along the highway struck Robert as exotic. While they wound their way through the back roads of Bessemer, they passed the curious Wigwam Motor Court with its tee-pee shaped rooms, then the refineries and furnaces, and in the distance the statue of Vulcan, Roman god of the forge, watching over the city from the top of Red Mountain. Finally, they came into Birmingham proper, with its huge stores and impressive movie theaters. The department stores were the same ones as those in Tuscaloosa but even larger. The art deco Alabama Theatre dwarfed the old Princess Theater back in Columbus. Birmingham was a city of giants.

Pop drove around until he found a large park downtown where many people were congregated in bright-colored clothes and church-going hats. Wally was so distracted by all the new sights and sounds, it was all Robert could do to keep him focused enough to get from the truck to the corner of the park without running into anything.

In the distance, enormous chimneys poured black smoke into the air. Robert rosined up his bow and set into "Angeline the Baker" while Wally pounded on that kick drum in time. The fiddle sound cut through the air that afternoon like never before, clear and effortless as if it were Robert's natural voice singing out. The jaunty melody caught the attention of several passersby who formed a semicircle around them. Hands clapped and feet stomped. When the melody came around again, Wally started bleating out the words:

Angeline the baker lives in our village green
The way I always loved her beats all you ever seen.

They went through all six verses, each interspersed by a fiddle solo. Wally had his eyes closed and sang out to the sky:

Angeline the baker; her age is forty-three.
I bought her candy by the peck, and she won't marry me.

Not a bad warm up tune, Robert thought after they wound it down. A pretty young white lady passing by put a dollar in the jar, raising his hopes and confidence. The girl's red hair was cut short and mussed as if she'd just taken off a hat, and she wore a white dress with green flowers. Robert watched her watch them as they launched into Robert's previous nemesis, "Old Joe Clark." The tune went by with only some minor errors, so they then tried some other old-timey standards. The girl's eyes were focused on

Robert's fingers, those usually awkward, stubby fingers that today only could dance.

She kissed a five-dollar bill before putting it into the coffee can, never losing eye contact with Robert. After another long gaze, the girl traipsed away. Robert thought about Edwina Hunter, and he felt a little bit guilty being intrigued by another girl. But Edwina had gone to the Princess Theatre with that other boy, so he figured he must have missed his chance with her. He wondered if he'd ever have a chance again—with any girl.

Lying in a motel bed later that night, he couldn't help but think of the red-haired girl who had watched them that afternoon and the strange effect she seemed to have on him. As he drowsed, he thought he could hear her voice, softly singing:

My heart beat like a hammer.
My arms wrapped around you tight.
Stars fell on Alabama last night.

He had never heard her speak, but in this half dream her voice was as dark and sultry as the July air outside.

In the middle of the night, he made Wally get up so he could get a handkerchief and put it by the bed, adding that he was feeling a little bit of hay fever. When Wally was snoring away again, he then relieved the pressure that had built up in his loins with a few gentle tugs. It didn't take much. He tucked the soiled handkerchief under the mattress in case he needed it again later.

The words from the song resonated in his skull, churned over and over in his mind as he drifted in and out of sleep. The heart beating like a hammer. The arms wrapped around him. Wally's arm. His heart.

Driving south, the skyline of Birmingham soon faded into quarries where iron ore and marble had been chewed out of the earth and then into verdant hills dotted with cows. The land flattened and chameleoned from red to brown to green until they reached Montgomery, where all was mud and concrete. The state capital was small compared to Birmingham, more like downtown Tuscaloosa but without the vibrancy or the charm. The capital building itself, which they had seen in passing, was a pristine Greek temple, kept bright and shining since before the Civil War.

Downtown was more faded and gray but just as lost in time. Everything looked a hundred years old, and the air had the odor of must and mothballs. Lawyers scuttled from their offices to the courthouse and back again. Nobody stopped to watch when the boys set up to play.

Before they'd finished even one song, a police officer interrupted and said, "Y'all can't do this here. Move along. You're disrupting foot traffic."

The boys submissively backed away toward the truck, but Pop edged up closer to the officer. His voice was calm and clear, and he spoke slowly, with tense control.

"This is a public sidewalk. We got as much right to stand here as anywhere else."

Mama had come from the truck by now, having noticed the squabble. "Dewey, what's going on here?"

"Pop," Robert said. "It isn't worth it. Nobody's stopping anyway. Let's find another spot. Or just move on to the next town." Pop could look physically intimidating with his wiry frame and stern face, though he probably wouldn't follow through. Robert was afraid the cop would misunderstand. He could already see the officer eyeing Pop's holstered gun, watching his hands.

The officer said, "Sir, you should listen to your son. Ma'am, is this your husband? Perhaps you could convince him…"

"Now listen here," Pop said, getting more aggressive. "Unless you can tell us just what it is we're doing wrong, all I'm convinced of is that you think this sailor suit you're wearing gives you the right to make up rules. We ain't in nobody's way. If we were blocking the way, how could two dozen people have just walked past us?"

"We've got enough trouble around here. We don't need some freak show causing a ruckus downtown in the middle of the workday."

Pop punched the cop, knocking him flat on the ground. Before anything else could happen, two other officers came out of the shadows and had Pop in handcuffs. They took his Colt away too. Robert had never seen Pop actually hit anybody. Even when the boys had been punished for something when they were younger, whether it was talking back or refusing to do some chore, the worst they got was a couple of hard swats on the backside with Pop's belt. Robert was still dazed with disbelief when Pop was pushed into a squad car. Mama was clinging to him, begging the officers not to take him away. "Back off, ma'am. Don't make us take you in too."

When the car drove off, Mama was left sitting on the sidewalk gasping helplessly for breath, her asthmatic lungs refusing to take in needed oxygen. Robert and Wally helped her up and walked her to the truck where she quickly pulled her Benzedrine inhaler from her purse and took a long hit from it. Afterward, she hugged them both. Wiping the tears from their eyes and then from her own she said, "Let's hope they let him off with a fine and that we have enough money to pay it."

They spent the rest of the afternoon on a wooden bench in the smoky gray police station ignoring the curious stares of passersby. At the very least, they were told, Pop would spend the night in jail. They could hope for a quick hearing and a light sentence, but assaulting a police officer was a serious offense, so they had no idea what to expect.

Heavily discouraged, they found a cheap motel near the station where Mama and the boys slept in the same bed just like when Robert and Wally were babies. For distraction, they turned on the television set. Ed Sullivan's show was just ending, and a program called "The Hate that Hate Produced" began, hosted by an affable interviewer named Mike Wallace, whose voice sounded familiar, comforting, and authoritative, but the subject matter he introduced was clearly, to Robert's ears, designed to arouse fear and anger. A Negro preacher began shouting to an enormous congregation: "I charge the white man with being the greatest liar on earth! I charge the white man with being the greatest drunkard on earth... I charge the white man with being the greatest gambler on earth. I charge the white man, ladies and gentlemen of the jury, with being the greatest murderer on earth."

These men spoke of the evil of "the white man" in the same spitting rhetoric as some travelling preachers he'd heard in Columbus talk of other imaginary devils, the way people like Colonel Whitehouse talked about communists. It hurt his heart to hear people talk like this. Robert knew much was not right in the world, but he couldn't reconcile a lot of this. At one point in his life, he might have taken offense at it, as he knew probably most white people in the country did. But since he'd spent the last few weeks as an outcast, a freak of nature, there was something changed

82

about his sensibilities now that made these speeches feel like a reasonable response to their experience of "the white man."

Mama said she found the program tiresome and switched it off after about ten minutes. Wally was already snoring.

Even after the television was shut off, city noises kept Robert awake most of the night, and he could see that Mama wasn't sleeping either. Mama's face at this close range, with every wrinkle and crack exposed, seemed foreign and worn like a relic from some ancient statuary. Red lesions of eczema from stress and lack of sleep populated her neck line and marched down below the borders of her flannel nightgown. Still she held onto them, and none of them spoke. Robert knew they were all thinking of the worst case scenario and what they would do if Pop had to go to prison.

Out of the silence, Mama began softly singing a lullaby she'd sung to them as small children, in almost a whisper. It was by Robert Burns, of course, "Highland Balou." Most of the lyrics were Scottish, and Robert had never learned the meaning behind them. The melody, he suspected, was something Mama had made up herself. But the warm, earthy sound of it soon put him to sleep, just as it had done so many nights when he was a baby.

First thing the next morning, they dressed, shuffled back into the station, and sat on the same bench. Mama still wore no make-up, and her hair sprung out in disheveled half-curls. They were told that there would be a hearing in the afternoon. Until then, the morning passed slowly. Mama bought the boys doughnuts and drank endless cups of hot coffee. Mama's skin was the color of an under-ripe tomato. She said, "I'm gonna walk around the parking lot a little bit. Let me know if you hear anything."

Not a minute after Mama left, Munford Coldwater shuffled in the door and sat down next to the boys, wearing that same oversized brown suit and tie with a fedora now to match, carrying his pocket notepad along with a folder full of other sundry papers. "I come to talk to you about your Dr. Montalto."

Wally was snoring lightly behind Robert's ear. "Just keep it down," Robert said.

"Er, look, I can't prove Montalto is a charlatan. His background checks out. He probably could have become a successful and respected surgeon, but he ran into some troubles."

After shuffling through some of the papers in his file folder, Coldwater said that Dr. Nicholas Montalto was raised in New Orleans. His father was a veterinarian, and his mother was a night club singer whose father was a butcher. As a teenager, young Nicholas had assisted with both his father's animal surgery and his grandfather's butcher shop. He was smart and well-rounded in his education, went to medical school at Tulane, and then served as a medic during World War I. When he came back from the war, he met a precocious girl named SueBell, who was a singer like his mother. Every night that she sang at a little place in the French Quarter called Zelenko's, he sat in the front row to watch, and he'd send flowers backstage. Once in a while, she'd see him for a few minutes, but he always got chased off by her manager, a perpetually drunk Creole named Fontaine. This was back during Prohibition, and it was thought that Fontaine was an enforcer for a gang of bootleggers. She always insisted Fontaine wasn't her boyfriend, but he kept a tight watch on her like a jealous husband nonetheless.

Coldwater licked his fingers, turned the page and started in again. He said that one night, Montalto and SueBell had arranged to sneak out the back before Fontaine caught up with them, just so they could talk. But she didn't show up at the rendezvous point. Montalto went back to her dressing room to check on her and even from down the hall, he heard yelling and furniture crashing. He ran for the door and burst in a moment too late. Fontaine had hit Sue-Bell with a crowbar. She was dead before Montalto could do anything to help her. When Montalto turned around, he was surprised that Fontaine was still standing there, perhaps in shock himself at what he had done.

"And this is the part that I'm not sure I believe," Coldwater said. "But it's there in the court records."

Montalto remained composed as he walked slowly up to the murderer, saying, "Well, you look just like the cat who ate the canary." When he got within arm's length, he went for Fontaine's throat, ended up knocking him unconscious, but he didn't kill him. When Fontaine came to, in some back alley of the French quarter, he was desolately naked. His hands had been replaced with tiny little cat paws, and a long furry tail now surfaced out from the small of his back and limped down between his legs.

So, Coldwater continued, Dr. Montalto then spent twenty years in prison, and his medical license was stripped away. While he was in there, he met a man who had been in the travelling circus business, and they eventually talked about what had landed them each behind bars. The man said, "Well, I know some people who would want to have surgery like that on purpose." After they were freed, they went into business together, and Montalto looked after all the medical needs of the performers, including enhancing any deformities they might already have to make them more spectacular. He didn't just create freaks though; once in a while, a deformity would be so problematic for the performer's health that he would feel obligated to remove it, if possible.

"What happened to Fontaine?" Robert asked, looking at his own hands.

"Oh, he just put his tail between his legs and ran off somewhere."

Robert laughed. "You're putting me on."

"Like the string said to the bartender, I'm a frayed knot."

"I don't get it."

"Anyway," Coldwater concluded. "I just wanted you to know the story. No reason you can't go through with the surgery if you really want to." With that, he tipped his hat and left the room.

"What the hell was that?" Wally said, groggy. Robert realized his brother had slept through most of Coldwater's speech.

Robert said, "Just another thing we didn't need to hear. But it doesn't really change anything." The thought of the man with cat paws for hands didn't even sound real to him. He started to wonder if Coldwater had even been there, had even told that story, or if it had all been a dream, Coldwater a ghost.

Finally, Mama came back, and it was time for the hearing. The courtroom was half empty, and the family sat on a pew just behind Pop and his public defender. Coldwater lurked in the back of the room. The officer Pop hit was there also, sitting on the opposite aisle. The policeman told his side of things, that the family was obstructing foot traffic. When asked to move, the suspect became irritable and eventually violent, he said. Pop pled guilty, said the officer had insulted his family, but he was sorry for reacting the way he did. The judge was an old man, bald and rotund with a bulbous nose. "This is your family behind you?"

"Yes, your honor," Pop said.

"From what condition do your sons suffer?"

Sulfur in the air…blood in the water…A white light…white lab coats…all the doctors in Birmingham…a promise in New Orleans…

Robert could feel how pathetic they looked, as if he were outside of himself, looking at them from the judge's bench. Two greasy sons, stuck together like frozen meat, wearing a double shirt made of flour sacks, ragged and dirty. A bedraggled mother who clearly hadn't slept properly since long before her husband got in trouble here. The judge took pity on them. He asked if they had any money. "You struck a police officer on duty. We don't take that lightly. But you have no previous record, and your family has already suffered greatly. You'll pay a fifty-dollar fine and spend four nights in the city jail."

The bailiff led Pop away, and Mama cried. They paid the fine out of the cash they'd made the past couple of days. Later, when they visited him in jail, Pop said to continue on without him. They'd have better luck with Mama's relatives anyway, he said. He'd join them when he got out. He'd hitchhike or something, he said.

Mama said, "When they let you out of here, we will come get you. And then we will never set foot in this horrible city again."

FOURTEEN

The Montgomery County Jail was no worse than a lot of places Dewey Mackintosh had slept, except for the permeating smell of urine. He tried to think of it like camping, his jail mates just the local wildlife. He ignored them as much as possible, though he never stopped watching them amble in the jaundiced fluorescent light. So far he was alone in his cell, but he knew it wouldn't be that way long. There were adjacent cages and others across the way. Three to four inmates slept in each, drooled, laughed at nothing in particular, talked to themselves, or preached at each other.

Bunch of hyenas, just like all those jackasses he had to be around when he was in the service. He had always been a quiet man, and the sound of other people talking got on his nerves, especially when they had nothing really to say. That was why he decided to stick with farming after the war instead of going and getting a mechanic job like he'd done in the army. Take a wife, have a couple of kids, spend most of your time alone with your thoughts—making things, growing things, killing things; that was all he ever wanted to do.

They had taken his gun so he couldn't shoot anybody, his boots so he couldn't kick anybody, and his belt so he couldn't hang himself. Nothing to do but ignore the hyenas and think. He tried to visualize his in-laws in Mobile seeing the boys for the first time and being moved to help, though they had never helped before. Even in fantasy, the vision was fogged and blurry, but it was as close a thing to praying as he knew how to do. Back during the war, a Filipino priest had very nearly converted him—a weak moment when nine thousand miles away his oldest son was being born. All his life, he had avoided being ensnared in the constant entrapments of this Jesus-haunted world. It was something he and Lucretia had agreed on from the start; they weren't going to push Jesus on the boys, which was hard because everybody else pushed it on them, from their school teachers to their friends. One reason he'd volunteered for service was to see a part of the world where Jesus wasn't hiding behind every bush and cornstalk. It was all just talk, like most everything else people talked about, a lot of nothing. He hoped that in the South Pacific, he'd find people who only spoke when they had something to say, and then he met Manuel de Rosario, a tiny yellow man in black, a wasp of a man, who sat next to him in a *pulutan* bar drinking shots of the local liquor, *lambanog*, distilled from coconut flowers. Sometimes he would mix it with *tuba*, the juice of a young coconut. Dewey wouldn't touch anything but the beer in those places, and he drank so much of it there that he never touched it again after he got back stateside. Now he only drank shine, or bonded whiskey if he could get his hands on some.

Manuel de Rosario had been educated by Jesuits in the States and spoke English with only an occasional hint of an accent. The Filipino Father didn't like talking either, so he and the American soldier sat next to each other at the bar in silence—ten, maybe twelve times—before a word was spoken between them. If Rosario looked like a wasp, he also spoke like one, in short, quick stings. The first time it happened, he had emptied his glass and was waiting for a refill. In the other corner of the bar, a fat local woman was singing American songs to pre-recorded music in broken English. Rosario looked over at Dewey and said, "So…what's matter with you then?"

"Nothing time and space can't fix," Dewey said, surprised at his own obscure words. Unsure why he chose to phrase his condition in that particular way, he started to explain further, but the priest interrupted him.

"Time and space are illusions, and if the solution to your problem is an illusion, problem is probably an illusion as well."

"What do you mean?" Dewey said.

"What do *you* mean?" Rosario said.

"You're drunk," Dewey said.

"Look. One way to talk about space is space between you and me. Mathematician talk about space, mean something different, has to do with three dimensions and infinite possible points. Scientist talk about space, mean something else. It mean everything around us as far as we can imagine. Philosopher talk about space, it created by the mind. Intuition tells us there is space, but really it just a construct used to talk about something theoretical. An illusion."

"That's nonsense. My wife and son are *nine thousand miles*

away, on the other side of the earth. That's no illusion."

"Ah, I see," Rosario said. "It not the distance that bothers you. It's the powerlessness."

Dewey admitted that was a better way of putting it. They talked for hours that night, laying their life stories on the bar like bamboo mats. No subject was off limits for Rosario—sex, politics, religion, philosophy, even sports. He seemed to have an informed but distanced view about every topic under the Manila sun. Gradually, Dewey began asking Father Rosario about his faith, about saints and ceremony and all the things that his Southern Baptist folks had said was medieval hokum. Rosario painted a beautiful picture of it all, but it came just short of making Dewey into a believer.

"Look," Rosario said. "Father, Son, Holy Ghost are all basically three ways of talking about same thing under different conditions. Like water, ice, and vapor—all the same type of molecules but under different conditions, so we have different names. American, German, Japanese—all basically the same, but different conditions, so different names. See?"

One night, some three months later, the priest was mugged while he was walking home from the *pulutan*, beaten badly and stabbed. He died the next day. Rosario was the only friend Dewey had during his time overseas, perhaps the only friend he had ever had. It was another three months before he was discharged, and he spent a lot of that time thinking about Rosario. The priest had also spoken to him of death and of the afterlife, which Dewey had also called nonsense, but of course Rosario had an explanation for everything.

"Look," Rosario had said. "You can talk about heaven, or reincarnation, or ghosts, or say you just turn off the lights and get eaten by bugs. All just different ways of talking about the same thing. What really matter is what you do *before* you die. All afterlife idea is a way of giving context and meaning to what you do. The spirit *does* live on because the spirit is not a part of your biology. It is the sum of all your actions, the memories other people have of you, the results of your having lived."

The one thing the priest had given Dewey Mackintosh, which he still carried to that day was this idea of the spirit equaling action and knowledge. And that's how he got through the rest of the war, knowing that he had a son back at home who as yet didn't know who his father was. He had to live through the war so his son could know who he was, and so he could know his son.

His remembrances were interrupted when two uniformed officers brought in another prisoner, a stout, cream-mustached man in an expensive but dusty gray suit, and roughly tossed him into the cell with Dewey. The man lit up when he saw Dewey, who asked him what he was smiling at. "Nothing worth smiling at in here."

"I saw you," the man said dumbly. "In the courtroom. You got those boys."

"Still ain't nothing to smile about," Dewey said.

"I saw you earlier too, on the street. Tell you what I see when I look at those boys. *Money.* I'd know how to make me some *money* if I had them boys."

Dewey took a step back to get a wider look at his cellmate. When he wasn't talking, he chewed on his tongue like it was bubble gum. He was the sort that always had to be grinding his teeth on something. Though there wasn't much of it, his blond hair was plastered against his head, and he smelled faintly of licorice. "What, specifically, would you do?"

"Well, let's just say I have some contacts in show business. I could introduce you. You'd be set up. Travel the country in style."

The man was getting too close, so Dewey backed away and turned his shoulder, hoping the man would keep his distance. "Seems you know more than enough of my business," Dewey said. "But I don't know enough of yours. What'd you get pulled in for?"

"Aw, it was just a lil' misunderstanding. I'll be out of here before long."

"A misunderstanding." Dewey was getting sleepy and tired of talking. His interlocutor was no Manuel de Rosario. The man nodded, noncommittally. "Well, what do they *think* you done?"

"Long story really. Working for a travelling show, not unlike yourself in some ways. Someone wanted their money back. Misunderstanding. Altercation. Continued misunderstanding. You know how it is. Now, I *know* what you did. I saw it myself. Tell you what, son. I don't want to get on your bad side. You have a hell of a left hook!"

"Then I guess you won't mind if I take the top bunk?"

"Eh, help yourself," the man said.

Dewey fell asleep, and by the time he woke up, he was alone again. The man had already been released. Good for him, Dewey thought, and quickly drifted back into dreams of Manila.

FIFTEEN

They left Montgomery straight from the jailhouse, Mama driving the old pickup truck as fast as it would carry them. They passed through more cow pastures and cotton fields, all separated by one little town after another, and Robert wondered about them all, how the people there lived and why. He assumed, for some reason, that Wally was thinking of something similar and was surprised when Wally asked him if he thought there really was life in space, on other planets.

"I don't know," he said. "I suppose there could be."

"Do you think God lives in space?"

Robert said, "If there is a God, he's supposed to be everywhere, space included."

"Don't you believe in God?" Wally asked, his voice revealing some concern. In Robert's chest, he could feel Wally's desire to pull away in his disbelief, like Wally wanted to see the look on Robert's face to make sure he wasn't pulling his leg.

"You know I don't," Robert said.

"Do you believe in the devil?"

"Nope."

Wally was thoughtful and relaxed again. "Maybe God lives in space, and it was God that joined us together."

"If he did," Robert said, "I sure would like to know why."

After a long pause, Wally said, "Funny how it is called just space. Like emptiness. But it ain't all emptiness. There are planets and stars and meteors and who knows what else?" Robert thought he knew what he meant. It also included whatever had filled him and his brother, which was the opposite of empty.

Wally didn't ask any more questions then. As they approached Mobile, Robert could smell salt air. They passed a marina on the bay that housed everything from little fishing skiffs to princely houseboats. Now, that would be freedom, he thought—not even the land to tie you down. But it was only a brief fantasy that he used to fill the time, and it was soon disrupted.

Wally said, "Is that the ocean?"

"That's Mobile Bay, and beyond that is the Gulf of Mexico."

Wally thought a minute. "How long would it take to swim to Mexico from here?"

"Long time the way you dog paddle," Robert said, ribbing him. Wally laughed.

Gray beards of Spanish moss hung down over the sidewalks. Before they would visit Mama's family, she insisted they check into a motel to freshen themselves up and change clothes, though she had to spend a good chunk of their remaining money to do so. "We will not let them see us looking defeated, no matter what we've gone through."

Bathing was always an ordeal, so they often skipped it. The boys had to stand in the tub with the shower running. Mama would reach in through the curtain to help scrub them so water wouldn't go everywhere. At home, Pop had installed a bar to help them both when they had to turn around. Here on the road, they just had to move slowly to keep from slipping.

While Mama helped the boys wash, Wally said, "So…we're going to see your parents?"

Mama scrubbed Wally's back and said, "My mother, Donna May Dean Dollar. She's your grandmother. Donna May's husband, my stepfather, is named Harry Dollar. Mister Dollar is a preacher. My aunt Eunice might be there as well."

"Is he a 'piscopalian preacher?" Wally asked.

"No, he, uh, basically made up his own church. Ok, turn."

Wally screwed up his nose. "You can do that?"

"People do it all the time," Mama said. Robert stared at the square white tile of the motel bathroom so as to not look at Mama looking at his nakedness. He had to concentrate to not think about Edwina or the girl in Birmingham or much of anything else to keep himself in check. Getting washed was probably the thing he hated most about his life.

Mama's family home was in a modest neighborhood with a mix of modern and historic homes. Theirs was a two-story white colonial style, old but not well kept. The porch and columns were overrun with ivy, and paint peeled from every surface. A window on the second floor was boarded up, as if they were expecting a hurricane.

"Is this where you grew up?" Wally said to Mama.

"Yes. It used to be beautiful."

Mama's mama, Donna May, met them at the door. With her bright orange hair and green eyes, it was easy to see the resemblance to Mama, but Donna May was much heavier, both physically and in spirit. Her hair fell down in long youthful braids that belied her sour expression. She greeted them with an unsurprised scowl wearing a formal looking dress with blue ruffles. "Oh, it's you. When I heard the noise that truck was making, I thought it was the gardener. Have you finally left that…character you call a husband?" Her accent was patrician, with an affect that sounded almost British.

"No, Mother. He's home working the farm. Somebody's got to keep the boll weevils out of the fields." Robert thought she was doing a pretty good job of covering up, all things considered. She was probably accustomed to this kind of distance with her mother, never quite being honest about things.

"I thought that was what the niggers were for," said a deep voice behind her. Mr. Dollar revealed himself chuckling at his joke. He was a very tall man, about six and a half feet, burly, and clean-shaven. He was in shirt sleeves and suspenders with a loosened tie, as if he had just returned from church and was settling in for the afternoon.

Mama didn't acknowledge Mr. Dollar's effort at humor. She asked if they'd received her letters.

Donna May said sternly, "Yes, we got them. Come in, I suppose. Eunice, can you make some tea?"

Robert didn't get much of a look at his great aunt Eunice before she slunk away to the kitchen. All the furniture in the house looked like it had come from a museum, dark wood with an ancient unpolished look and ornate carvings. The chairs were all embroidered. Robert found an ottoman wide enough for him and Wally to share. Mr. Dollar sat in a large blue chair, and Mama sat on the sofa at the opposite end from where Donna May sat. The room was dimly lit, and there were cobwebs in the corners of the high ceilings, as well as on the gaudy chandelier that was directly overhead. Mama looked at Donna May, who looked at Mr. Dollar, who looked mostly at his watch or a place on the floor between his feet. Nobody looked at Robert and Wally.

"Well," Donna May said, still not making eye contact. "What do you want?"

"Want?" Mama said. "Well Mother, I…We are on our way to New Orleans to see a doctor who might could help us. We thought we'd visit our family."

"'Might could?' I suppose you've picked up that mode of speech from the barbarian. Never mind, though," said Donna May. "But let's not be distracted by trivia. That's the doctor you mentioned in your letter, I presume. And you know very well there's a reason we seldom see you. I admit, though, I appreciate this chance to see my grandchildren once before I die, such as they are, even if it is only to induce guilt and petty coins from my old heart." She put her hands over her heart and closed her eyes dramatically as she said this.

Eunice came in then with a tray of tea. She was an older lady in a gingham housedress, with gray braids in the same shape as Donna May's. She nearly dropped the tea when she got a good look at Robert and Wally. "Oh, you poor—"

Donna May cut her off. "Eunice, don't make a scene."

After putting the tray down in front of Donna May, Eunice slipped into a chair in the corner. She never took her eyes off the boys. Robert wasn't sure what was more uncomfortable, the steady gaze of his great aunt or the wall put up by his grandmother.

"Boys—" It seemed as if Mama wanted to talk privately with Donna May, but she couldn't just send the boys outside to play like little kids. Robert turned his face away, observing the faded birds of paradise in large Oriental ceramic pots by a back door. Through the window of this door, he could see a backyard overrun with weeds.

"Mother, about these boys."

"That's what you get for having boys. They're always into something."

Mr. Dollar so far had been observing quietly but now stepped in. "Look at it this way, Lucretia. You say no doctor or scientist understands why these boys are stuck together. Well? Isn't it obvious? Who or what has the power to do such a thing. Only God. If God made this happen, he made it happen for a reason."

Mama said, "Maybe the reason was so we could reconcile our differences."

"Or," Donna May said, "perhaps He has cursed you for marrying that un-Christian barbarian. The bottom line, though, is that we are poor. I said earlier I thought you were the gardener, and I was just being facetious. We have no gardener, obviously. We are as poor as you are, poorer probably. We've nothing to give you."

For another half hour or so, Mama tried to make small talk and catch up on family happenings with not much success. At one point, Wally said to Mr. Dollar, "I heard you made up your own church. What's that like?"

"Oh," Mr. Dollar said looking at Mama, "Where did you hear that?"

Mama came to his defense. "The Fellowship of Levi is somewhat difficult to explain to a child who has grown up Episcopalian."

At the mention of that word *Episcopalian*, still somewhat new to them both, Wally seemed to take the hint that he should drop the matter. From things Mama had said in the past, Robert had pieced together that Mr. Dollar held "church" meetings at people's houses. They would feed him and give him money, and he would speak to them about all the things they needed to stop doing to avoid going to Hell. According to Mama, he was strict and mean. After he came along and married Donna May, he didn't let them eat pork or celebrate Christmas or cut their hair.

Furthermore, whatever Robert knew of grandmothers, he only knew from fairy tales, and in those they were kindly old ladies unfairly eaten by wolves. He wasn't much impressed with this Donna May, and he wouldn't be too disappointed if some big bad wolf came around to eat her up. And where Mama got all this about being Episcopalian was beyond him. Maybe she had grown up Episcopalian before Donna May took up with this ornery minister, or maybe it was just something she said to keep people out of their business. He'd never set foot in any church in all his life, Episcopalian or otherwise. But he knew the Episcopal church in Columbus had pretty stained glass windows and was one of the oldest buildings in town.

Finally, having given up on getting any money out of her mother and stepfather, Mama began winding up the visit. She said, "It was good to see y'all. Really it was. Stay in touch." They all knew neither side would stay in touch.

As they were leaving, Eunice hugged them both despite protests from Donna May that she "stop being so dramatic." She smelled like baby powder and whispered something in Robert's ear that sounded like "gas."

Once they were back in the truck, Wally revealed that Eunice had slipped him ten dollars. When he handed it over to Mama, she regarded it curiously for a moment and then added it to the coffee can.

SIXTEEN

It was a narrow highway they took from Mobile to New Orleans. Once they passed the gray beaches of the Mississippi coast, they entered the delta, and then the bayou, where the water seemed to take gargantuan crocodile bites out of the land and the rusted skeletons of abandoned automobiles littered the sides of the road. They came into New Orleans just after dark, and the laces of wrought iron and shuttered windows made Robert feel as if he were in the middle of some hundred-year-old French novel off Mama's bookshelf.

As they crossed over Esplanade Avenue, a small parade approached them, a dozen motley-dressed men and women pumping parasols in the air and dancing in bounce step to a four-piece brass band. Everywhere they turned there were people drinking and shouting, some literally dancing in the street.

Despite the celebratory ambience, Robert had some trepidation about the city because of Coldwater's crazy story about Montalto, which he still hadn't told anyone about. He half expected to see the gutters flowing with blood, like a scene out of the French revolution, with satyrs and other mythic monsters running amok. Instead, what they found was music. The air here was thick and felt like an extra layer of clothing, and the city smelled like rotting garbage, but none of that mattered.

"I think I'll like this place," Wally said. There were musicians on the streets, on every street, and Robert was amazed that they were all so good. He and Wally would have a difficult time competing in this environment. There was a black kid who couldn't have been older than six playing an amazing jazz trumpet solo on one corner. A group of teenagers played a syncopated drum line on upturned buckets. Once in a while, Mama stopped the truck and just watched for a little while. In the rear view mirror, Robert could see her eyes watering. She'd told him that she'd spent a lot of time here as a girl, at least until her mother married that false preacher, and those had been some of her happiest memories. After Mr. Dollar, there had been no more trips for her to the sinful city of New Orleans.

They drove around slowly for a little while, witnessing the frenzy of activity around the French Quarter before Mama reluctantly left that area of town. Though it was night now, the doctor was expecting them, and their plan was to see him before deciding where to spend the night.

Montalto's office sat on the second floor of a building on Chef Montour Highway west of downtown, above a dirty bookstore and next door to a neon-lit motel called the Halfway Inn. Despite the dinginess of the neighborhood, the office itself looked clean and freshly painted. French doors led from the spacious foyer to the waiting room and from the waiting room to what they presumed was either the examination room or office.

While Mama sat down on a brown naugahyde sofa in the waiting room, Robert and Wally perused the dozen or so framed photos that decorated the walls. They displayed all manners of human oddities—men who were half wolf, women who were half fish, a boy with the legs of a goat, even a couple of pairs of apparently conjoined twins. In many of the photos, a man Robert presumed was the doctor stood shaking hands, or paws, with the subjects.

"I wonder if these pictures are before or after," Wally said. Robert was thinking about the story Coldwater had told him and didn't respond.

The French doors flew open, and the doctor emerged—short, round, and tanned like a Christmas turkey—from the room beyond. He greeted them expectantly as welcome guests, shaking hands with all three members of the family who were present. "And the father?" he asked.

"Unfortunately detained," Mama said without any irony.

Montalto wore thick glasses and had long wisps of gray hair that he frequently had to brush out of his eyes. "Oh, that is too bad. Well, boys, let me take a look at you here," he said.

He examined the seam, just as all those many doctors had previously done, the whole time muttering notes to himself.

"At some inconvenience to myself," he said while continuing the examination, "I took the liberty of obtaining your records from the hospital in Birmingham. I agree with them that there are some risks, but they can be mitigated." He gestured toward the waiting room. "You can see from my gallery that I've taken on many unusual cases in my career. Nothing exactly like this, but I'm confident that it can be done."

"I was wondering about those," Robert said. He wasn't sure what else he could say about the curious display. Wally's hand sat there on his chest as always, a dead weight. He put his own hand on top of it, which startled Wally for a moment, but then he relaxed.

"Obviously," Montalto said, "not everyone in the medical community is willing to take the same kinds of chances that I am. And needless to say, many of them have not been supportive of my work. But I do have a very good success rate."

Mama's hands trembled as she took a hit of Benzedrine from her inhaler.

Robert said, "Can I ask you about Fontaine?"

Montalto laughed, an exuberant laugh that caught Robert off guard. "Somebody's been telling stories about me, have they? Well, let me assure you that old chestnut has been greatly exaggerated." Apparently answering a questioning look from Mama, he added, "A youthful indiscretion that made the newspapers. Your son has apparently been doing some research."

Mama's face registered surprise but seemed incapable of formulating a verbal response to this news.

Robert said, "I have been doing some reading up, and I think you ought to explain yourself before we go any further."

The doctor launched into a story that didn't exactly contradict Coldwater's but left out some of the more spectacular details. He said he had gotten into an altercation with someone and used his position as a surgeon to get revenge. He'd done his time, and that was all behind him.

Mama and Wally seemed satisfied, but Robert wasn't convinced. He couldn't get much more information out of Montalto either. "Well, let's get back to business then," he said. "What all would be involved? And how long would it be before we could work again?"

"It's hard to say what's involved exactly, until we get in there and do it. I'd guess you could both be relatively active again within a few weeks. It might be longer before you can do strenuous labor though, several months." After a moment, Montalto added, "We should discuss my fee. I could do the operation for three thousand dollars."

The boys and Mama all gasped. She said, "Dr. Stanhope said

100

two thousand. He did say it was just an estimate, but still! We are barely getting by as it is! Can't you reconsider?"

He held out his tiny, sun-browned hands to calm her. "Mrs. Mackintosh, I understand. We can probably work something out if you fall a little short. However, you must realize that this is no ordinary procedure, and there is great risk involved."

Mama only said, "I'll consult with my husband when we return to Alabama. Unfortunately, he was unable to make the trip with us today."

With the exception of a few formalities, that was the end of the appointment. Currently, they had the ten dollars from Eunice and some change, much of which would be gone after staying in another motel overnight.

The Halfway Inn next door was reasonably priced, so they stayed there. Mama showered and the boys sat on the bed and practiced some new songs. While Robert was tuning and rosining, Wally said, "Do you think he can do it?"

"Only one way to find out."

"You sure you want to?"

Robert was surprised to hear his brother backpedaling. "We can't go on like this the rest of our lives. Not if we have a choice."

"Yeah, I guess not."

"Do you think we should just stay like this? You want to always be stuck with me, not being able to sleep or eat or even shit like a normal person? You can't even use your left hand. You can't go anywhere without me there."

Wally stayed silent for a moment. "No, I suppose we couldn't," he finally said.

Robert wasn't ready to let it go yet. "And what about girls?"

Before Wally could answer him, Mama came out of the shower in her butterfly night robe.

"Mama," Wally said, "You aren't getting ready for bed yet are you? We're in New Orleans!"

Mama had always talked about how much she loved coming here as a kid. She had even been a bit giddy about it earlier in the day when they sat watching some of the roadside musicians. "Yeah, Mama. Take us out on the town."

She said, "Oh, but it's so late..." She was smiling.

"How often do we get to come here?" Robert said, getting excited. "Come on. Let's just park in the French Quarter and walk around. Maybe we could even make some money."

She removed her robe and revealed a red dress underneath. "I thought you'd never ask."

They parked just west of Canal, and the Quarter was just like it had seemed as they drove through it at dusk, but even more so. At night the streets were filled with people. Bourbon Street was so crowded, they could hardly push through the throng. Nude dancing girls were brazenly advertised in neon, and people not much older than Robert stumbled around spilling beer from plastic cups. Bands and musicians were everywhere. Robert held the fiddle close to his chest, protecting it from the drunken hordes surrounding them. Wally had brought only a tambourine. Half fascinated and half repulsed at the excess, Robert hardly knew where to look for the greatest spectacle. He knew he wanted to come here sometime without Mama so he could explore more.

They found a spot on Royal, close to Esplanade, where the nearest jazz band was enough muffled by bodies and buildings that they could do their own show. Wally counted off, and they started into a tune. Across the street was a quaint three-story white house, perhaps a hotel, adorned with Greek columns and black wrought iron. Purple and white flowers covered the iron railings of both balconies. A small circle of people amassed around them and gradually grew. Mama danced and passed the coffee can around, saying "Those are my boys" and "Please help out. We're raising money for their operation."

They played about an hour and made almost ten dollars. They passed back through the pulsating beast of Bourbon Street. More than once, Robert had to duck and cover to prevent the fiddle from getting smashed. When they finally reached the Halfway Inn Motel again, it was well after midnight. Sweaty, exhausted, and half-dreaming already, even Mama slept in her clothes. They'd had so much fun, Mama suggested that they stay one more night so they could do it all over again the next day. They had another two days until Pop got let out of the Montgomery jail anyway, and they had to stay somewhere. Wally agreed right away, citing the money to be made playing on the street there. Robert didn't have any objections either, and the thing in his chest, the thing that seemed to hold him and Wally together seemed to loosen its grip just a hair.

SEVENTEEN

Coldwater needed to get from Montgomery to Mobile and then from Mobile to New Orleans, but the Eldorado wouldn't start. He'd never been one of those Southern boys that instinctively knew how to fix broken cars, so he'd had it towed to a garage a half mile away from his motel. The mechanic told him he needed a new starter, and there were a couple of other things wrong that he hadn't even known about, including a bad axle. If the car had started, his right front wheel might have flown off as he was going down the highway. It would take a few days to get all the parts. So now he found himself white-knuckling the armrests of a seat on the four o'clock train. He'd be in Mobile by seven, which was entirely too fast for a body to be able to make that trip. Trees, hills, farmland, and little towns flew by his window like the flash at the end of life. Every screech of the tracks re-enacted his parents' fiery screams of death.

Somewhere around the green and blue blur that he assumed was Greenville, he noticed he was being tailed. The stocky crew cut in a gray suit at the back of the car had also been in the train station in Montgomery, reading the same front page of the same newspaper. Either it was the most interesting front page ever devised in the history of journalism, or he wasn't really reading it. About every two minutes, the crew-cut looked up from the paper as if just stretching his eyes, but his eyes always landed on Munford Coldwater. To test his theory, Coldwater casually got up as if to find a restroom. When he opened the door at the end of the car, though, he found two feet of an open-air, thin, shaky walkway where his car joined up to the next one. The countryside blew by at a nightmare's pace, and the roar of the train was deafening. With a glance behind, he saw that the crew cut was poised to stand, but was waiting for Munford to continue through to the next car before he followed. There was nothing to do but finish what he started and fight his way through the hollering wind into the next car, which seemed to take forever. He gripped the handle of the next door while he still had hold of the first one. Logically, he knew it would probably be safer just to get it over with, but his feet refused to move other than to shuffle inch by inch toward the destination.

After seven eternities, he was finally safe inside the adjoining car. It was another passenger car, identical to the one he had just left. There was, thankfully, a restroom at the back of this car. Probably had been one in his original car, but he hadn't thought to go that direction. In any case, it couldn't have been better placed because he was sure he was going to puke, which he did. When he emerged from the toilet, crew-cut was waiting for him, sitting quietly in a seat near the back, just as he had in the other car. He recognized the guy now—the young soldier that Whitehouse had guarding the gate around the pond back in Pickens County, so he took the open seat beside the kid.

"Why is Whitehouse having me trailed?"

"I don't know what you mean. I have leave to visit my family in Mobile for the weekend."

"Without your uniform on? How will strangers know the service you've done for our country?"

"How I dress when I'm on leave isn't your business or anybody else's."

"Oh yeah. Then why'd you change cars at the same time I did?"

"It was too hot in that car. You felt it. I figured you were searching for someplace cooler, and it seemed like a good idea. Now I'm not so sure."

Come to think of it, it was much more comfortable in this car, but Coldwater still wasn't buying the soldier's story. There was also the matter of the newspaper, but it was clear that no matter how much he pushed it, the young guy wasn't going to tell him anything. He had an answer for everything.

"I don't want to run into you in Mobile," Coldwater said.

"You're not my idea of a hot date either."

Thankfully, the train arrived in Mobile soon after that. As far as he could tell, he and crew cut had gone their separate ways, but he had a feeling they would see each other again.

Coldwater put eyes on the Dollar homestead as soon as he

could after arriving in town. He didn't see any lights on anywhere. There didn't seem to be anybody home. Based on the state of repair, it looked like nobody had been home for twenty years. His mission, as he saw it, was to keep an eye on the Mackintoshes, especially now that the father was indisposed. He didn't trust the Dollars or Montalto either, and he had the idea that he might be able to dig up some dirt on one or both of them if he watched closely enough. He must have already missed Lucretia and the boys here, though. No sign of the Mackintosh vehicle, but there was a silver Pontiac Streamliner—pre-war or '41 at the latest—parked around back. Like the house, it had once been nice. Since he was on foot, he wasn't sure what he would do if he saw the Reverend go somewhere in the car. Which is exactly what happened, of course. The Streamliner pulled out of the driveway from the back of the house and headed north on Catherine Street. Coldwater was a little surprised it still ran. Resigned, he began walking in the same direction, toward Dauphin Street.

When he'd walked almost all the way to Springhill Avenue, he saw the car again, parked alongside several others outside a modest cottage. He lit his pipe and waited. He assumed it was a meeting of Dollar's congregation, The Fellowship of Levi. They had no central church or meeting place; they held meetings at members' houses. From what Glassworthy was able to tell him, it seemed like they were basically against anything that might be construed as fun. No drinking, no dancing, and no sex except for procreation. They didn't eat pork, and the women couldn't cut their hair. Coldwater's instinct told him that Dollar was making money from this venture somehow, but he didn't want anybody to know about it. Embezzlement, money laundering, something was certainly going on.

An hour later, when the party let out, he saw it was a group of all men at this meeting. Women likely had separate meetings. Instead of following Dollar himself—useless if he was just going home and near impossible if he was going anywhere else—Coldwater set his sights on one of the followers, a thin, sallow man in a dirty wrinkled suit. The sad sack was on foot and he was an easy mark. If he was reading the man right, he was suffering from the DTs, which meant he was going to find a place to go get a drink, despite the tenets of the fellowship, not to mention Alabama state law. It seemed to him a good time to take up drinking again himself, so he tailed the poor fellow at an easy pace back down to Dauphin Street, caught up with him just south of the old cathedral.

"'Scuse me, sir." Coldwater was straight with him, that he wanted to know about Reverend Dollar, and he was willing to foot the bill for some booze in exchange for some information. The well-worn creature said little but nodded assent, led him to a pharmacy down the street, where the quiet gentleman filled a prescription for a pint of bonded bourbon and two Dixie cups on Coldwater's dime.

"Ain't much to tell," were the first words the man spoke. His hands were shaking too much to pour the whiskey, so Coldwater did the honors. "I only been there twice't. Somebody told me they could hep me, you know, put myself back together."

The whiskey burned, but it was a good burn. What Coldwater learned from the man confirmed what he already knew about the Fellowship of Levi, but it didn't tie Dollar to any kind of fraud or cover-up. They had taken up a collection, but it couldn't have amounted to more than a few bucks, and there was nothing unusual about that.

When he and the drunkard parted ways, Coldwater found himself a little tipsy, so he decided to wait until morning to check in with Glassworthy. Since the Mackintoshes had apparently already moved along, he'd do the same. Tomorrow, he'd go on to New Orleans and see what he could find out about Dr. Montalto.

"You're going to New Orleans? Today? Hold please..."

Mozart's Requiem blasted in his ear for approximately six minutes, and then Glassworthy came back on the line.

"Okay, I'll meet you there on the 8:00 train. Pick me up at the train station. Where are you staying?"

"I don't know yet. How'd you get a train ticket so fast?"

"Hold please..."

It was the second movement now, he thought. A choir sang *kyrie eleison* in undulating harmonies. He was no expert when it came to classical music, but he'd taken some music appreciation classes in college, and he distinctly remembered studying this piece. Liked it enough that he'd bought himself a phonograph recording of it, which he sometimes played while smoking his pipe.

He was just about to get lost in it all over again when Glassworthy returned.

"We have reservations at the Frenchman. Lucky to get in there at the last minute."

"What, do you have some sort of psychic network there connected up to every person, place, and thing on the planet? And who's paying for all this?"

"Haven't I been telling you I needed a vacation? I can pay for my ticket easily enough. You can expense the hotel."

He didn't see any use in arguing with her. Another damn train. Not for him. He picked up the phone again and made arrangements to rent a car for the rest of the weekend.

After a few minutes of pacing alongside the platform, Coldwater saw her patiently standing in that doorway, wearing a shaggy coat that was multicolored but mostly orange and hung down past her knees, which were encased in black stockings. She was leaning in the doorway with a cigarette, looking like a surreal dandelion that the wind was about to blow to smithereens. She wore her straw-blonde hair straight to her shoulders and then it curled up and nestled under her chin. It looked like a very comfortable place to nestle. Her glasses had dark, wide plastic frames.

He walked up beside her and said, "Miss Glassworthy."

She turned to face him, and he hugged her shoulder. He led her to the rented car, a brand new Continental. When she sat in the passenger seat he had a chance to really look at her face, oval and symmetrical, clear and white as a snow-blanketed tundra, with nose, lips, and chin that tempted him to run his finger down the gentle slopes. She caught him staring.

"I could get used to this," he said.

"Me or the car?" she said.

"Both. You are...my wife for the weekend?"

"Editorial assistant," she said. "The Frenchman won't ask, though."

The Frenchman was on Frenchman Street, of course, just outside the French Quarter, a pink oasis among the ruins of what might have once been a respectable neighborhood. There was an old fire station across the street, and several large but neglected houses along the road nearby.

"Before we check in," he said, "I've got to do a little snooping down on the West Side."

They took the car down Chef Mentour Highway to a shabby, half-abandoned part of town. After he parked, she said she would check out the dirty bookstore while he looked around the building. It was Montalto's place alright. There was a faded sign on the door, half covered in wisteria, that said, "Nicholas Montalto / Medical Services." Probably wasn't legal to call himself a doctor. There wasn't much else to look at around there. You would almost think the place was abandoned. He didn't know quite what he was looking for, but he decidedly was not going to find it hidden among the weeds growing around the wrought iron bars that covered the windows.

He knocked on the door. No answer. Knocked again. After a minute, he heard footsteps, and then the door creaked open. Montalto was a smaller man than Coldwater had imagined, with small eyes, and a big round face. He kept brushing gray hair out of his face as he squinted into the bright sunlight. Coldwater put out his hand and proceeded straightforwardly.

"Good afternoon. My name is Munford Coldwater. I'm a reporter from the *Tupelo Daily Journal*, and I've been following the story of two boys from Alabama, Robert and Walter Mackintosh. I believe they are potential clients of yours. I wondered if you'd care to discuss the case."

"I'm sorry. My patient files are strictly confidential, as I'm sure you are aware, Mr. Coldwater."

"As I understand it, you are not a medical doctor, which means that patient/doctor confidentiality would not be a factor, at least legally. And I'm going to write about this whether you cooperate or not. Don't you want a chance to tell your side of the story?"

The door slammed shut. Coldwater stood there a minute or two thinking about whether to try a different approach. Straight shooting obviously wasn't going to work, so he'd have to come up with something sneakier. He went around back to check the garbage cans, but they'd already been emptied. Though the encounter with Montalto had been disappointing, his hope was rekindled when he noticed the Mackintosh truck parked in the lot of the Halfway Inn next door. Just about then, Glassworthy returned carrying a brown paper bag.

"Miss Glassworthy, I'm afraid we have to cancel our reservation at the Frenchman. We're staying right here."

She turned her mouth down but said okay. "I can't wait to show you what I found at that bookstore. We don't have bookstores like that in Birmingham."

Inside their room, he took off his shoes and turned on the television. When she removed her coat, he saw that she was wearing a cocktail dress with a black and white checker pattern. She removed her own shoes and joined him on the bed.

He looked her over. "Miss Glassworthy, why don't you see if you can find the ice machine," he said. She got up and put her shoes back on, and her crazy fuzzy coat. Off she went. He flipped through channels with the sound muted, looking more at the closed door than at the TV. Pretty soon it opened and she came through it with her full bucket. The next moment, there was a glass of ice water next to him on the bedside table. She was now bare legged, though she still wore the black and white dress.

"Your legs are beautiful," he said.

"Thank you," she said. "I got them from my mother."

He took a long drink of water and then he grazed his fingers down her thigh, over her kneecap, down the front of her shin, and back up. She touched his unshaven face and leaned in to kiss him.

"As your editorial assistant," she said, "I am going to suggest that you don't open your mouth so wide when you kiss. In my opinion, you should take it more slowly, and use more suction."

"I'll take that under advisement," he said, annoyed and amused at the same time. He took off her glasses and resumed kissing her, keeping her words in mind. Her lips fit snuggly against his, and their tongues played at one another gently.

"Also, you must shave before we go out."

"Out?"

"Much as I would love to hole up with you in the motel all weekend, my love, we're in New Orleans!"

They found a small bar on the edge of the Quarter. A jazz band was playing in the back room. They sat at the front bar, where they could hear both the band and one another. Though he wasn't used to drinking much, there was something about the combination of New Orleans and Gustie Glassworthy that made it impossible not to. He bought himself a scotch, and she had the same. She sat to his left, resting her right foot on a rung of his barstool. "Tell me about the last time you were in New Orleans," he said. She began, and while she talked he caressed her thigh with the hand that wasn't holding his drink.

As they drank more, his fingers crept higher, until she pushed his hand away again. He kissed her neck. "That couple has been looking our way," she said to him. She craned her head around in an unsubtle way and then looked down at her lap.

"I don't know about the girl, but that's the flathead that followed me on the train from Montgomery. He works for Colonel Whitehouse."

"Whitehouse is having you followed?"

"That's the up and down of it," Coldwater said. "Excuse me."

"What are you doing…"

Coldwater approached the man, who must have outweighed him by at least a hundred pounds, all of it lean muscle. "You some kind of pervert? Watching me with my girl? Why don't you pay some attention to your own girl here? Last thing you said to me was—and I quote—you're not my idea of a hot date. You seem to have changed your mind."

He felt his eyes burning. He really thought he might punch this guy. Really. Being with Glassworthy must have given him a testosterone boost. The soldier's date was not amused.

"Mr. Townsend, who is this man?"

"Just some crackpot I met on the train."

"You knew me before the train, soldier boy. You work for Colonel Whitehouse, and you followed me from Montgomery to Mobile, Mobile to New Orleans, and from my motel to this shabby bar."

"Who you calling shabby?" That was the bartender. Nice guy. Coldwater gave him an okay sign and returned to his tirade.

The soldier gathered up his date. "Come on, Myrtle. Let's just get out of here."

They left, but Coldwater spent the rest of the night looking over his shoulder until they got back to the motel. He checked to make sure the truck was still there, and it was. He'd have to get up early to keep watch on it. It might be better if he just didn't go to sleep. The allure of Glassworthy, however, prevented him from doing his due diligence, and when he did get up to check just before sunrise, the truck was gone.

EIGHTEEN

Mama faced down and gave out one of her loud Scots-Irish sighs. "He says he can do it, and Dr. Stanhope vouches for him. But he is…peculiar." She described Dr. Montalto's office and his manner. Robert and Wally listened with interest and did not disagree with anything she said. Pop remained expressionless and circumspect.

"And your family?"

"Unhelpful. Mean. Nothing has changed. But Eunice did give us some gas money."

"Goddamn hypocrites—" Pop muttered under his breath. He took a moment and pulled himself back together. "Boys, anything to add?"

Wally said, "We made some money in New Orleans."

"That's good news at least."

They brought Pop back his belongings, including the Colt, but not the bullets. Surprisingly, Pop didn't complain about it.

Robert couldn't get so excited about the money they'd made. New Orleans had been a bright spot of fun, but now they were back to the same situation they'd been in before the trip started. On the plus side, they had seen the mysterious Montalto, and he seemed eager to help. On the other side, they still had only the money they'd made in New Orleans since they spent most of what they had before on Pop's fine. Mama filled Pop in on the doctor visit, particularly on the promise of the boys being able to work again within a few weeks of the operation. Wally told him all about the performance in the French Quarter.

They wasted no time getting back on the road after leaving the Montgomery County jail. It was a long drive home, even though they took a more direct route instead of going through Birmingham. The narrow highway between Montgomery and Tuscaloosa curved over hills, past dozens of farms and pastures not unlike home. Only the little railroad village of Centerville briefly interrupted the bucolic greenery and the earthy scent of flatulent cows that filled the space between the capital and the college town. Wally somehow dozed through most of the trip.

They stopped in Tuscaloosa only to get a late supper from a diner downtown. Tuscaloosa seemed different, lonelier, in the cool night air than it had been during the day. Pop bought burgers in sacks and brought them back to the truck. During the remaining fifty miles back to Pickens County, the boys picked at their burgers, neither of them especially hungry, even though they hadn't eaten since their dawn breakfast of beignets in New Orleans. Their shirt was still covered in powdered sugar, and the sweet airy taste was still in Robert's mouth. Wally's hand on Robert's chest filled both of their stomachs with the weight of the situation they were in and the choice they had to make. The bumpy road made it difficult to feed themselves.

At home, Pop spread out the Cities Service map once again and said, "Bottom line is that you can't do farm work. Irregardless of whether you eventually have the surgery, you gotta do something with yourselves. Might as well play music, make some money."

Mama flinched at 'irregardless,' a pet peeve. She'd long ago stopped correcting Pop about such things, but Robert knew better than to say that or any number of other verboten words in front of her. Pop didn't notice and continued tracing some of the lines on the map that stretched out from Columbus like so many spider legs. The hounds had been let inside and circled the family at the table like a wagon train.

Robert's eye traced the route they had taken to New Orleans and back. There were so many black dots along the way that they had passed through in a blur. "Maybe we should try more small towns this time," he said.

Pop looked up with a smile and said, "Good eye, son. I was gonna say the same thing." Robert basked in the compliment for a moment before Pop continued. "We can start in Columbus like before and head north on 45. We need to hit every little town along the way. When we think we can't make any more money one place, we move on to the next one. We should be able to get to several each day. Once we get to Tupelo, we can cut over to 78 and make our way to Memphis. Then we come south through Oxford and circle our way back home."

Everyone in the family nodded as if this were the understood plan all along, as if any of them had any say in the matter.

"Next trip, we can go south from Columbus or east through Tuscaloosa and back through Birmingham. What do y'all think?"

Mama said, "Do we have to go right away? I don't feel ready to travel again so soon." The trip they had just taken, Robert noted, had been especially hard on Mama. She looked like a ravaged scarecrow.

"Maybe it makes the most sense for you to stay put here and take care of the house," Pop said. "We leave first thing in the morning. And no motels this time. That's eating up our profits."

Unsure if he himself was ready to go out again this soon, Robert looked for Mama's reaction to the announcement. She seemed to be holding her breath to prevent herself from saying anything.

The road this time seemed less daunting to Robert. By now, there was a routine, and the boys' repertoire was growing by the day. The little towns of West Point, Aberdeen, and Okolona were not so profitable, but they made a few dollars and moved on. They stayed in Tupelo for a couple of days, looking for the best part of town to perform in. Knowing Tupelo was where Munford Coldwater was from, Robert expected to see the reporter lurking around every corner, but he never materialized, even when they performed downtown just a few blocks from the newspaper office.

Walking back to the truck with another thirty dollars or so added to the coffee can, they passed a store with a huge window display of color television sets. Wally made them stop and look. They'd read about color television for a couple of years, but it was their first time seeing it in person. "It's just like being at the movies," Wally said.

Robert wasn't so impressed, and in fact he found the colors less than lifelike, and the wall of sets overwhelmed him, made him dizzy. He tried to focus his eyes on one set at a time. The program being aired seemed to be about the history of rockets, which did in fact interest him. A room full of scientists referred to a series of charts and graphs, which transformed into animations that explained how an explosion in the back of the rocket forces energy in one direction, propelling the rocket in the other direction. All the men in white lab coats reminded Robert of Whitehouse's men and the team of doctors at the hospital in Birmingham. The sound was either turned off, or they couldn't hear it through the window. After a couple of minutes, Robert tried to pull away, but Wally held fast to the spot in front of the window.

Pop said, "Come on, Wally. Let's move along."

After a moment of resistance, Wally demurred, but as they turned to go, the person Robert most didn't want to run into in Tupelo was standing before them saying, "Well, look who dropped into town for a visit."

Coldwater re-introduced himself to Pop while Robert rolled his eyes.

"I sure would be interested in catching up with y'all. Can I buy you lunch? There's a diner across the street that does cheeseburgers with pimiento cheese."

"That sounds gross," Wally said.

"That's one thing Wally and I agree on," Robert said. He looked to Pop for a clue as to what the decision would be, but his expression was as wooden as usual.

"Well," Coldwater said. "They have other things. I'm sure you could find something you'd like."

Pop said, "We'll go, but we'll pay our own way."

"Now, Mr. Mackintosh. This ain't charity; it's simple hospitality. You're in my town, and so you are my guests. Besides, it's well worth it if I get another article or two about it. I can call it a business expense, and the paper will pick up the tab."

The diner smelled of hot grease and coffee, all of which made Robert's stomach bark angrily. The ugly, black-haired lady who took their orders was familiar with Coldwater—called him by name and touched him on the shoulder as he sat down in a corner away from other customers. It took a minute for Robert and Wally to get situated comfortably. Since Robert and Wally could not sit facing the same direction, the waitress set a small table in front of Wally for his food. Pop ordered steak and eggs, which sounded good, so Robert ordered the same. Coldwater said he would have "the special." Wally had a burger "but not with no pimiento cheese."

"So," Coldwater started in right away. "You boys look like

you are holding up pretty well, all things considered." Robert didn't know what to say to that, so he didn't say anything. Coldwater looked at them expectantly for a moment and then continued. "You've been to see the doctor in New Orleans?"

"We have," Robert said. He took a moment then to take a look around. There were a few other bloated pale customers sitting at the counter and a few others at a table on the opposite end. Faded prints of Greek landmarks—he recognized the Parthenon from pictures in the encyclopedia they had at home—accented the otherwise white walls. The black side cook was the only thing breaking up the stark monotone of the place. It reminded him of the hospital in Birmingham.

"Mr. Mackintosh, what was your impression of the doctor?"

Pop reddened a little, not an angry red. "Well...I..."

Robert exploded, pointing his finger across the table and nearly pulling Wally out of his seat. "Coldwater, you know damn well he didn't go to New Orleans with us. You know what happened in Montgomery because you were there."

Pop calmed a little and pushed Robert's arm now. "You were in Montgomery?"

Wally said, "I didn't see him."

"You were sleeping. He followed us," Robert said.

"Were you following us, Mr. Coldwater?"

"Well..." It was Coldwater turning pink now. The waitress brought the food over, and the aroma of steak, even if it was overdone, momentarily took Robert's mind off the accusation he had just made. He hadn't eaten this well in weeks.

"Don't really bother me if you were," Pop said. "Nothing we can do about it, so there's no use complaining. Anyway, somebody *should* probably document what these boys are doing. Kind of nice knowing somebody is watching."

Munford said, "Boys, what was your impression of the doctor?"

Robert was still looking at Pop, not quite believing. Wally said, "He was weird."

Having recovered a little, Robert added, "Mama trusts him."

"Do *you* trust him?"

"I don't trust anybody outside this family, least of all you," he said.

"Whoa, now. What did I do?" Munford put up his hands.

"I just don't trust you. I don't have any reason to. But I do thank you for the steak and eggs."

Pop smiled at this, and Robert felt like he had represented the family well. At that point, as if by mutual agreement, they all dug hungrily into their lunches.

That afternoon, they travelled about sixty miles west along U.S. Highway 78 to the small town of Holly Springs, Mississippi. It was approaching early evening when they got there. As was Pop's pattern, they located a street corner near what they assumed was the center of commerce and simply began to play. It was much like street corners in other small towns. Brick and concrete buildings bunched together behind an uneven canopy: a grocer, a hardware store, a post office, a bank, a barber shop. Down the road were churches that loomed over the main drag like judgmental parents.

However, nobody seemed to be out and about at all. A blue-green Plymouth pulled up across the street from them, and a man stepped out. He was small and round with a bushy oversized ginger mustache that seemed to take over his otherwise cherubic face. A brown suitcase matched the color of his seersucker suit where dark sweat stains crept out from the armpits and other crevices.

The man watched them for two songs, smiling and tapping his foot along, chewing on a mahogany brown cigar as thick as Wally's wrist. While the boys were discussing what to play next, he called out to Pop, "New at this, are you?"

"Now look here mister—" Pop said. Robert watched closely, not wanting a repeat of the Montgomery incident.

"No, no. Sorry. It isn't the performance. But I take it you haven't been doing a road show for long."

"And *how* do you take *that*?" Pop asked, his voice elevating.

The man introduced himself then. He was a travelling salesman named Charlie Cannaday. "I used to be involved in a road show of sorts, though it was more of what you call a 'medicine show' and not a musical act. At any rate, would you be willing to take some advice? I'll accompany it with a monetary donation of course."

"Go ahead, Chuck Canada," Pop said, holding the tip can forward.

Cannaday put a dollar in the can. He smacked at the cigar the way obnoxious old ladies kiss at babies. "Well, you can't just show up in a hick town like this and expect people to come around. That might work in a big city where people are always walking around anyway. But in a little old place like this, you have to announce yourself. You have to make some noise."

Robert said, "How are you supposed to do that?"

"I'm listening," Pop said.

"Well, in the old days, we had a gentleman, who would go ahead of us, put up posters, spread the word in the taverns and such, the general store or what have you and announce us. Though there aren't any taverns in this forsaken state. Which makes it especially easy to sell these particular wares," he looked toward his briefcase. "We would show up the next day at noon, and practically the entire town would come out just for the novelty."

Wally said, "We ain't got anybody that can do that. It's just us three."

"I see. Well, still. You have to go where the people are. Go to the, er, the locals here call it a *jook*."

"Where's that?" Robert said.

"*What's* that?" Wally said.

"Follow me. I'm on my way to one now." With a mischievous skip in his step, Charlie Cannaday returned to the Plymouth. Pop shrugged and gestured for the boys to hop into the truck. They followed to a remote shack at a crossroads just outside of town. There were about a dozen cars outside, and they could hear music coming from within half a block away.

Charlie conspired with Pop and the boys outside his car before they went inside. "Now look," he said. "Be prepared. You know this is a colored town?"

They hadn't known that.

"Mostly colored anyway. They have a colored college here, in town there. So it's not all sharecroppers at this place. They have plenty of disposable income, so don't worry about that. I'll go in and do my routine. When I'm finished, I'll introduce you. You can play your music while I sell my products, and we should both be able to make some money here. Okay?"

Pop looked dubious but said okay.

"How shall I introduce you then?"

Robert thought maybe they could use their story to their advantage. He was almost shocked he'd never thought of it before now. "Call us the Pickens County Fireball Brothers."

"Just the Fireball Brothers," Wally corrected, "from Pickens County, Alabama."

Pop nodded approval.

Charlie said, "I get the brothers part, but why fireball?"

Sulfur in the air...blood in the water ...A white light...white lab coats...all the doctors in Birmingham...a promise in New Orleans ...

Charlie smiled, impressed. "And so you shall be named."

They waited for a lull in the music, and then they walked inside.

"Ladies and gentlemen," Charlie began. Dark faces turned toward them. Some had been playing cards and others were just sitting talking, sipping moonshine. The décor was bare walls. Charlie gesticulated with his cigar as he spoke. "I have been travelling across this great state of yours and many others. I've come all the way from across the country in San Francisco, Californ-eye-aye to bring you Doctor Schaff's genuine all-purpose bitter tonic. Now Doctor Schaff himself passed on some time back at the age of one hundred and three, and that's all due to a strict regimen of this here tonic. It'll bring you up from down and down from up. It'll ease whatever ails you from indigestion to rheumatism. Doctor Schaff's company is gone and doesn't make this stuff anymore. What I have here and in the trunk of my car is the last of the stock."

A man who seemed to be the proprietor of the place held up a mason jar and said, "Hey white man, get on outta here. These folks got all the medicine they need right here."

Cannaday was not fazed. "Sir, if you'll hold for just a moment. Don't be hasty." He punctuated *moment* and *hasty* with the burning cigar, which had now developed a long head of ash. "A few drops of this tonic, dissolved in an ounce or two of that there medicine will not only improve the taste, but you'll feel better the next day. Try it."

The salesman added a few rust-colored drops of his product to a glass of shine for the man, all the while continuing his spiel.

"Doctor Schaff devised this unique blend of herbs and roots back in 1815, and the formula has been passed down through six generations of his family so that I can offer it to you today for fifty cent a bottle. If you'll line up, I've got some sipping cups, and y'all can each one of you have a sample if you like. And you sir, since you are an entrepreneur yourself, I'm happy to let go of an entire case of the stuff at a twenty…no, thirty percent discount."

The proprietor took a sip and declared it good. "Fifty percent discount," he said.

"Make it forty, and you have a deal." Cannaday shook his hand and then continued. "My travelling companions here are the Fireball Brothers from Pickens County, Alabama. Called so because a fireball straight from outer space is responsible for the condition they are in today. It fell upon them while they swam innocently in a pond near their farm. Please enjoy the tonic. Enjoy the music. They seek to raise money for an operation, so please show these young'uns some kindness as well."

The boys then launched into "Old Joe Clark." With the taste of their shine apparently much improved with Cannaday's bitter tonic, the customers drank up and became lively. After an hour, the boys had played everything they knew, and Robert's arms were sore. But more people had come in and were partaking of the new shine cocktails with the proprietor's encouragement, so the boys started over from the beginning. By the time they had finished a second set, Robert and Wally could barely stand.

Outside afterward, Cannaday shook their hands and said that was the greatest sale he'd had in weeks. He'd convinced the owner to buy a second case of the stuff by the time it was all done. Pop looked at the pile of coins in his coffee can and agreed that it had been mutually beneficial.

"Where are y'all headed next?"

Pop said, "Memphis, I reckon."

"Aw, shoot," Cannaday said. "I just came from that way, but I tell you what. I'll head that way if you think we could work together. I'll make a few posters and head into Memphis tonight. Nothing fancy, of course, but later on we can get something professionally made." He wrote some notes down for Pop. "I'll meet you on the corner of Beale and South Fourth at noon tomorrow. Sound good?"

Pop nodded. "How much did you say that there bitter tonic costs?"

"Have a bottle on me," Cannaday said, pulling one from the pocket of his coat.

"Thankee."

As the salesman was turning back toward his Plymouth, Wally said, "Hey Canada. Thanks for giving us a name." Cannaday tipped his hat.

After he left, Robert prodded Wally, "Hey now. I thought of the name."

"Oh, yeah. That's right. Sorry, Bubba."

With a new name and a new confidence, the Fireball Brothers took on Beale Street in Memphis to an enthusiastic crowd, introduced by Cannaday. They then followed the Mississippi down through Clarksdale, Cleveland, and Greenville. Pop always found a couple of dollars to celebrate with some local moonshine, which he was somehow always able to find. He took to using a few splashes of Cannaday's tonic to enhance it.

In Yazoo city, Pop got drunk and disappeared for a day. When Robert and Wally woke up in the back of the truck, he was just gone. Cannaday had run out of his product and had to go his own way, but he promised to meet up with them again as soon as he could. At first, they assumed Pop had gone hunting, but his rifle was still in the back of the truck, and he didn't hunt with the Colt. The day passed into the evening, and they stayed huddled up in the back of the truck. A breeze crept in through the drafty hutch after dark.

Robert said, "If he doesn't come back, do you think we can figure out how to drive the truck?"

"What you mean if he doesn't come back?"

He'd driven the truck before, but not since the fireball. It might be possible if he sat on Wally's lap, but it would be damned uncomfortable. But he was already uncomfortable. When Wally got excited like this, Robert's whole body would heat up like it was filled with coals, and he felt like that burning tree stump on the fourth of July, like anybody passing by could see right through him into the fire. What images they would see in the flames might depend on the person, but the right person, with the right sensitivity, might see right through to the secrets of the fireball itself.

"I'm just saying we should know what we're gonna do if anything happens to Pop. It's good to have a plan."

"I don't know," Wally said. "I don't want to talk about that no more."

So they sat in silence, their hutch in the back of the truck getting warmer even as the night got cooler. The next morning, a blonde lady in a Thunderbird dropped Pop off. He was still tanked, and they didn't get started to the next town until afternoon. Robert would be damned if he was going to ask Pop anything about it. They headed back east through Greenwood, Winona, Starkville, and Columbus until they were back at home in Pickens County with more than two hundred dollars saved up.

Mama ran to them while Pop was still helping the boys down from the back of the truck. "My young adventurers," she said. "Tell me what sights you've seen."

Wally told her about the jook and the tonic salesman, and about their new name.

"The Fireball Brothers...It has a ring to it," she admitted after some thought.

"We'll take a couple of days to rest up," Pop said, "but then we need to get back to work."

"Dewey," Mama said, following inside. "What's the hurry? You don't have a schedule."

"We're making good money. Can't get lazy." He showed her the money in the can. "I'm going to put this somewhere safe, just take out a little seed money for next time."

"Just a few days, Dewey. I miss the boys. I miss you," she said.

Robert had been noticing her becoming more emotional since Montgomery, sleeping less and less. Pop never did like to look emotion in the face. He was rousing the dogs. "Going hunting," Pop said. "We can talk about it later."

That night, Mama sulked over rabbit stew, and she didn't ask Pop for more time. While trying to sleep, Robert heard them arguing. "Admit it," Mama said, crying. "You don't love me anymore. You're bored here."

"I ain't admitting to nothing," Pop said.

Robert drifted back to sleep after that, though uneasily. He understood that Pop just wanted to get out and make more money so everything could return to normal sooner. Mama only wanted everybody together, at least for a few days or a couple of weeks at a time.

Over breakfast the next morning, Mama and Pop glared at one another like sworn enemies at the signing of a treaty that neither side favors. The very air was poisoned with mistrust and intolerance. "We leave day after tomorrow," Pop said. Mama cleared the dishes that they were still eating and slammed them into the sink. Pop spent the rest of the afternoon and evening in the barn working on his instruments and tweaking the boys' custom seat in the back of the truck.

NINETEEN

With the boys and husband gone again, Lucretia occupied herself with cleaning the house, feeding the dogs, re-reading every book in the house, and cleaning some more. She was stranded with no vehicle and no money on a farm that wasn't producing anything. She barely slept, after they left. "Sleeping" was what she called it when, every other day or so, she suddenly stirred and realized that two or three or six hours had gone by in a blackout. Every sound of the dogs or birds outside trampled her nerves. The patterns in the kitchen wallpaper seemed to develop eyes. If she left the kitchen, it was the radio that watched her. And in the bedroom, it was the patterns in the knotted pine wall panels that transformed into spies tracking her every move.

When Munford Coldwater pulled up in his long brown Eldorado to check in with her, it might have been a relief from the boredom, but it was also just one more set of eyes tracing her, judging her as a wife, mother, and home keeper. Her lack of ability to keep it together. Maybe her parents were right and she had let Dewey steal away all the potential she'd once had. She would have been a Mardi Gras queen, would have married into some other elite Mobile family, sheared off the tail of her grandmother's royal train to tack on to the end of her own.

"What I don't get," he said over a cup of shamefully weak tea, "is your folks down in Mobile."

"What d'you mean?" She asked, discombobulated because he'd mentioned her parents just when she was thinking of them, like he was looking into her thoughts. He was in his shirt sleeves, rolled up. She didn't know how the skin on his arms could be so dark when he was always wearing that suit. Perhaps he was part Indian. His arms had a scaly look to them, like snake skin.

"Well, your daddy, he owned some sort of shipping company, right? And then he passed, and your mama sold the business. There was money then, plenty of it. Then she married that preacher, Mr. Dollar, whose collection plate does just fine. Where did all the money go? They either spent it or gave it away, or they still have it."

Lucretia shrugged. She didn't have any concept of money then, how much there was or wasn't. There had been money for jewels and crystals and ermine, a custom mantle in the high Elizabethan style that weighed forty pounds. "I don't know, Mr. Coldwater. I just don't know. All I know is they cut me off when I married Dewey, and they apparently don't feel obligated to do me any favors."

"That's a damn shame," Coldwater said. "A damn shame."

They stared at the tea cups for a while longer, looking for something else to talk about. Then Coldwater stood and said, "Well, I'll be on my way. Thank you for the tea, ma'am."

The tea had been far too weak, appallingly weak. Just another thing her mother would be ashamed of if she could see it. The kitchen walls might be reporting it back to her. She had to get out of the house. She asked Coldwater if he would be willing to give her a ride into town; she wanted to go to the library and run some other errands. She'd find a ride back, or maybe just walk.

"That's ten miles. It'll take you three hours!"

"I…I don't mind. It will be cool this evening, and I'm in no hurry to come back to this empty house. The walk will help me sleep tonight."

"You do look like you could use some sleep," he said.

On the way into Columbus, Coldwater said again that he thought there was something strange going on with Lucretia's relatives, and did she mind if he went down there to look into it. She didn't mind, but she thought it would be fruitless. Then a few moments later, she remembered the ark.

"The ark," she said suddenly. "There was some project that he called the ark."

"What was it?"

She didn't know anything but the name of it. She always imagined it to be a boat, like Noah's. Her father's business had been boats, so it had not seemed at all strange that her new stepfather also had an interest in boats. Mobile was a coastal town, after all, and lots of people had an interest in boats.

Before she thought of anything else she could say, they'd arrived in front of the women's college, her alma mater—or it would have been if she hadn't dropped out. She thanked him as she exited the car. He thanked her back, for some reason she couldn't quite figure, and left her standing on the sidewalk. The wisteria was still in bloom, even this late in the year. It was getting toward the end August now, and the cafeteria would be brimming with song come supper time. She could almost smell the estrogen.

There were students everywhere, reading and picnicking in the late afternoon shade of the magnolia trees. She had been sitting under one of those very trees reading Robert Burns when Dewey Mackintosh came crashing into her life.

The version of events she told other people, especially the children, was heavily censored. In fact, what Dewey had said to her was not that he would be back later to take her to dinner, but that he'd be back later to take her to bed. The actual words he'd used were, "I'll be back in an hour and we'll have ourselves a nice time."

She'd surprised herself by saying, "Alright." She'd further surprised herself by waiting for him. He'd been true to his word and she had shed her virginity in the cab of his pickup truck. He picked her up every afternoon for weeks. She'd never met a man who was so rude or presumptuous, who cursed so brazenly, who took what he wanted. At the time, it had been a thrill. Then she'd found out she was pregnant with Robert, and it was Easter Break so they drove to the coast to ask her family for their blessing. When they didn't get it, they found a justice of the peace in Fort Walton Beach to perform the ceremony for them, and then it was done.

The library was still a few blocks away, but she'd asked Coldwater to drop her off here so she could stroll around the campus. None of the girls even looked at her. She wandered freely past her old dormitory where she had roomed with a girl from Jackson who was scandalized when she once walked in on them—Dewey down on his knees, her with her legs spread and his face buried in her. God, they had done it all over this campus and even in the Confederate graveyard down the road. They had done it every day, multiple times a day, until the war. When he came back, he'd changed, become more distant. They still had sex, obviously—they had Wally—but not as often and not as passionately.

She passed Painter Hall, home of the Humanities Department,

126

where she would have spent much more time if...no use on dwelling. She wondered if any of her old professors were still there. It had only been fifteen years, and some had been quite young, though they didn't seem that way at the time.

Having had enough reminiscence, she trekked through a residential neighborhood toward the library. Just west of the school was a row of ostentatious antebellum houses that she remembered admiring when she was a student. Now, they just seemed pretentious. Along Second Avenue, she passed the funeral home and flower shop, the small Catholic cathedral, the beauty shop, the dairy bar, and the photographer's, before turning down Fourth Street to the old Victorian house that housed the Columbus and Lowndes County Public Library collection. It was a temporary measure; the county was in the process of building a permanent library up the hill. The library she'd grown up with back in Mobile had always struck her as Egyptian with its square white temple design. She hoped the new library would be something more like that.

Inside, the dim light of the library pleased her tired eyes. The marble foyer led her to the stacks where she ran her hand along the spines of random books, like caressing the rib cage of some giant dog or cat, a faithful companion. She lingered there, floating through the aisles, in awe of the amassed knowledge that surrounded her.

As a girl, she'd spent countless weekends and afternoons poring through book after book in the Mobile library, losing herself in the romance of some bygone age. The sweeping stairway up to the fiction section, overseen by a grand gas-lit chandelier, had been a transport. Miss Emma, the dowager empress of the library, had greeted her by name every week. If she hadn't married Dewey, perhaps she would have become a librarian herself. She would have lived there if they had let her, that library.

At the front of the large room, near the checkout desk, she found a display of best sellers. In the back of this section, behind some other books, not exactly hidden but also not in plain view, she found the two she wanted: *Lady Chatterly's Lover* and *Lolita*.

"Them's saucy ones, Mrs. Mac. Better hide them from the mister," said the old lady behind the counter with a chortle. Lucretia didn't know the old woman's name, though her wrinkled face was as familiar to her as those of her own family. She was no Miss

Emma. She imagined her own face behind that counter, in that alternative universe in which she did not get married and have babies, and babies didn't have freakish accidents in ponds with meteorites and subsequently travel around playing music, leaving her as alone as she would have been if none of that had ever happened.

"Thanks for the warning. I'll keep it in mind." Maybe what she and Dewey needed was a little inspiration. When he returned, she'd read to him in bed, just the dirty parts.

She slipped the books into her handbag and prepared herself to re-enter the bright sun. The air outside stank of fried fish due to a concentration of fry houses on the next block down. They called it Catfish Alley, where the local blacks ate, drank, gambled, and played music, and white folks left them alone to their business.

The Episcopal church down the block, St. Paul's, promised relief from the brightness and the odors of Catfish Alley. She had been in this church many times to rest her feet when running errands in town. It was her refuge, even though she had never been especially religious, not even as a child growing up in a highly religious household. Though the similarities were superficial, it reminded her a little of the old Episcopal Church in Mobile, the oldest one in the state. More similar was the old Spanish Cathedral with its shrines and crucifixes. Crucifeces, she thought? No, that couldn't be right. Somehow, she'd always been too cerebral to buy into the magical thinking of it. But something about the stained glass windows and the deliberate angles of the architecture helped her to process her thoughts, and she did think about God in an abstract sense.

She was overwhelmed, in fact, by the vast complexities involved in her personal concept of God. She thought of the mythological figure everyone calls God as...well, as a mythological figure. The word was a useful label because she couldn't wrap her head around all that the idea of God encompassed. Using the name God was the only way she knew of to talk about such an idea. It was just so complicated.

A well-built church, she thought, raised her awareness about the complex metaphor that was her idea of God, how it revealed itself in everything. The lighting and incense and the architecture were designed to enhance that feeling of awareness, the sense of mystery. As she sat in the pew, she thought about how there are always water molecules in the air, but a mechanism like a shower is designed to concentrate those particles in a stream, and there she was showering in the love and serenity of God's warmth. She felt good afterwards, comparatively, and somehow grateful.

While looking for a shady place to stroll after she left the church, Lucretia found herself in the residential neighborhood that lay between the college and the downtown shopping area. Dr. Stanhope's old Victorian. She didn't need anything from him but considered a social call, which only further proved to her how lonely she really was. Normally, his unkempt yard grew wild in motley patches, but someone had cleaned it up, discarded the weeds, and organized the remaining wild flowers into distinctly designed beds. There were wild orchids the same purple color as his house. From the street, she could see some movement inside, but it didn't appear to be the doctor. Had he hired a maid? That would be disappointing, she thought.

Against her better judgment, she edged closer to the window until she saw more movement, but then it was too late to remove the vision from her mind—Dr. Stanhope's bare, bright, alabaster bottom with a pair of dark legs wrapped around it. She wasn't sure if it was that maid he was doing it with, but she couldn't think who else it could be. She turned and walked quickly in the other direction, laughing harder than she could remember having laughed in months.

She walked through downtown, past the Bell Café and Alford Drugs. Again, she thought of downtown Mobile, as a teenager going to the movies on Dauphin Street, dressing like Vivien Leigh for opening night of *Gone with the Wind*. The Mardi Gras balls, raising Joe Cain, the Order of Mystics, chasing death around a broken column that somehow was supposed to stand for the defeated South. Imagine Robert getting roped into all that elitist nonsense. He'd hate it! That other life, if there'd been no Dewey, no babies, no fireball, seemed so distant and bizarre. Alien even.

There wasn't anything else she wanted to do in town, so she began the long walk home. It was late afternoon now and the day was beginning to cool. Lucretia continued her stroll casually, taking in the early autumn foliage that grew wild along the side of the road. But before she had gone very far, Martha Jean's car pulled up beside her.

Lucretia considered saying no to Martha Jean's offer to give her a lift, since her walk had only just started, but after a moment of reflection, she acquiesced. It was only further proof of her solitude that she was willing to sit in an enclosed space with her overly talkative neighbor, even if it was only for the fifteen minutes it would take to get back to the farm. But then the first thing out of her own mouth guaranteed that their visit would be extended quite a bit longer.

"Did you know that Dr. Stanhope has hired a maid? A live-in maid?"

TWENTY

"Introducing, the Fireball Brothers from Pickens County, Alabama. Fused together by a fireball from outer space! Step up, folks. Gather around."

Doing his best to imitate the bravado of Charlie Cannaday during Charlie's absence, Pop seemed to have found his voice, hawking for the boys on street corners all over Alabama, Mississippi, Tennessee, and even further away. At a junk shop in eastern Kentucky, Wally had picked up a trumpet. He learned how to play it quickly, though not quickly enough for Robert, who had to hear every sputter and blare of the thing as they travelled from town to town. Once Wally got the hang of it, Robert had to admit that it added an interesting dimension to the act. Wally could play harmonies with Robert's fiddle lines, making them sound at times like a full band, rather than two skinny boys stuck to one another.

Wally also thought it would help if Robert learned guitar, an instrument more suited to accompaniment than fiddle. "The strings are bigger, and it won't cramp your hands so much," Wally said. Robert brought along one that was sitting around Pop's workshop, but it was too different from what he was used to, and he didn't spend the time working on it that Wally spent with his trumpet.

In Houma, Louisiana, Robert noted a weasel-eyed roughneck, watching the tip jar a little too closely as Pop passed it through the crowd. Covered in oil stains, he probably worked on one of the oil rigs parked offshore. A patchwork scruff of black beard lived on his face like moss on a rock, and he was circling them like a stray cur homing in on its dinner. He was a scrawny guy that Robert could have easily taken down in his prime, but attached to Wally, he would be useless in any kind of fight. Pop saw him too and kept a tight grip on the coffee can when he crossed in front of the man with it. He kept his other hand on the handle of his Colt.

Robert's main concern was what would happen to Pop if he shot the roughneck in a tussle over the can. It was going to be Montgomery all over again, but worse if they killed a man and dumped him in the swamp. Distracted, he missed a cue from Wally, but he caught up again on the next verse. The man was moving through the crowd as Pop moved through it, always only one or two bodies away.

After three or four songs, the man backed away and sat down on a bench across the street, began rolling himself a cigarette, relieving Robert of his vigilance.

It was a clear night, and they were planning to camp off the road somewhere on the way to Lafayette. Pop had his hands full, loading Wally's kick drum into the back when suddenly the roughneck was there by them, waving a knife at Pop, telling him to keep his hands on the drum and make the boys hand over the money. Robert thought about how much money was in the coffee can now. A few hundred dollars he thought. Probably more even than what they had stashed at home.

"They're already strapped into their special seat, mister. I have to help them out of it. You can see, they can't sit in no regular seat."

"Don't even try to bullshit me," the man said. "They may be freaks, but they are able-bodied. I've been watching them."

Wally said, "I think I can reach it from here, Pop. Through the cab window."

The window between the truck bed and the cab was unlocked, but Robert could see that the coffee can was far out of reach, underneath the seat. He asked Wally what he was doing but was ignored. Then he saw. Wally stretched his arm over to the gun rack just below the window. The roughneck couldn't see what he was doing until it was too late, and Wally was pointing the barrel straight at the man's head.

Robert knew that if he actually pulled the trigger with his one good arm, there was almost no chance he'd hit his target, and he'd probably blow the windows out of the truck. Not to mention the kick would hurt like hell. But he held steady, and the roughneck backed away enough that Pop was able to drop the drum (which wrecked the attached cymbal) and unholster his sidearm.

As the man ran off, Wally set the shotgun down and picked up his trumpet. He played the bugle call of the cavalry charge, and Pop fired a shot into the air. Wally laughed his head off all the way to Lafayette.

They returned from the road newly encouraged with another coffee can full of cash, almost six hundred this time. Though he liked seeing new places and new sorts of people, Robert was tired of sitting in their hutch on back of the truck and longed for the open air of home, to lounge on the porch and drink lemonade. When they pulled into the driveway, the usual sound of barking dogs did not greet them. In fact, the dog pen was empty. A moment later, they heard muffled barking inside the house.

When they went inside they saw that the dogs were running in circles around the living room, and Mama was coming at them with a shotgun pointed at them. The dogs were barking, not at them, but at Mama. She growled at Pop, "Don't come near me, you...you Lothario."

"Whoa, now Lucretia," Pop said. "How about you put that down and tell me what this is about. And what are the fucking dogs doing in the house?"

She didn't lower the gun when she answered, "You fucked that blonde whore of Babylon next door, and who knows how many others. It's no wonder you were so eager to get back out on the road. You probably have one in every town by now."

"Now, Lucretia. You know that's all crazy talk. When's the last time you slept?"

Robert and Wally crept into the background, ducking behind the kitchen counter. But Mama then directed them to get to the bedroom. "I want you safe behind me just in case I end up shooting your father. He's done enough damage to you already."

"Lucretia, the dogs."

"I needed company."

The boys went behind their mother, as they were told, but they didn't retreat to the bedroom. Instead, they stood in the hallway just a few feet behind her. Pop had shown her how to shoot, but she was no expert. Robert hoped he'd get to a spot where he could easily grab the gun away from her, hoping Wally would instinctively go along.

"Lucretia," Pop said. Mama had suffered some anxiety attacks in the past, though nothing quite like this. When Pop called her by name repeatedly, it was always in an attempt to calm her down from one of her episodes. Today, it didn't seem to be working.

"Yes, I talked to Martha Jean. We were both bored and lonely, I guess, and she brought over a bottle of whiskey someone had left at her party. Halfway through the bottle, she was crying. She admitted everything."

"What did she say?"

"She had to get this off her conscience, even though it happened years ago."

"Lucretia, I thought we straightened all that out back then. Nothing happened."

"That's what you told me, and I made myself believe you. Now I know that you lied." She was crying now, and her words became shapeless caterwauls where only the occasional "liar" and "bastard" were understandable. Robert nudged Wally a little closer. Then came the blast.

A lamp was destroyed, the same one Robert and Wally had nearly knocked over several times when trying to fit themselves through the kitchen door. The dogs barked louder now. Pop and the boys descended on Mama before she had time to reload. It took a good while to calm her down, Robert, Wally, and Pop all holding onto her tight. Robert felt their four hearts beating hard. Wally's hand heated up Robert's chest and slowed his heartbeat down, but he could still hear everyone else panting. The dogs gradually settled down.

Pop said, "A'ight now. We gonna talk this over as calm as we can, and we gonna figure out what has to happen."

They decided to wait a while before going back out on the road, and Pop agreed to sleep in the barn in the meantime. Stanhope brought over some medicine to help Mama sleep, and if she hardly slept before, she was now the opposite. They barely saw her over the next week and a half. Robert and Wally made their meals with whatever they could scrape up around the kitchen or the yard, a lot of beans and some squirrels. On the rare occasions when she came moping out of the bedroom, Mama always just said she wasn't hungry. They brought their food out to the barn to share it with Pop, who didn't come into the house if he could help it.

One of those beans-in-the-barn mornings, Pop said, "Let me explain about Martha Jean."

Robert said he didn't want to hear it, but Wally did. Pop's

explanation was nothing more or less than Robert expected it to be. She was lonely then, with Eddie away at the war, and she'd always had someone to take care of her before that. Pop had let himself be tempted, and he always regretted it. But it didn't seem to hurt anybody at the time, so he thought if they never told anybody, it would never matter.

Later Wally said, "I always knew something was going on between them."

"No you didn't," Robert said. He didn't think any less of his father for it. He didn't think less of Martha Jean either, though it was true he didn't think much of her in the first place.

At night, Robert and Wally talked in their room about whether their parents were going to get divorced. Robert was of the opinion that they wouldn't. Wally wasn't so sure.

Wally said, "Do you think they still love each other?"

"Love is just another word for disappointment." This was a thought that had come to him on the road. He had not always been so philosophical, but in the back of the truck there was often nothing to do but think. He had thought about his frustration with Edwina and even with the other infatuations of his youth, which now seemed so distant. Even the pretty girl in Birmingham that had captured his imagination, whose name he did not even know, was an unsatisfying mystery with no conclusion. He saw further disillusionment in his parents, in the Van Chukkers, in the faces of practically everyone he saw. In the long term, nobody was actually happy, it seemed to him, when it came to the subject of love.

TWENTY-ONE

The highway through east Tennessee took Charlie Cannaday through a winding gap in the mountainside. His cigar trailed
smoke, which mingled with the damp Appalachian air out the
open window. The Plymouth Savoy sailed over the curves and
hills. Had he been born in another time and place, he'd have been
a seafaring man, and he liked to consider himself anyway a sort of
buccaneer of the road. Not so much a highwayman or road agent,
stand and deliver, your money or your life type of thing, though
perhaps highwayman was an appropriate term for one who cruised
the road, living by his wits, seeking opportunities. He was a wily
fox. He liked that idea. Maybe he'd begin to call himself "The
Fox." Charlie "The Fox" Cannaday.

Between Birmingham and Nashville, he had sold all but the
last three bottles of his product, and this old lady in Monteagle
would supposedly be able to help him make some more. His recent good luck notwithstanding, he would have sold out even faster if he could have convinced those Fireball Brothers to travel
east with him instead of going their own way. He'd already exhausted Memphis and everything else along the river right up to
St. Paul over the past few weeks, and it was his policy to never
visit the same region twice in six months. Three months was about
how long it would take most people to run out of the tonic, and
they could spend three months pining after more, so that when he
showed up again, he'd be welcome. Alternatively, if he had made
a less favorable impression, perhaps it would be forgotten by then,
or there would be a crop of new customers that had moved into
town since his last visit.

At any rate, there were always more highways, more roads,
more towns. The little towns interested him too—old mining vil-
lages, county seats of farming communities, towns founded by
religious exiles, once-thriving railroad towns and port towns that
were losing their relevance now that travel was cheaper and easier. All roads went somewhere, and every place had some reason
for existing, each one its own treasure. Next to him on the pas-

136

senger seat was his treasure map, produced by the Cities Service Company of Bartlesville, Oklahoma. Even though he practically knew every square inch of it by rote, it was still comforting to have it there beside him, a guiding force. Some nights at a motel or campground, he would revisit it as one might revisit a favorite novel, poring over every crooked line. He knew each town by smell and could invoke that scent from the little black dot that represented it on the map.

Outside his window, green hills and streams flashed by him like images in a film. It almost didn't look real, like when actors stand in front of a blue screen, and then they are later projected in front of the Alps or the Eiffel Tower. He puffed at his cigar and gazed down the silver ribbon of road winding through the mountains. The woman, a toothless vestal virgin no doubt, lived outside Monteagle and was the only person he knew of in the area that would have something like the ingredients: gentian root, angostura bark, wormwood, grains of paradise, devil's club root. Other things he'd never even heard of or would assume were poisonous just from the sound of the names. Let it steep in alcohol for a couple of weeks. Add some cinnamon and clove for flavor. Sugar to help it go down.

Gilmore Scott gave him the name and address of the hillbilly lady, said she knew how to make these old-fashioned tinctures. He imagined that she used them to cast spells or something, probably lived in a cave on the side of the mountain.

The combined pungency of cigar smoke and green countryside. The car itself smelled of the tonic he'd been pedaling across the country for more than a year now—it smelled of the Caribbean Sea, the jungles of the West Indies, the Amazon. Sure, it had been a good run, and he supposed if he couldn't get more of it, or something similar, he'd just find something else to sell. He could sell anything. But he'd never get that scent out of his system, even if he got it out of the car. It was the scent of adventure and the scent of wonder. It was that scent that drove him onward.

At a diner outside Winchester, he filled his belly with chicken fried steak and tea as sweet as maple syrup. On the next table over, someone had left a newspaper so Charlie thumbed through it, glancing over the local news and grocery store specials. Page three had a feature that had been picked up from the Tupelo paper about those damn boys, and even mentioned them by that name, the Fireball Brothers. The ungrateful imps had been all over the Southeast since he last saw them. He tore out the page and stuffed it in his jacket pocket. The whole thing turned his stomach.

Watching those boys play their music was like watching a coon hound stand up and say the Pledge of Allegiance. The results were about what you would expect from a small child, but you were amazed they could do it at all. They sounded like a broken hurdy-gurdy. That screechy fiddle and the thunderous bass drum would have been an assault on the ear drums played by anyone else, but they still managed to captivate. They moved as one body and appeared to think as one body, and so you tended to look at them as a single thing and not as two boys who happened to be welded together by some invisible force. Privately, he had pleaded with the father to go back along 78 to Birmingham, but there was no talking him into it.

If the Fireball Brothers had come along with him, it wouldn't matter that he'd run out of product. By then, he could have convinced the father to let him help manage the boys. He could have taught them so much about how to talk to a crowd, how to sell themselves. They all could have made a lot more money.

The directions Gilmore had given him took him down a paved country road and then to a dirt road. The woods imposed themselves over the clay path, giving it the feel of a tunnel. After turning into the gate and passing some cleared fields, he came to a little white house with a red roof and brick chimney, alone in the field.

A small woman in a blue checked dress and kerchief answered the door. Her eyes were green, not emerald, but grass green, a dark spinach green, and he stood before her stunned by her beauty some moments before finding his voice.

"Excuse me, ma'am. I was looking for, eh," he squinted at the slip of paper in his hand. "See Oh Bain…"

"I'm Siobhon," she said. Pronounced she-von. One of those damned unsayable Celtic names.

"Your grandmother, maybe?" She cocked her head. "Gilmore Scott sent me. I need a certain tonic."

"It's me you want." She invited him into the house, which was not at all cavelike but was decorated in a simple country fashion. Far as he could tell, she wasn't toothless either, though her East Tennessee drawl was thick. "How much of it d'you need?"

"Much as you can spare. A couple of gallons would do for now. I can come back in two weeks and get more."

Though the inside of her home was unlike what he had pictured in his mind, the balmy medicinal odor of herbs and roots was precisely as he had imagined, primitive. She turned and examined him, her green eyes scanning over him. "Mr. Scott sent word ahead, but…it takes a few weeks to make it. The botanicals need to sit in the solution for at least two weeks, and then there are some other steps. I have about a quart right now."

"A quart?" Charlie heard his voice rise and calmed down by petting himself, pretending to brush some dust off the front of his jacket. "Well, miss, I don't think you quite understand my situation. A mere quart wouldn't last me a day."

"I'm sorry, sir…I didn't catch your name."

"And I didn't give it to you. You can call me the Fox." He aimed his pistol at her. It had not been his plan to rob her, and Gilmore Scott wasn't going to like it. But he would just have to understand. Filled with the invigorating vegetal perfumes around him, he was a conqueror, a conquistador. He would have his quarry. She would stand and deliver.

Siobhan remained calm, staring back at him with the green eyes of a leviathan. "Sir, I don't know what Mr. Scott told you about me, but I ain't a commercial producer. I provide these tonics medicinally for people in my community. I don't make anything in large batches."

"Just give me the raw materials then. Tell me how to do it, I'll do it myself."

"I wouldn't advise that," she said.

"Well, you don't have any choice." He waved his arm at her. "Go on, get the shit together. Since I won't be coming back here, I'll take whatever you've got, long as it will fit in the trunk of my car."

She sighed. After a pause, she gathered some mason jars of various items off the shelf and carefully packed them in a box, and the aroma of the botanicals washed over him in waves as she gathered them from their individual jars. He put his foot up on a chair and stood over her, inhaling the fragrance, holding the pistol casually, thinking himself a highwayman now in every sense. The Fox strikes again. He lit up another cigar.

Charlie set up his lab in a motel room outside of Chattanooga. He'd made her write out the recipe, but he'd forgotten to get her to label the jars. He didn't know what half of these herbs and roots were, much less what to do with them. Even going to the library in Chattanooga hadn't been any help since he couldn't identify any of the ingredients he had in his possession. She'd told him that he'd need a good amount of ethanol. She didn't have any on-hand and wouldn't tell him where to get it. "Right, so you can go rob him too?" He'd slapped her for that one, but she wouldn't relent. It didn't matter. If a little hillbilly girl like that could learn to make this stuff, he could figure it out for himself.

After making about a hundred telephone calls, he found a supplier that would sell him ethanol in bulk. It would take a lot of his cash on hand, but he'd make it back. He got funnels and cheese cloth and a carton of little glass bottles. Gilmore Scott would know what to do about labels. They had parted ways a week ago outside Nashville. Scott wouldn't have gone far since then and arranged to meet up in Atlanta at the end of the month.

The mason jars all sat open before him, some filled a quarter or halfway with whatever it was, some filled more. He poured the alcohol into each jar, enough to cover all the solids and decided to just let them marinate there for a two weeks. In the meantime, there was nothing to do but wait.

A short walk down the two-lane highway where his motel sat, there was a small roadhouse with nothing identifying it but a blinking pink neon sign that said "Beer," except the B was out, causing it to actually read as "eer." He took it as an invitation. A basic roadside bar with a jukebox, bottled beer, and a ragged pool table. Usually, he'd go in a place like this and order a whiskey, make sure the barkeep saw him put the tonic in there. Barely even had to make a pitch if you get their curiosity up. "Oh, I take it for my health, but it really improves the flavor too," he'd say. "I have a few bottles stored away, but I can always get more."

Here, there wasn't enough of a crowd to bother with the routine, and he didn't have product yet anyway. The bartender, a gray mustached man in a blue checked shirt, made like he was wiping the bar down just to give himself something to do. Two younger fellows in denim bibs and long beards were so absorbed in a game of billiards that they didn't even look up when he walked in.

"Your finest Pabst Blue Ribbon, sir," he said, finding a seat.

Barkeep nodded, pulled a beer bottle from the cooler, opened it, and emptied it into a glass all in one swift motion. A lady emerged from the washroom and plopped down on the next stool over without saying a word. Mid-thirties, he guessed, maybe the older sister or young aunt of Romulus and Remus at the pool table. Or could be the barkeep's daughter. No, that look he gave her when he lit her cigarette…maybe the barkeep's wife. He mouthed something to her, a lover's secret. Her hair formed a blonde puff. She wore a white halter top and knee-high pants.

When he finished his first beer in silence and started another, she said, "Aren't you even going to say hello?"

"Didn't want to presume, ma'am."

"I ain't wearing no ring, and I ain't attached at the hip."

He permitted himself to look. She had probably been pretty once, still held together pretty well for a hillbilly. Muscular thighs. He imagined them squeezing like a boa around his neck. Might be looking for compensation, and he didn't have a lot of cash with him. But he was the Fox after all, and the Fox could take what he wanted. Considered taking it from Siobhan back in the hills; she'd have been feisty.

After another beer's worth of innocent banter, he mentioned he was staying at the motel next door.

"Let me guess," she said. "You want to show me your stamp collection. I thought you'd never ask. Do you mind?" She gestured toward her glass. Wants me to pay for her drink, he thought. He put a five down on the bar. More than he had wanted to let go of, but made him look like a hot shot. Maybe he'd be able to move some product here when it finished cooking.

She took his arm, and he escorted her out. Footsteps behind him, but then they stopped. Nothing to worry about. Once in the door though, he heard them rushing up. Either Romulus or Remus hit him hard, and then it was dark. He woke in his room, but it was empty. No roots or herbs. No mason jars. No experiments. No money. No pants. Only a note on the mirror. It said, "Dear Fox. Sorry I had to sour your grapes. I hope your head feels better soon. –Siobhan."

TWENTY-TWO

One Tuesday, Mama came out of the bedroom, fully dressed and made up like she was going out. She had lost a lot of weight, not that she had much to spare, but she had covered it up well, in high heel shoes and that same red dress she had worn into the French Quarter that night that now seemed so long ago. There was a lightness to her walk, and she hummed a bright Celtic tune. "Boys," she said, still brushing her hair out while she walked. "Please retrieve your father from the barn."

"Are you feeling better, Mama?" Wally said.

She looked up at them and paused, blinking. "Yes. Yes, I am. Thank you for asking. Now get your father for me, will you?"

When Pop came in, the two of them retired to the bedroom. Robert and Wally tried to listen through the door, but they couldn't hear anything. Their parents didn't come out for hours. Finally, the boys gave up and went to sleep. When they woke the next morning, Mama was making flapjacks, and Pop was sitting at the breakfast table.

"Morning, boys," he said. "Sit down. We need to have a family talk."

He told them that he and Mama had worked some things out. The crux of it was that they would be going out on the road again, starting the next morning, and that when they got back this next time, things were going to return to normal.

Robert was skeptical. "Normal?" Nothing had been normal since that fireball came down out of the sky.

"It means after breakfast, y'all get your heifer fucking bags packed and do some rehearsing."

They stayed on the road this time for more than a month. Pop said it was to give Mama the time she needed to rest and think things over. He didn't act concerned and so Robert didn't act concerned either, though he was. Right about seven or eight each morning, the truck would roll into a town square or a farmers' market and find a place to park for the day. Today it was Anniston. Tomorrow it would be someplace in Tennessee. They travelled all over, as far west as Oklahoma City, and as far north as Charlottesville, Virginia. Pop had fitted a mattress for the back, so that the boys could sleep comfortably there. He'd sleep in the cab with his feet out the window.

With only his right arm and his feet at his disposal, Wally would mostly just pedal that kick drum and sometimes play the harmonica or trumpet. He picked up new instruments with ease. For Robert, with the exception of that one time in Birmingham, the fiddle still always felt foreign and delicate in his hands, hands more suited to throwing baseballs, pulling weeds, and chopping wood. They both knew they weren't very good, but the novelty always attracted people. They improved a little each time they played, and they always collected at least a few dollars.

They passed through Birmingham several times in their travels, and Robert always hoped to see that girl again. He knew it wasn't rational to think it likely. Birmingham was a big place.

On an afternoon in late August, somewhere in eastern Tennessee, the mountains bloomed green and gold above the road where Pop had parked the truck while he went off to find a campsite and build a fire. Robert and Wally remained strapped in the truck bed. A long, red Pontiac Bonneville with the top down rolled up behind them, and with some apparent difficulty, a round man with a gray suit, top hat, and half chewed cigar pulled himself out of the driver's seat.

His voice full of brio and barbecue sauce, the man said, "Damn, your daddy makes good time getting down the road. I've been trying to catch up with y'all since Shelbyville."

The stranger introduced himself as Gilmore T. Scott of the Gilmore T. Scott Travelling Circus and Sideshow. One of his employees had seen them perform the previous day, but by the time Mr. Scott got there, they were gone. A waitress tipped him off about what direction the Fireball Brothers had been headed, and here they were. "I have a business proposition for you," he finally said.

Pop, who by then had returned from the brush, invited the man to come sit down by the fire and talk it over. Scott repeated the backstory about his travelling circus and offered them forty dollars a week to join up.

"Oh, it's you," Pop said.

Gilmore T. Scott clapped his hands together. "Of course, of course. We spent a few hours together in the Montgomery jail back in July. I've been looking for you ever since then. It was serendipitous that I crossed your path again back in Maryville. Now what do you say to a hundred a week. You can't be making a forty a week on your own."

Pop said. "Some weeks are better than others, but we ain't splitting with anybody."

Robert calculated how long it would take to make what they needed at that rate. It was a gamble, so Robert understood why Pop held firm, even when Scott upped the offer to forty each. "That's over a hundred dollars a week," he said.

Under his breath, Wally said, "Take it, Pop."

"Hush up," Robert said. "Pop knows what he's doing."

Pop was impassive, and eventually the man gave up. A rustling in the bushes caused Pop to grab his gun. "If that's a rabbit we'll have a nice dinner. I'll be right back."

When Pop disappeared into the brush, Scott pulled a flask out of his jacket pocket, had a slug of it, and offered it to Robert. He declined, but Wally took it eagerly. Robert side-eyed him best he could without breaking his own neck.

Scott said, "I don't suppose y'all have worked with a Dr. Montalto?"

Robert answered, "You know Montalto?"

"Know him," the man said. "Hell yes, I know that backstabbing sumbitch. Well, you just keep on working for him, and see what that gets you. Good luck."

"We don't work for him," Robert said. "But he's going to help us, after we save up the money."

"Help you do what? Attach a third?"

Wally said, "He's going to split us up again."

"Split you? You have a good thing going here. If I were you, I'd keep working this. Y'all could be famous."

Robert shrugged.

"To each his own," Scott said.

Robert stared up at the sky beginning to go dark. A handful of distant fireballs twinkled through the pink dusk. It occurred to him, you could spend your whole life analyzing a moment, trying to understand it from every angle, observing how every previous moment in your life led up to that one and how every moment since then has been changed by that moment, how every detail that radiates out of that moment has an almost infinite number of people, places, and things that it touches and alters. But that was no way to live.

Scott started at the sound of two shots from the brush behind them. Robert and Wally were used to it. On this trip, they'd eaten rabbit, squirrel, possum, and even snake. Anything was fine if you salted and cooked it enough over a campfire. When Pop returned, carrying two bloody rabbit carcasses, he offered to let Scott stay and eat.

"Appreciate it," Scott said. "But I have dinner waiting for me at my own camp." With that, the man had another slug of his whiskey and departed.

Afterward, Pop explained to the boys that not only was Scott's offer not enough, he didn't trust anyone who drove a convertible.

"I've no doubt," Pop said, "that man would have robbed back every penny he'd paid us and then some the first chance he got. And I don't want to get tricked into no kind of contract neither. When we're ready to go home, I want to be able to go home. Your Mama's waiting on me."

A couple of days later, they were passing back through Birmingham. They were all weary of the road but wanted to make a little more cash on the way back to the farm. They managed to find that same little patch of park across from the barbershops where they had played the first time they were there, and the same kind of crowd showed up. Robert's entire body was vibrating with anxiety, and the first couple of songs were rough. But then he saw her there, again, the red-haired girl now wearing a floppy straw hat, jeans, and a short-sleeved checkered shirt. All that had happened the last few days was so overwhelming, Robert had forgotten to be excited at the prospect of possibly seeing her again. He felt something in his chest begin to hum with energy.

Music then flowed from his fingers as if from a spring. Wally seemed to be infected by it also, and sang with rare gusto. The girl stayed and watched until they took a break almost an hour later.

Robert wiped down his instrument, and found himself only a little startled when he saw the girl standing directly in front of him. She was so small, maybe not even five feet, and thin as a pixie.

"Y'all, that was phenomenal. Simply phenomenal. I loved watching you play. Are you playing more, or maybe a set somewhere tonight?"

Wally was drinking water from his mason jar. Pop had gone back to the truck to count the money.

"Uh, thank you, uh, ma'am." Robert said. Compliments were rare in his experience, and usually they came from someone who wanted something in return. She was grinning. "I think we are going to look for a place to stay, or else move on to Tuscaloosa, and find a place there. We might play a little more after we take a little rest, if there are still people around."

"Phenomenal. Do you have a gig in Tuscaloosa?"

He hadn't thought of it as "gigs" exactly. They just showed up and played. Nobody ever asked them to, even if they did occasionally stop at a honky tonk or jook joint. Pop came back over toward them, the pickle jar now empty again except for a couple of teaser dollars to make sure people got the idea. He was hunched over and holding onto his back. He'd been sleeping in the truck cab for several nights in a row.

"Not exactly," Robert said, to answer the girl. "Pop, are you okay?"

"Just a little stiff," he said, the pain in his back showing through his voice. "Be alright in a little while. Can't wait to get home though."

She said, "Where's home?"

She seemed genuinely interested. Wally said, "We live in Pickens County, on the other side of Tuscaloosa, near the state line."

"That's a long drive," she said. "Do you ever play in night clubs?"

"No ma'am," Robert said. "We just play on the streets."

"Oh, stop calling me ma'am, silly boy. My name is Elizabeth, but you can call me Izzy."

Pop said, "Izzy don't seem like a proper name for a girl, specially one so pretty." He tried to smile, but ended up grimacing again, holding his back.

"That settles it," Izzy said. "Y'all need to just stay with me tonight. I've got some extra mattresses because my roommates just moved out. And I know some Chinese massage techniques that'll take care of that back so you can get home comfortably tomorrow."

She hopped into the passenger seat of the truck and gave Pop directions. It wasn't far. The apartment was dark and smelled like smoke. When she flipped on the switch, a few cockroaches skittered away into the walls. Two small floor lamps revealed minimal furniture, a floor covered in throw pillows of various sizes and shapes. Diaphanous cotton sheets billowed out from the open windows, casting ghostly shadows on dark walls where uneven stacks of books formed skeletal spines. There was a small functional kitchen on the right and a hallway that led to the bedrooms on the left.

"I can't believe you haven't read Norman Mailer," she said. "He's simply phenomenal." Along the short walk to her place, she had talked mostly about books and jazz musicians, none of which Robert or Wally had ever heard of.

She directed Pop to a mattress so he could lie down. Then she dragged a second mattress in from another room so Robert and Wally could do the same. Izzy said she was going to fix Pop's back, and gave Robert a stack of magazines to peruse. The first one Robert picked up was a *Life* magazine, with a bookmarked article titled, "Squaresville USA vs. Beatsville." Music from a record player materialized from somewhere near the back and played a sultry saxophone tune. He read the article out loud to Wally, which was apparently an open letter from some girls in Kansas to a poet in San Francisco, pleading him to come stir up some excitement in their dull town. They both laughed at the weird language used in the article—"This town is Squaresville itself, so we as its future citizens want to be cooled in."

Wally, still laughing, said, "I don't get it."

Izzy retrieved a colorful wooden box from the kitchen cabinet. From the box she took a thin cigarette, lit it, and took a long drag. She gestured for Pop to do the same. "It'll relax your back muscles," she said.

Robert couldn't quite place what the smoke smelled like, but he knew it wasn't tobacco. The closest thing he could equate to it was the scent of a cow field after a long rain. His mind wandered to the fields of Pickens County. When he was younger, maybe

147

about seven, he had been wandering around some of the fields near their farm and came across a dead cow on the other side of a wooden fence. Having never seen a dead cow, he was naturally curious about it and began climbing the fence to get a closer look when the carcass began to bulge and pulsate. Suddenly the cow's stomach burst open and a family of possums, covered in slime and blood, erupted from the body, grinning and screeching. It was the first evil thing Robert remembered ever seeing.

The dead cow in his mind began to low, and then he realized the moan was coming from Pop. Robert worried for a moment. "He's fine," Izzy said. "Massage is pretty intense if you've never had it." She filled a glass with water from the sink and went back over to Pop.

Wally said his legs were falling asleep, so they stood up to stretch. Robert perused some of the books lining the walls—so many authors he'd never heard of. It was mostly poetry, from what he could figure. He lost track of time flipping through several ragged volumes, while Wally looked on over his shoulder.

"Ha—I love that one," Izzy said, looking over at them. The book in Robert's hand then was a book of poetry by Allen Ginsberg. She was closer than Robert had realized, and Pop was laid out on the mattress with his shirt off, looking a bit like Eddie Van Chukker's roasted pig. "Your daddy's asleep," she said. "Let's let him rest. Want to go see some jazz? The Owl's Club is right down the street. Sun Ra is playing; he's phenomenal."

"What's a Sun Ra?" Wally said.

"Maybe just for a little bit," Robert said. "We're pretty tired ourselves. But we want to be cooled in." He grinned.

She took them through the parking lot of the dirty concrete block apartment complex she lived in. On the other side, there was a square building painted blue with the windows boarded and no sign outside.

There were eight people in the band, more than the number in the audience, which doubled when the three of them arrived. They were the only three white faces in the small crowd. The musicians were all dressed up in Egyptian regalia and played something that sounded more like a riot of chickens than any music Robert had ever heard. The drums played a fast swing beat, and two bass players in the corner thumped out a mystical minor scale. The horn section blasted harmonic punches while the saxophonist screeched out what Robert might call the melody if it were less chaotic. On some sort of electronic organ, the band leader was playing an erratic counter solo to the saxophone. He was an enormous colored man, looked like a pharaoh from outer space, and in fact he was singing—or rather more like ranting—something about being from Saturn.

My whole body changed into something else.

I could see through myself. I went up.

I wasn't in human form.

I landed on a planet that I identified as Saturn.

They teleported me and wanted to talk with me.

They had one little antenna on each ear. A little antenna over each eye.

They told me to stop going to school because there was going to be great trouble in schools.

The world was going into complete chaos.

I would speak through music, and the world would listen. That's what they told me.

Robert didn't know what to think of this giant Negro from Saturn or of the red-headed girl. She was fascinating but confusing. He couldn't understand half of what she said. As for Sun Ra, Robert thought he might be dreaming it all.

"Isn't he phenomenal?" Izzy said, bringing them both beers. "He's from Birmingham, but he moved to Chicago a while back. He never shows up back here. It's a fluke you even got to see him."

The beer tasted sharp and sweet at the same time. Wally gulped his down in one swallow. Robert sipped on his, slipping into the strange Pentecostal mood.

Sun Ra stood from his organ and marched around the room, physically lifting up each person from their chair, giving them an intense bear hug, and setting them back down. When he came to Robert and Wally, he stopped and waved his arms. The band came to a sudden halt. Robert felt himself tremble. Even Wally, who obviously couldn't see, could sense the man towering over them, his giant white eyes gazing down upon them from a countenance dark as space itself.

Sun Ra said, "Rise up."

Wally mumbled, "It's in us."

Robert felt Wally's hand on his chest growing hot. He remembered the day in the barn when he had cut the seam with a violin knife, the white light that shined through his skin and then cauterized the wound. How had he forgotten it? Wally was right. It's in us, he thought. That's why they couldn't find anything at the pond.

"It's in us," he said out loud. Nobody seemed to have heard him.

Sun Ra said again, "That's right. It's in you. Rise up." They did. "Follow me."

The band started up again, and they followed Sun Ra as he marched around the perimeter of the room. As they passed each table, patrons joined the parade. They went around the room perhaps a dozen times. Robert was dizzy by the time it was over. The band took a break after forty minutes. Robert, Wally, and Izzy stumbled outside. While Robert had nursed that one beer through the set, Wally had drunk three of them, throwing their mutual coordination off kilter.

"This Birmingham of yours is a strange place," Robert said.

"Is it not the same Birmingham as everyone else's?"

"I don't know. You expect people to be a certain way, but they never are." She smiled at him. "It's all new to me," he said, "but something tells me your Birmingham is different."

She said, "Every place is strange if you look close enough. Do you know what a tapir is?"

Robert scratched his head and said no. They had stopped in a park and sat on the grass, which was cool and moist under their legs. It was just after midnight, and the moon was just shy of full, like an orange disk of butterscotch candy hanging over them, dripping sweetness. Wally fidgeted, trying to make himself comfortable. The best thing seemed to be to try and lie down, spooning like they did when they slept. Izzy shifted herself in under Robert's arm, so he was now in the middle, spooning her. Izzy's hair still smelled like sweet, earthy smoke. His hand was on her belly, and he was getting an erection. Izzy only bore deeper into him, her backside pressed up against him. He was afraid he might burst.

"It's a beast that can't decide if it's a pig or an anteater, but in fact it's more closely related to a horse," Izzy said.

Robert had almost forgotten what they were talking about, and this drew him out of his thoughts. He laughed and said, "I know a doctor that might have invented that beast."

"Birmingham is like a tapir," she said. "It's a big city by Alabama standards, but still rather unsophisticated. I think it has more in common with the Old West than the Old South." She took Robert's hand from her belly and casually placed it on her breast. "More comfortable now?"

It wasn't the first time he had held a breast in his hand. A girl named Maggie Williams had let him touch hers after school one afternoon the previous year. She had lured him into the woods and taken off her shirt, and he had just stood there holding it. It had been warm and small in his hand like a hard tangerine. He and Maggie didn't do anything else, and after a very long-seeming five minutes, she pushed his hand off, put her shirt back on, and ran away. Izzy's was larger and soft like a ball of unbaked bread.

Izzy reached behind, touching his still rigid crotch, and said, "Oh, nice." She then, much to Robert's surprise, unbuttoned his pants and pulled out his prick. Shifting her own pants and panties down, she pulled him closer and inside.

Wally said, "Hey, what are y'all doing?"

"Nothing," Robert said. "You're just dreaming. Or maybe I am."

She pulled his hand down so his fingers touched the small bump between her legs, just above where he was inside her. It felt like nothing he knew, like something warm and buttered. The scent of peaches filled his head.

"Slower," Izzy said. In a few moments, her body shivered, and so did Robert's.

"What is happening?" Wally said.

"Hush," Robert said.

It didn't take long before he discharged with another shudder. Izzy turned, smiling, and kissed him lightly on the cheek. She pulled up her pants and then helped Robert with his.

"I should probably get y'all back to my apartment so you can get some sleep."

They came back in quietly so as to not wake Pop. As they did anytime they slept in a regular bed, Robert hurled Wally over his back and then flopped over him and into position. Wally's body was tense and stiff, but Robert's was loose, almost liquid. He knew what was bothering Wally, but he was in no shape to address it.

Izzy said, "You're just so...*existential*. So in the moment."

"Thanks," Robert said drowsily. "You are too." He fell asleep before his face touched the pillow, and he dreamed about baking bread.

151

The drive back to Pickens County went by quickly. Robert was in a daze, still thinking about lying down in the park with Izzy. He had almost forgotten for those few minutes that Wally was there behind him. During the trip, Wally talked incessantly, but even this did not disturb Robert from his daydreaming.

"Izzy was so nice. Didn't you think she was nice? How old did you think she was? Maybe twenty? Twenty-one? And that Sun Ra, what was he? About eight feet tall? At least seven feet."

Robert just said uh huh and sure.

Mama was buttoning up her housecoat when they walked in. It was now the end of September, and the heat of summer had not yet relented, but a fog had settled in, which had cooled the air by a few degrees. Even with the weather getting milder, Mama looked flushed and sticky as if it were a humid day in August.

"You look hotter than a baked potato," Pop said.

"I was just doing some cleaning up in the bedroom. I heard you pull up and ran out to greet you. Like I always have. So sit down. I'll make some coffee. Tell me all about your adventures."

Wally told her about the different towns, the camping, and the travelling circus. In turn, she told them that Eddie Van Chukker was still being held by the military folks down at the pond. Some people were starting to say he was a Communist spy. She'd been doing some housework in Columbus for grocery money, and people had been real nice to her. There was some crazy talk about a wolf lady running around town after midnight, but she hadn't seen anything of it herself. And that Munford Coldwater had been by a few times to talk. He wasn't so bad as she'd imagined at first, and in fact, he'd helped her get some perspective on things.

Also, she said, Doctor Stanhope had given her something that helped her to sleep. A little white pill. She didn't know why she hadn't thought of it before. Insomnia had made her such a wreck, she'd been losing touch with reality. She felt a hundred percent better now.

"Most importantly," she said, "Dewey, I want you to know I'm not mad at you anymore. I've had the time I needed, and the most important thing to me is that the family stays together. I'm not even mad at Martha Jean."

Robert thought she was altogether too calm about everything to be believed. But if she claimed she was happy, he supposed he had no choice but to take her word for it. He and Wally got up to unpack their bags. From their bedroom window, Robert saw a brown Eldorado speeding away through a clearing in the field.

"Wally," he said. "I've said it a dozen times…"

"I know, you hope you never fall in love. I'm tired of hearing it. Listen, Bubba. You shouldn't let all this shit between Mama and Pop mess with you so much. Just because they are damaged doesn't mean you have to be."

"How'd you know that was what I was going to say?"

Wally said, "You really think I'm stupid, don't you? It's true that you've always been smarter than me, but I notice things that you don't. I saw Coldwater's car just now. I've seen him sneaking away from here more than once. The way I figure it, Mama thinks she's getting even with Pop, and that makes her feel better about everything."

They stayed home for a few days, and everything was routine. Pop checked on the fields; it had all gone to seed in his absence. All he could do was plan better for next year. He picked some corn every day, so Mama could use it. In the early mornings, he tried to hunt so they'd have some kind of meat. He left Mama with some of the money they had earned so she could buy supplies and dog food.

The road, too, became routine, and nothing much changed either there or at home for the next couple of months except the color of the trees.

TWENTY-THREE

By thumbing through his pocket notebook, Munford reminded himself of what he already knew about Reverend Dollar and the Fellowship of Levi. Unsure of where exactly to begin, he decided to go down to the marina. After all, if the ark was a boat, it made sense for it to be docked somewhere nearby. There were dozens, perhaps hundreds of boats there, though: from fishing schooners to yachts. It was not difficult to imagine himself cruising away aboard one of these stately vessels, to vanish at sea, no other soul for miles, perhaps eventually landing on some remote island or some other continent, or perhaps relenting to the power of the sea itself. He tried to read all the names to see if one happened to be called the S.S. Ark or some variation thereof, quickly realizing it was probably a ridiculously common name for a boat and not necessarily even the name that Dollar would pick.

Today's job would call for some good old-fashioned tailing and perhaps a little acting. To the Dollar household he went then, parking the Eldorado down the block. Nothing happened for several hours, but then around eight, Dollar came out of the house, wearing a wide-brimmed hat and long coat. Munford checked the sky for clouds and saw nothing but stars. Dollar started on foot down the street, first down the avenue that connected the residential neighborhood to downtown and then down the middle of Church Street toward the ruins of the old Spanish fort. He appeared to be meeting someone there, but Munford couldn't get a good look at the guy from this distance. The reporter edged in closer, peeking out from behind a Confederate monument. If he wasn't mistaken, the man to whom Dollar was speaking was none other than Colonel Whitehouse, some 200 miles south of where he should have been, at his station by Bobo's Pond in Pickens County.

If the plot got any thicker, Munford thought, you could build a brick house with it. Whitehouse wasn't in uniform, and the men only spoke for a few minutes. When they went their separate ways, Munford was torn about which one to follow. He decided on Dollar. When there was a respectable distance between Dollar and Whitehouse, he made his move.

"Reverend, can I have a word?"

Dollar turned and looked quizzically at the reporter. "Do I know you?"

"Not yet, but I know you. And I know the man you were just talking to. I need to ask you about the ark."

He mumbled something about not knowing what Munford was talking about and began edging away, but then Munford said "It has to do with your grandkids, or your wife's grandkids. It's important."

"Now, what could they possibly have to do with the…"

"So you admit there's an ark?"

"Look mister, um…"

"Coldwater. Munford Coldwater." He flashed something from his wallet, which, in the dark, could pass for a detective license.

"Whether there is or isn't some such thing, I don't know what it could have to do with Lucretia's unfortunate savage boys."

"Well, what is it then?"

"What is what?"

"Maybe you could tell me what you and Colonel Whitehouse were talking about down by the wharf a few minutes ago."

Reverend Dollar took a moment and quieted his voice. "I was providing him with spiritual advice of a personal nature, the details of which are none of your damned business."

"Salty language for a preacher, Reverend."

"I bid you good evening."

At that, the Reverend left the scene so quickly, that Munford didn't have time to try and stop him. An all-night coffee shop was open down the road. The reporter sat at the counter staring at his notes, trying to think of another angle, a way to get into the Reverend's private business.

"Aha," he said out loud. The waitress gave him a look. "The aunt!"

The next morning, he sat in his usual spot, waiting for Eunice to leave the house. She never did. But, the reverend had taken the car that morning, and where he went Munford no longer cared.

In the late afternoon, Mrs. Dollar had left on foot, and Munford seized the opportunity to ring the doorbell.

"Afternoon, ma'am. My name is Munford Coldwater. I wonder if you have a few moments to chat. It's about your niece. I'm a friend of her family."

The worried frown that Eunice's face bore as a rule became even more pronounced.

He attempted to put her at ease, assuring her that nothing tragic had befallen Mrs. Mackintosh—nothing new at least. When he asked if he could come inside, Eunice looked even more panicked than before. "Tell you what," he said. "I can see you're nervous that your sister will come home. We can just sit and talk in the kitchen, and if anybody comes in, I'll slip out the back before anybody has a chance to know that I'm here. I just have a few questions to ask you." During his vigil, Munford had already mapped out the house's exits and entrances, so he knew this was possible. Eunice reluctantly let him in.

"Now, Miss...er..."

"Dean."

"Miss Dean, can you tell me something about a project of the Reverend's called the Ark?"

"Ark? Do you mean the A. R. C.?"

He hadn't considered that it could be spelled with a C, much less that it was an acronym of some kind. She explained that it was a research center, that he had been a biologist before he started his ministry. "As far as I know, it's no longer operational," she said. "What could it possibly have to do with Lucretia?"

"That's what I'm trying to figure out."

The two of them had more time to talk than he had expected, and he asked her about the ministry's financial situation, about her own involvement in the ministry, and about whether Donna May's first husband had left any money. On the first point, she had no knowledge at all; on the second, she admitted that she was skeptical about the religion and was secretly still a Methodist, though not practicing. It was clear she was scared to death of both her sister and brother-in-law. About Lucretia's father, she was certain he had left some money for Lucretia, but she probably never received it because the Dollars had blocked off her trust fund when she married Dewey. Otherwise, she would have received anything that was left over after her college education once she

156

turned twenty-one.

"I was never sure that it was legal, what they did," she said.

"This might be a strange question," Munford offered, taking a sip of his tea. It was very strong tea. "Has the reverend ever concerned himself with what they call extraterrestrial life, either in his former or current occupation?"

"Extraterr..." She paused without finishing the word and cocked her head to the side, struggling to follow him.

"Alien. Unearthly. From space."

"Oh that!" She waved her hand like it was the simplest question in the world now, and then explained. It had been the reason for his religious conversion, what inspired him to start his ministry. She had heard the reverend sermonize on it many times. One night as he lay down to sleep, he was enveloped in a white light. Next thing he knew, he was in a vessel looking down on the earth, and a voice told him that he had a purpose, and that was to spread the word that Jesus would someday deliver the righteous to salvation on a distant planet. It was his belief that Jesus and the angels of the Old Testament were in fact ancient aliens, and that mankind was being groomed to help repopulate the home planet.

Classic abduction story, Munford thought. These tales were a dime a dozen ever since that weather balloon was shot down in New Mexico back in '47. They multiplied when Sputnik went up two year ago, and they were growing exponentially. Usually attached to a near-death experience. The most likely explanation was that the reverend had a heart attack just as he was drifting off to sleep that night. Coldwater kept this opinion to himself, though, and just nodded as he jotted down notes from the conversation.

He heard someone coming in the front door. As promised, he slipped out the back and made his way down the road. He hoped Eunice had the sense to hide the tea cups. As he left, he told her he would be in touch soon. He thought he had all the puzzle pieces now, but they were scattered and out of order.

TWENTY-FOUR

They brought the guitar with them again. For some songs, it did sound better than the fiddle, but they had to adjust the key to fit the chords Robert knew. He switched back to the fiddle often, and he could tell he was getting better.

Outside of Atlanta, they stopped at a public campground for the night. Pop built a fire, and the boys sat around it working through exercises in the guitar instruction book while Wally advised him that it sounded like "a herd of cats walking across piano strings."

"Ease up, Wally. I'm still getting used to it."

A voice behind them said, "Well if it ain't the Fireball Brothers from Pickens County, Alabama."

"Chuck Canada," Pop said. "I almost didn't recognize you."

Wally gasped audibly when they turned around and saw him. Cannaday's eyes were bloodshot, his seersucker suit was mud stained, and the ginger mustache had sprouted a wild and prickly beard. He told them he was still hawking the same formula, though it looked to Robert like he'd been drinking it more than selling it.

"I admit, sales have not been coming as easily as they used to," he said. "Mind if we try the old act again for a while? Maybe changing things up will bring new luck. I've been up the coast, and now I'm headed west again."

Pop had no objection to travelling together, and in the morning they went toward the next town up the highway together, the Mackintosh truck caravanning behind Cannaday's blue-green Plymouth. They came to an unmarked tavern not much different from the one in Holly Springs where the salesman first christened them the Fireball Brothers. Unlike Holly Springs, this was a white establishment, but it was just as ramshackle.

However, upon entering the establishment, a huge mule of a man instantly grabbed Cannaday by the lapels and said, "Oh no. We done heard about you a'ready." The man dropped Cannaday onto the gravel outside, leaving Pop and the boys wondering what to do. "If you with him, you got to go too."

Pop spat when the big man had left them. "What in hell was that about?"

Cannaday said, "I…I don't know. I've never been here before." He was still sitting on the ground. Pop rolled his eyes and held out a hand to help him up. Then he went to the truck and came back with his map.

"Tell you what," Pop said. "Why don't you go on to…looks like Buchanan…and start spreading the word around. We'll meet you there this afternoon. That's the sort of thing you said worked best in little towns, right?"

"You've got a good memory, Mr. Fireball."

Once Cannaday's car was on the road, Pop went back inside the tavern and announced, "We are not travelling with that scalawag, whoever he was. We just come here to play some music."

The show went on as usual, and they made about twenty dollars. While they were playing Pop was talking to the bartender that had thrown them out earlier. He told the boys afterward about the conversation.

"Listen up," he said as he strapped them in. "Chuck ain't selling the same product as before. It's in the same bottles, but it ain't the same medicine. What he had before might've been snake oil, but it tasted good and didn't hurt nobody."

"Snake oil?" Wally wasn't familiar with the term.

Robert said, "It means it wasn't really medicine. It was just alcohol."

Pop nodded and continued. "Some folks over in Kennesaw got sick from drinking this new product he's selling, and the word has spread around all over. We need to disassociate ourselves from that man."

"What happened to the people that got sick? Did they die?" Wally said.

"They say one died, but that could just be rumor. Hard to tell what the real truth is at some point."

Wally's grip on Robert's chest tightened. "What'll we do?"

"We'll take the road north to Rockmart and try to lose him. His bad luck is catching, looks like."

159

They worked their way through northwest Georgia and eastern Tennessee with no more sign of Cannaday until they began heading south again and came to Oxford, Alabama. When the crowd dispersed after their performance, the salesman from Arkansas remained standing in front of them, staring.

"Meet me in Buchanan, you said. No, there's no need to explain. My decline and fall became obvious to you. I would drag you down the same depths to which I have dragged myself." He spoke in a monotone and he held his hat in front of his paunch.

"Did you know you poisoned those people in Kennesaw?" Pop said.

Cannaday shielded his face. He admitted he had used up his stock of Dr. Schaff's formula, and he had refilled the bottles with his own experimental concoction. He shrugged. "Some turned out better than others." The travelling salesman had been lingering there in Oxford for a while, regrouping, making a new batch of product, and hoping the Mackintoshes would come through at some point. "Come on back to my motel," he said. "I rented a place with a kitchen, and I'll make you something to eat. It's just down the road from here."

Wally whispered in Robert's ear that this seemed like a bad idea, and Robert agreed that he didn't have the best feeling about it. Pop must have been hungry though and said, "I suppose I don't see no harm in talking things over."

They followed Cannaday to a place called the Dewdrop Inn— not as shabby a place as Robert had pictured. In the parking lot, Robert saw a red Pontiac Bonneville that looked familiar, along with a convoy of airstream trailers that had set up camp in the empty lot next to the motel. It was the Gilmore T. Scott Travelling Circus, he soon realized, just able to make out the faded sign on the side of one of the closest trailers. He pointed it out to Wally.

"I ain't surprised," Wally said. "Things that happen once always come back around again."

"Sometimes sooner than you'd think, though," Robert added.

Distracted by the spectacle down the way, they almost didn't notice that when they entered the room, Pop had his hands in the air, and Cannaday was pointing a pistol at him. "Stand and deliver, boys. Stand and deliver. Now, very carefully, put that Colt of yours down on the table."

Pop did as he was told.

"Now how much cash have you got on you?"

Robert calculated how much they had, a few hundred surely. It had been a lucrative couple of weeks.

"Whatever we have is locked up in the truck," Pop said.

A toilet flushed, and a minute later, Gilmore T. Scott came bumbling out of the restroom. "Well, look who is paying us a visit. Interesting how things work out, ain't it?"

"Mr. Scott, you've arrived, just in time," said Cannaday. "Can you check the gentleman's pockets for keys and anything else of interest?"

Scott complied, found the keys, and was soon rummaging through the truck. He came back with the shotgun and the wad of cash that Pop had stowed in the glove box.

Cannaday said, "Well, Fireball Brothers and Mr. Fireball. Your good luck has run out." He hit Pop hard in the back of the head with the butt of his pistol, knocking him out cold. There was nothing Robert could do but stand there and watch it, with Scott pointing the shotgun at him.

"Boys," Cannaday continued, circling around behind them, "I'm sorry to do this to you too."

Robert heard the thunk of the gun on Wally's head, and then a moment later, the room faded into a liquid, and Robert felt himself plunging down into it.

Robert came to, but Wally was still unconscious, rendering both of them immobile. He soon discovered it wasn't just because Wally was weighing him down; they had been tied to a chair. It seemed they were still in Cannaday's motel room, but Pop was not anywhere in Robert's line of sight. A crack of light indicated that the door had opened, and in a moment, someone was untying them. He heard Coldwater's voice saying, apparently to someone outside, "Get some ice. And then call the police."

When Robert was able to turn his head, he saw Pop on the other side of the room. Coldwater was getting him untied as well. A little brown lady in a white uniform came in with a bucket of ice and said, "Manager has already called the police."

The next thing Robert knew, the police were already there, asking Pop what happened. The boys were in the truck, and Coldwater was sitting on the edge of the opened tailgate. "You boys just take it easy, now."

Robert's head still hurt, and everything around him was still fuzzy.

"They won't get far," Coldwater said. "As criminals, they weren't exactly masterminds. Seems like an act of desperation leaving you like that. Something happened that made them decide to leave in a hurry. Almost like…whatever it is…this energy, let's call it, that binds you together, was protecting you."

Wally stirred then. "Could have started protecting me before they hit me in the back of the head—"

"So wait," Robert tried to lean forward, but Wally was still focusing his weight in the opposite direction. "You are suggesting that a fireball from space was somehow protecting us in that motel room even after we were knocked out?"

Coldwater shrugged. "Just speculation, but maybe. Cannaday is already wanted for poisoning those people in Georgia. Scott abandoned his circus with no warning. For a couple hundred dollars? Just seems strange. I don't know what else could have scared them off like that."

Ever since the fireball, they were a part of something that was bigger than themselves, and it was somehow protecting them. But the specifics of it were too mysterious, and he couldn't hold the thought for long. It made his head hurt more.

When they pulled into the driveway, the house was silent. The dogs weren't even barking. Even the wind was mute. Pop must have sensed that something was wrong and went inside without helping the boys out of the back of the truck. They waited for a little while and then worked their way out of the seat. Wally was able to open the hatch, and they rolled and squirmed and somehow landed with all four feet on the ground.

As they struggled up to the front door, Pop came back out, pale as the sky was, and redirected them back to the truck. His hand covered Wally's hand on Robert's chest. "Wait out here, boys."

"What's wrong?" Robert said.

"Just wait by the truck until I tell you."

They did as they were told. Wally was shaking, making both

of their bodies vibrate so much the very ground they stood on seemed to be rattling. They leaned against the side of the truck for additional support. Robert put his hand over Wally's, where his father's hand had been a few moments earlier, and he took Wally's other hand in his to try and steady him.

In a few minutes, the sheriff arrived. A siren wailed in the distance and drew closer and closer until an ambulance came speeding into the lawn, nearly crashing into them. Dr. Stanhope jumped out of the back and ran inside with two white-coated technicians. There was no denying then what Robert had already suspected from the moment they had arrived.

"Mama!" Wally shouted, trying to run.

"Hold on. You're going to hurt yourself."

The boys made their way as quickly as they could over to the stretcher that was being carried out. Wally nearly knocked himself and Robert over into a pile of logs that had gone uncut since the winter before. Pop went to talk to the sheriff, but Robert had already seen that Mama was covered in a sheet.

When Pop caught sight of Stanhope standing around by the ambulance, he ran after the doctor screaming that Mama had overdosed on those "fucking lot of pills" he'd given her. Stanhope ran around to the back of the house, and Robert lost sight of them by then. A couple of sheriff's deputies had to separate them. It took three of them to keep Pop from snapping Stanhope's neck. They cuffed him and put him in a car to wait for him to calm down. Another deputy helped Robert and Wally off the ground.

Both of them were sobbing so hard they could barely remain standing.

TWENTY-FIVE

Stanhope came out of a blind reverie, otherwise known as a blackout. He found himself at the small writing desk that had always been the cornerstone of the living room, an empty glass and a nearly empty bottle of Old Forester at his elbow. The vision of Lucretia Mackintosh, pale green, laid out on that gurney like a slab of rotted meat, still haunted his memory. His face still ached under his eye where Dewey had struck him. His stomach gargled boiling acid that came up his neck and spilled out onto the cool tile with a sickening splash. He rinsed his mouth with tap water and spit it out into the sink. A dish towel, crusty with dry oil, was all he could find to clean the floor. He covered the mess and swished it around with his foot. A window was open in the kitchen, and the frilled green curtains billowed inward and reminded him of dancing marionettes. The autumnal breeze from outside also invited in the odor of burned food. A ruined frying pan full of char sat atop the stove.

He heard sounds of movement from upstairs, furniture creaking across the floor and thumping back into place. Nell doing some cleaning. She had been adding her unique touch to the place. There had been some incidents over the summer. Whenever there was a full moon, walls couldn't contain her, and she'd run down the streets of downtown Columbus in the middle of the night, not returning until daylight. So for her protection, they returned to New Orleans those times. They would go out to the bayou where she could run free without the suspicious eyes of neighbors. Whenever they made these trips, she would bring back little trinkets and souvenirs.

The Mardi Gras masks and beads had been fine. They added color and brought an atmosphere, a feeling of gaiety to the old place. It was a welcome change. There were some old brass instruments, a trumpet and a trombone, that she found in a junk shop and just had to have. Those too were fine. After all, everyone likes music. This last trip though, she had brought back this wall hanging with skeletons and other frightful things. She had bought a doll and a stick pin, and she told him she needed a hunk of his hair. Joking but not joking.

She was acting out. It was all to get back at him for bringing up the surgery again. He wanted her to at least have a consultation with Montalto, but she wouldn't budge on it. They'd had a row, and she gave him the hairy shoulder for the rest of the weekend. She was still mad at him.

Stanhope sat again, feeling careworn. He filled his glass with what was left of the Old Forester—another souvenir from last weekend's trip. After a few small sips, his eyes cleared some more, and his mouth tasted better. She hadn't put the voodoo shit up in the living room, at least not yet. In fact, he didn't see the Mardi Gras masks or the brass. A shadow of dust had already formed a ghost on the wall where these items had hung earlier that morning. Stanhope stood, or tried to. More frantic banging upstairs, and Nell coming down the stairs, dragging his two largest suitcases behind her.

A chair tumbled to the floor under his feet as he stumbled diagonally toward the foot of the stairs. The suitcases fallumped from step to step. With no small amount of effort, he made it there. "Nell, baby…"

"You don't love who I am. You love somebody you wish I was. It's always been like that, Henry. I can't take it no more." Her voice had never been so clear. She enunciated every syllable like she had rehearsed it.

"But Nell…Don't be ridiculous. Where will you go? You've never been on your own."

"I don't know yet. I got a little saved up from gifts you give me. I'll go back to New Orleans and find some work there."

"Let's talk this over, can't we? I know you're mad about me bringing up Dr. Montalto. I'll never mention the man's name to you again." He could feel his breath falling out of him in green sweeps. His stomach ached, and his head throbbed. It would kill him if he didn't have Nell to take care of, to take care of him. They needed each other.

"It ain't just that, Henry. You know…" She emitted a groan and sat on the stairs with her head in her hands. "This green gingham dress is just like the red one. Just like the blue one. You've bought me other dresses, finer dresses, but I never wear them because we never go anywhere."

"What do you mean? We go back to Louisiana every month."

"But we don't go into the city. What do we do there? What do we do here? We hide in the woods like savages, or we hide in the house like church mice. I need some freedom. I need to be who I am. And look at you. You nearly burned the house down earlier trying to cook bacon for yourself. You act like I'm the one that needs taking care of, but you can't take care of yourself. And I ain't gonna be your mama anymore."

A car honked its horn outside.

"That's my taxi, Henry. Now you best move out of my way."

TWENTY-SIX

Martha Jean's head hung as Colonel Whitehouse spoke from across the little black table in words as patchy as a fog. *I know it's difficult. Don't worry. Your duty. Cooperation.* The lounge where they sat was louche with decadence—velvet, brass, and stained oak. She had come here sometimes when Eddie was overseas, and she had been coming back more and more since his latest arrest. Her wedding ring was safely tucked into her purse. The drive to Nashville, though long, gave her time to think, and by the time she reached the bar at the Hermitage Hotel, the solitude of driving had transformed her into another person, the person she might have been if she'd never met Eddie, a sophisticated working girl in the city. Upon arriving, she always ordered a very dry vodka martini and smoked her cigarettes through a stemmed holder she'd found in an antique shop.

She even smoked cigarettes in the house now. Eddie had made her smoke outside. She heard herself speaking banalities about the house seeming so big without him. His personality took up so much space. It wasn't supposed to be like that. They were going to have a quiet, comfortable life in the country, but the only time she'd been comfortable there was with Dewey. Yes, Eddie had come back from Korea half mad and half the man he'd been before, but even before the war, it hadn't been comfortable. Quiet yes—entirely too quiet. They almost never spoke. It was not actually Eddie's personality that took up so much space; it was the silence that he carried.

"That funny-named reporter has been to see me," she said. She was not even taking care to divert her smoke away from the colonel, and she felt this was fair after the six months of smoke in which she had been immersed ever since Whitehouse and his team came into town. "He's been to the house a couple of times."

"Coldwater. What did he ask you?" Whitehouse was wearing his dress uniform, an eagle sparkling from his chest through the cloud of cigarette smoke. He could be a good-looking man if he were a little taller, she thought.

The reporter had asked about where she had come from, about how a sorority girl from Jackson ended up married to a hillbilly peach farmer. It was something she'd had in common with Lucretia; they'd both been educated city girls who married country boys. They had both been seeking that quiet comfort that never quite materialized. Dewey was quiet too, quiet but purposeful. When he spoke, he had something to say. Sharing a man with Lucretia had not felt like any kind of betrayal at the time; they shared so many other things, and Dewey had plenty of energy to spare. When she finally admitted it all to Lucretia, all these years later, she'd first approached it as a theoretical. "What if it had been true?" Lucretia had not been fooled by this ruse for even a second, however.

Before the war, Eddie had been clever, even funny. If there was anything that had seduced her into this country life, it had been his humor. Just little observations and connections he made that were cute and sometimes downright hilarious. Later these connections manifested as conspiracies. Oddly, she couldn't think of one example of those cute observations now. That had been poisoned by Korea and everything that came afterward.

Coldwater had also asked her what she knew about that, what Eddie thought he saw at the pond. It was all madness as far as Martha Jean was concerned. She read somewhere once that the Koreans had used lights and sounds and fireworks as intimidation tactics. Since the fireball, nothing had made sense. Two boys she had once rocked on her knee were now tangled together like wisteria vines. Her dumb, hillbilly husband had been whisked away in the interest of national security. Since Eddie was gone, Martha Jean had been spending more time in Columbus—not exactly a metropolis, but there was a movie theater and a couple of decent restaurants, plus the occasional cultural event at the women's college. For a while, she'd also taken refuge in her religion, in her church. But there was a limit to how much she could let Christ comfort her, and people in Columbus were starting to howl at the moon. So now, she found herself two or three times a week driving to Nashville, getting herself a nice hotel for the night, spending her evening at the hotel bar drinking vodka martinis, feeling a little rebellious for choosing the communist liquor.

The bar was quiet tonight, and she was sitting with the Colonel at a table in the corner. Ricky, the bartender, always kept his eye on her, made sure nobody took advantage. When she stayed late, until he closed down, he would help her to her room upstairs. He never made a pass though, even when she wanted him to. It was just as well. Soon after, she would be sleeping heavily.

"Coldwater didn't ask me anything he didn't already know the answer to. And I didn't tell him anything he didn't already know."

"Can you please be more specific?" Whitehouse took off his glasses and polished them on his sleeve as he asked.

"The questions were quite general and open-ended."

In fact, the reporter had been more than a little prying, asking about her relationship with the Mackintoshes, about her past with Dewey. She didn't know how he found out about it, but if one tilled the fields of gossip in just the right places, rumors from decades past would come springing up like May flowers.

"Just so you know," Whitehouse said, "Your husband, Eddie…He's not under arrest. He's been cooperating with the investigation. He's rather comfortable. His basic needs are being met and beyond."

Which changed everything, really. The concrete cell in her mind suddenly became a luxury suite. Why, they could have him in a room in this very hotel, she thought. And here she was carrying on like the merry widow, smoking in the house, drinking martinis, talking to strange men in hotel lounges in Nashville. Or perhaps she was even more justified now. If he was having such a good time talking about space aliens and such nonsense, why should she neglect herself? The contradictions made her dizzy. She caught her breath and gestured to Ricky for another martini.

Then Whitehouse told her about Lucretia Mackintosh.

"What?" she said, though she had heard him plainly. She'd last seen her neighbor when she'd picked her up walking along the side of the road in Columbus looking a little haggard and sunburned. At first, Martha Jean had barely recognized the woman who'd lived a quarter mile away from her for more than a decade and a half. There was a feral abstractness about her, like she was a discombobulate sprite looking for her portal in the forest. They'd laughed about the doctor's lover, which led to laughing about other things. She didn't know why she then decided to bring up the old unpleasantness. It was selfish, she knew, to want to unburden herself and place that burden on poor Lucretia. Something about that situation, drinking whiskey that belonged to their husbands, with all that had gone on, she thought that now Lucretia would find it—she didn't know…amusing. Did she really think Lucretia had known the truth that whole time and had simply forgiven her? In the haze of that moment, she supposed she did think that.

During the long drive home from Tennessee, she relived that last conversation with Lucretia again and again. At first, Lucretia had simply been quiet, reflective, quizzical, and later enraged. She threw the whiskey jar against the wall and walked out. Martha Jean had called after her, said she was sorry and that it was so long ago and that she had meant no harm by bringing it up. But Lucretia didn't turn back.

The next day, there had been a note tacked to the door. "It will be a long time, if ever, before I can speak to you again. –L.M." The childlike scrawl had been written with a hurried and trembling hand.

When she got home, she looked at that note again. "A long time, if ever…" While her husband had been off on some secret mission, chasing down extraterrestrials, she had managed to poison the environment around her home, just as she'd done when he had been away at war. Could anyone ever trust her? She didn't trust herself. That was why, she supposed, she always had to escape, to go to Nashville and be someone else for a few hours or for a night. Now, in her bed, still wearing her cocktail dress, she pulled the covers over her head and wept. No amount of tears would wash away her guilt and misery, but it soon wore her down enough to sleep.

TWENTY-SEVEN

They buried Mama in an open field behind the old barn, under an ancient white oak tree. Pop built the coffin and dug the hole himself. Robert and Wally couldn't do much to assist and merely looked on. When they'd finished with the burial, they all bathed and put on their best clothes. Mama had made the boys suits while they were on the road, in case they had the opportunity to perform somewhere fancy; they were powder blue with white Western trim like the real stars wore at the Grand Ole Opry. The clothes fit imperfectly, but it felt good to them just to put on something new, and they looked smart. Pop wore his best shirt and the bolo tie that he always wore when they were on the road. He washed and pressed his outfit the day before so it would be in top condition.

The day of the funeral was breezy and clear. In the distance, a cool chorus of frogs addressed the early dusk. The freshly dug earth of the grave perfumed the air. The grass was still mushy under their feet from a morning rain that had briefly interrupted their project.

They hadn't invited anyone else to attend the ceremony, such as it was. Robert played "Amazing Grace" and "The Red Haired Girl from Tulloch." Pop read poems from Mama's two favorite books—a collection of poetry by Robert Burns and another by Sir Walter Scott. He stumbled over some of the pronunciation, and a couple of times, he bit his lip before pulling himself together and continuing. Afterwards, he placed the two books on top of the grave and sprinkled the best loam from the field over them, as if they were seeds. He marked the grave site with a large rock, intending to replace it with a proper grave stone later.

Coldwater's Eldorado pulled into the driveway, and Robert's chest burned with anger. "What's he doing here?"

Wally said, "It's alright. Let's go talk to him."

Pop stayed behind, kneeling beside the grave site while the boys walked across the field to confront Coldwater. He was wearing that same overlarge brown suit he always wore and carrying a newspaper with him. "Boys," he said, "before you say anything, I just wanted to show you something." He handed over the folded up paper. "I hope y'all don't mind, but I took the liberty of writing up a brief obituary for the Columbus paper. I also had it printed in Mobile, so that your mama's family attorney could see it."

Robert snatched the paper from his hand without looking at it. "How could you write an obituary? What do you know about her?"

"If you are implying something…untoward…think again. I have taken an interest in your family, an interest that seriously goes beyond my professional duties as a reporter. I've spent a lot of time and a great deal of personal expense trying to help you boys."

Robert thought about accusing Coldwater outright of having an affair with Mama, but the timing didn't seem right, not with her just put in the ground, not with Pop within earshot. "Only seems to me you've been spying on us."

"Tell you what, son. There's a lot you don't know, and there's a lot I could tell you, but I think it'll be better if you figure it out for yourself. All I'm gonna say for now is that when you decide you're ready to travel again, go back through Mobile and talk to your great aunt Eunice. You will be received differently this time, I can assure you. With that, I bid you adieu and Godspeed."

Coldwater got back into his car and drove away.

That night, they ate their beans, sitting at the kitchen table surrounded by reminders of Mama. It was Wally that brought up the idea of getting back on the road. "Not right away," Pop said.

Robert said, "You're right. Let's wait until the New Year. We can make it until then on what we have."

Robert sensed his younger brother growing wiser by the day. With so little for his body to do, his mind must have been working in another gear than before. He almost couldn't wait to see what Wally was going to say next, a feeling that was impossible to imagine only six months ago. Had it only been six months? It felt like a lifetime had passed, but it had only been that last summer when the fireball came down, and here it was not even December yet.

Pop wasn't responsive. He'd said very little since Mama passed other than his few words at the graveside. Robert and Wally discussed what Coldwater had said about Mobile, whether that meant there would be money for them there, maybe even enough for their surgery.

Robert didn't want to get his hopes up, and he also was in no hurry to travel again. Mama's set of cast iron skillets still sat on the stovetop, the midsize one not even cleaned since she last used it a few days before. Pop had heated the beans in a small copper pot or soup pan maybe. Robert didn't even know the proper names for these instruments of Mama's milieu. Even the wallpaper pattern, a creamy yellow background with small and delicate white flowers, belonged to Mama. The very wooden spoon Pop had used to stir the beans had her own floured fingerprints on the handle.

"A'ight," Pop said, finally. "New Years. But the first damn week of January, we are getting to back to work, God damnit. Gotta do something in the meantime. Help me clean this place up. Your mama's already rolling in her grave at this mess."

Thanksgiving was less than a week after the burial. Martha Jean showed up at the front door, timidly holding a pie. When she saw the boys, she started crying and almost dropped it. "I'm so sorry," she kept saying. Her face, which was not so made up as usual, burrowed into Robert's shoulder, the shoulder he shared with Wally. A few large tear drops glaciered down into the shallow crevice between Robert's torso and Wally's arm and settled there, burning on his skin. Robert wasn't sure if she was apologizing for Mama being dead or for her screwing around with Pop a decade ago. Or if she thought one event had something to do with the other, a thought that had also crossed Robert's mind. Maybe Mama wouldn't have gone so crazy with the pills if the affair hadn't happened. Either way, Martha Jean's presence irked him, but he decided to keep his mouth shut about it for now.

Pop greeted her with the same indifference he always had. It occurred to Robert that he might still be covering up the fact that he had once, and perhaps still, had feelings for her—might even be hiding the fact from himself. Without looking her in the eye, Pop invited her to sit her ass down. She was still holding the pie in her hands. It smelled like pumpkin. Robert hadn't eaten anything but beans for weeks, and the aroma of the spices almost made him forget that he was angry at her.

Martha Jean sat down at the dining room table with them.

"I don't know what they've done with Eddie. He's not a spy, of course. This whole thing with the fireball just set something off in him. It's like he's back in the war. I don't know what to do."

Her voice was not emotional, but after she spoke, she started in crying again. Robert didn't know what to say to this. Apparently nobody did, since they all remained silent.

"Y'all are eating beans?" Martha Jean finally said, recovering herself. "That won't do. It's Thanksgiving. Come on over to my house. I'll whip up something. It won't be much, but it'll be better than this."

"We'll eat beans, and we'll fucking like it," Pop said. Martha Jean looked back at him. Robert, too, was surprised at how he sounded. He must have surprised himself also because he soon softened. "It's been a rough fucking month. You're welcome to some beans. There's plenty to go 'round."

He passed the pot of beans to her. Tentatively, she put the large metal spoon to her lips for a taste.

"Not bad," she said.

Before December was half over, they found they couldn't stand being in the house, so they went back out on the road. This also gave the boys an opportunity to wear their new suits again. They headed west this time, with the first stop being Columbus, Mississippi. The plan was then to head down Highway 45 to Mobile. They hoped it being close to Christmas time might be a point in their favor when then checked in on Mama's family and tested what Coldwater had told them. From Mobile, they would head to New Orleans, where Pop would threaten Montalto's life if he didn't go ahead and perform the surgery for whatever money they had with them. They'd all agreed—Robert, Wally, and Pop—that this was the only way they could proceed from here, to move on from Mama's death and attempt to put this horrible farce to an end.

As usual, they set up across the street from the Princess Theater during the Saturday matinee, a showing of *Pillow Talk* with Rock Hudson and Doris Day. They had been to Columbus many times since that terrible first performance, and Robert was always nervous he would see Edwina again and get spooked. However, she had never appeared and so his nerves remained untested. He knew, though, that the odds were good she would be watching that movie on its first weekend. He wasn't at all surprised to see Edwina come out of the theater with three other girls, a couple of whom he recognized from school. The girls watched from a distance at first, and Robert was surprised to find himself unfazed.

A few other townies began to gather around them, many dressed in overcoats and mufflers. Some carried arms full of Christmas shopping bags. There had been no snow yet, but it was quite cold out. Robert was never cold though, even spending hours outdoors in the bitterest weather. Wally was always there curled around him like another skin, and the fireball always burned in his heart. In the new suit, he was even beginning to sweat. They played their usual trio of reels to warm up. Robert's fingers limbered and somehow found their places on the strings. Wally stomped and whooped and banged the tambourine. A couple in the front row kicked up their heels and danced. The boys were swept up in the cheerful mood and launched straight into "Angeline the Baker" and then "Old Joe Clark" and then some contemporary country tunes. Song after song filled the cold air with life.

Soon, Edwina was up front, putting a quarter in the bucket that Pop was carrying through the crowd. She had ditched her friends and stood alone, gazing at them with her head cocked in curiosity. They finally took a break after a half hour, and she approached them.

"Y'all have gotten a lot better since I saw you this summer," she said.

"Thanks," Robert said. "We've been practicing, you could say. How's school been?"

She looked surprised to think about school. "Oh, I've been working. The phone company? Remember? I had to drop out. We had a bad crop this year, and my parents needed me to help out."

"Oh, I thought that was just a summer job. But I see. We had to drop out too." She was still a very pretty girl, Robert thought. But he no longer felt out of sorts around her. He wondered what Wally thought of her now, how sweet she looked in her green coat and felt hat. It occurred to him that it would be polite to introduce them.

"You remember my brother, Wally."

They both said hello. Among the throng that surrounded them,

175

Robert recognized Dr. Stanhope, accompanied by a dark, hooded figure so swathed in scarves that he could not see a face. It seemed that the doctor and this person were holding hands.

"Well," Edwina said. "I'm supposed to be doing Christmas shopping with my cousins. I should probably catch up with them. I just wanted to say hello. Call me sometime. I'm always on the other end of the line." She made a telephone pantomime, smiled, and ran off.

A lot had changed, and he wasn't sure he felt the same way about Edwina anymore. Her gesture had not stirred him the way it had in the past. There was no guarantee he'd ever see that girl Izzy again, but what had happened in Birmingham had changed things, and the scales had fallen from his eyes. She was a giggling teenage girl whose fancies changed with the wind. Her youthful softness had already started to harden after working for a living. But she was still good looking, and in a couple more years, she might turn out to be a reliable girl. He would consider calling on her again then.

The boys stayed on the corner for a couple of hours and then made their way down through Brooksville and Meridian, and then they spent the night in the truck outside of Quitman. They would hit Waynesboro, and Citronelle on their way to Mobile.

During the drive, it crossed Robert's mind more than once that they could make a go of it in Nashville, Atlanta, Birmingham, or even New Orleans, and never look back. In fact, it was Birmingham that was the most appealing because Izzy was there. They could forget about the surgery and rent a little house. Pop could set up an instrument repair shop and do that full time. But Robert kept this fantasy to himself. Pop had his plan, and they'd all agreed to it.

The Dollar household looked much as he remembered it. Its peeling paint and antebellum architecture were faded reminders of an already gone world. Pop elected to remain in the truck while the boys went to the door. Eunice answered the door, wearing a low-cut blue dress, a fashionable curly hair-do, and red lipstick. Robert almost didn't recognize her. She energetically invited the boys inside. Robert could feel Wally's reluctance, though it could have equally been his own. It was becoming hard to tell Wally's instincts from his, even to distinguish Wally's thoughts from his.

"Where's your father?"

"Waiting in the truck," Wally said. "Where's everybody else?"

"Oh, didn't Mr. Coldwater tell you?"

Coldwater had told them precious little except that they should show up here and that they would be welcomed. Robert explained this to Eunice in the most polite way he could conjure.

"You most certainly are welcome," she said, clapping her hands. "So it's a surprise, then!" She bid them to have a seat and asked if they wanted anything. "I have a paper here that you need to sign. It's a rather long story. Are you sure you don't want to get Dewey? My unfortunate sister and brother-in-law will not be here to interrupt, as they are currently incarcerated."

"Incarcerated?" Robert nearly jumped, not that it would have been possible with Wally there on him. "Maybe you should just tell us what's going on first, and we can fill in Pop later."

Eunice explained that Mr. Coldwater had helped her to prove two things, the first of which was that the Dollars had illegally blocked an inheritance that should have gone to Lucretia and subsequently to them, the boys. The second was that Mr. Dollar was hiding a considerable amount of money—tens, maybe hundreds of thousands that he had embezzled from the Fellowship of Levi.

"It seemed he was just waiting for the right moment to slip away with it, leaving your grandmother and me in the lurch," she said. Coldwater had tracked down the lawyer that had handled the family's estate, and there was a trust fund that had been set up in Mama's name. Papers to sign. "It isn't a lot, but perhaps it will help. Of course, y'all will stay here for a couple of days while I make arrangements to get you the check."

"Yeah," Wally said. "You'd better go get Pop."

They stayed with Eunice through Christmas, and for Christmas dinner, she made turkey, ham, dressing, and fancy vegetables, with pie and ice cream for dessert.

The bedrooms were all up an impossible set of stairs, so Eunice set up a pallet for the boys in the living room. Though they were used to camping out in random places, the dainty, genteel

177

Victorian dressings in the house were strangely unsettling. Robert was constantly afraid of breaking some frail porcelain statuette or another. He was perhaps more afraid that Pop would break something and not be able to properly apologize, thus proving his genetic inferiority to the Deans.

Pop kept mostly to himself, barely spoke except when spoken to. By the third day, Pop had found tools, nails, and paint, and he began fixing up the outside of the house. He simply couldn't exist unless he had something to do.

The family's attorney was a tall aristocrat, of the old French aristocracy of Mobile. His name was Ned Pate. His mother had been a descendent of the illustrious De Foy dynasty of Mobile industrialists. His grandfather had been in the business of landscaping and landscaping tools—De Foy Grass. Ned's own father had joined his wife's family business and worked his way up to president, whereupon he changed the name to Pate-De Foy Grass. They later sold the company to his brother-in-law Martin, who saw fit to rename the company after himself, Marty Grass. This story all came tumbling out when Ned Pate showed up at the house with the paperwork for the Mackintoshes to sign and a check. Robert didn't look to see how much it was for, but Pop got cash for it at the earliest opportunity, and they made plans for New Orleans.

The trip in to New Orleans had filled Robert with a strange nostalgia, but Pop didn't spend time driving through the Quarter. He went straight down the highway to the dirty, depressed west side of town where the doctor's office was located. Even here though, the dishwater smell of the city filled Robert's mind with the sound of clarinets and trombones.

Montalto reminded them of the risks and had Pop sign several waivers, and then he asked for payment. He took the envelope into a room in the back. When he returned, a few minutes later, he instructed them to skip dinner that night and to come back at seven the next morning. For their convenience, he arranged accommodations for the family next door at the Halfway Inn, where they spent an unquiet and unrestful night.

Just when Wally's breathing had stilled, and Robert was sure he was asleep, he said, "Bubba, what will we do after this?"

"All the things we couldn't do the last few months. Go back to school. Help Pop with the farm. Go fishing. You can play the fiddle again. I'm still not as good as you are, I bet."

"No, you aren't." They both laughed. "But what I mean is, how can we go back? Haven't we changed? Can't we keep playing music and travelling? I don't know if I can go back to the same life we had before."

"Maybe we won't have to," Robert said. "Remember when we threw ourselves in that pond thinking it would reverse the process?"

"You mean when *I* threw us in the pond. That was my idea."

"That's right, it was. That was pretty brave, Wally. And when you pulled the rifle out of the back of the truck on that roughneck that was trying to rob us?"

"It was the only thing I could think to do."

"Point is," Robert said, "when we get through this, I think you can do just about whatever you want to."

"But what do *you* want to do?"

"I don't know yet, Wally. I just don't know."

All through what little remained of the night, the parking lot outside their room bustled with the sounds of loud arguments, music from car radios, glass breaking, and other unseemly activities they couldn't quite identify. As Robert lay trying to sleep, Wally's hand twitched like a fish on the end of a line.

At the operating table, they were both given masks that fed sweet-smelling gas into their lungs. The next thing Robert knew, everything had turned white, and he was floating through a brightly lit void. He was conscious of Wally still there with him, holding on, just like that first day in the pond when that fireball fell out of the sky, and he swam, not understanding why Wally wouldn't just let go and swim with his own strength. But here they were floating through air—not even air. They floated on nothingness into more nothingness, and they didn't have to swim. Some other force, some gravity, propelled them on deeper into the field of white.

Gradually, Robert became aware of shapes coming into view, shadows of soldiers in battle. Against what, he could not say. It was as if they fought the light itself. Dr. Montalto was among the warriors, in the front line. He carried a bayonet, and seemed to be charging straight for Robert and Wally. As he drew closer, Robert screamed and the white light exploded all over again. Next, they

179

were high above a bombed-out city, full of crumbled and charred buildings. A drab concrete block structure that was only partially collapsed, protected by armed guards, appeared before them. Behind its walls, Robert distinctly heard Eddie Van Chukker's voice. "It attacked us with rays of light. I know what I saw. And I saw it again that night. It was the same thing as Chorwon. I saw it. Don't tell me I didn't see it. Look, there it is again."

Eddie pointed up a mountain where the spacecraft was. They didn't see it, but then they were climbing the mountain, though not really climbing. As before, it was more like floating, and it required no physical effort on their part, though it did require deep and exhausting concentration. Robert and Wally were in the spacecraft that Eddie was pointing at, or maybe it was in them. The mountainside was red with blood that spilled down onto the city below. At the crest there was a giant statue, a pharaoh in golden regalia, ten stories high. The face of the pharaoh was that of Sun Ra, staring wide eyed, not at the earth below but at space above. Before long, space was the place where they were, in all its cold vastness. The earth was but a blue ball in the distance behind them. Past the moon, past Mars, past the asteroid belt and into the great eye of Jupiter, they continued straight through that planet's gaseous corpus. It smelled like butterscotch. Outside, there was a pale white girl, looking in the porthole. She came floating out of the middle of a black cloud, and she spoke to them, but Robert couldn't understand what she said.

Inside the ship, it was bright white, like in the hospital. A woman lay up in a hospital bed near them, nursing a pair of infants. Eddie Van Chukker was there too, pointing. He said, "That's what they're hiding. Alien babies." Robert looked again and saw that the infants had a green pallor, unusually large skulls, and deep black eyes that seemed to suck him deeper into space. Donna May and Mr. Dollar were there also, laughing maniacally. They were laughing at the antics of a clown, also a deep-eyed alien, on a tiny bicycle; it was Mr. Scott's travelling circus, and all of them were aliens. Something about them. Robert just knew. Even the caged lions and elephants had the scooped out alien eyes and a sickly lime tone.

As suddenly as they had been shot upward, they now reversed direction. Robert could only feel himself falling down, down, writhing uselessly in space as gravity pulled him back toward the earth. He burned with the hottest fever as he re-entered the atmo-sphere, tumbling through misty clouds where faceless angels blew trumpets in random blares and laughed. For a brief few seconds there were trees and then a splash, and he knew he was back in the pond, sinking to the bottom, and his lungs filled with water so he thought he would drown. Above him, the king lizard Basilosaurus soared, an enormous serpentine ship in its own right. A moment later, he shot back up to the surface and drew air.

When Robert awoke, he was covered in sweat as if he really had just emerged from a long swim. His memory of what he saw and felt came back only in flashes and bursts, and his back hurt like a mule.

Wally wasn't there.

Off and on, he was aware that he remained in a bed, though he wasn't sure what bed it was, or where. He stayed in bed for days, with ephemeral strains of groggy recognition floating past from time to time, diaphanous images of his father, doctors, nurs-es, and other mysterious figures that faded in and out. Gradually, he gained lucidity. He ate food. He asked about Wally.

Pop, with his rough, field-worked hands on Robert's chest where Wally's hand had been, told him that Wally had passed during the surgery. Though by now, this didn't come as a surprise, Robert closed his eyes and longed again for the fog. It wasn't fair. He should have been the one to die. It had been his heart that had been obstructed by whatever alien interference the fireball had planted in them.

He wondered now how he could go on alone—a thought he knew contradicted what he had felt almost every moment they had been together. At some point during the long, strange journey he knew Wally was no longer with him, but he couldn't say exactly when that point occurred.

As Robert's head cleared more, he realized they were no lon-ger at Montalto's office in New Orleans but in an actual hospital. He came to understand that it was the medical facility at the Air Force base outside of Columbus and that Colonel Whitehouse was now in charge of his recovery. From what Whitehouse had told him, it seemed that some sort of force had knocked Montalto unconscious during the procedure. Whitehouse and his men swept in then and took over. They never did explain what they were doing there in the first place. Even when they let Pop take him home, he hadn't regained enough lucidity to ask for more details. However, whenever he thought on it later, the long and short of it was that he had made it through but Wally had not. Nothing else about it seemed to matter.

Back at the farm, they bushhogged and tilled and planted and never spoke about that day when they lost Wally. Neither Robert nor Pop wanted to go into what they now called "Mama's house," and they both slept in the barn. Grandfather-built and father-resurrected, the old family place now convalesced, its two hollow window-eyes no longer showing light. Pop had given new life to the pine exoskeleton, already then half decomposed, adding the iron pipes, pink foam insulation, and sheet rock, life-blood and inner skip. The furniture Pop had built, and the old Philco radio, had brought it warmth. But now it sat cold and empty again, a cadaver on a yellow table of neglected grass.

Pop began digging holes for a foundation for a new house, hidden from passersby on the back end of their acreage, between turn rows of the corn field and the old tomato patch, and Robert helped with that also. After that next summer was gone, Robert was now sixteen, but he felt twice that age, or more. Pop told him he could go back to school, a grade behind after the year of travelling, or he could stay at home and work.

Robert said, "Neither sounds like what I want to do right now." He knew he was too restless to stay there. He wanted to go back out into the world and find his way. "I can find work—doing construction, washing dishes, anything."

"Reckon you're old enough to do whatever you want," Pop said.

Early one September morning, Robert walked away from the farm with a pack of clothes on his back. He walked down the long dirt road that led to their property, up to the county road that led to Aliceville and Macedonia. Then he walked a mile down that road to the cross road with U.S. 82, under a red and blue blanket of sky, and he stuck out his thumb.

For a couple years, he went from town to town, working a few days or a few weeks until he got the itch to wander again. He learned to drink whiskey and to talk to strangers, and he wrote letters back to Pop two or three times a month. He worked side by side with blacks in kitchens and on construction sites. He heard about bombings in Birmingham, and he thought about Izzy, but he did not go there. Like many white men, he did not have the right kind of courage to become a warrior in that battle. When a year had gone by, he was still not quite used to being alone, without Wally always there over his shoulder, talking in his ear, making it hard to sit or lie down. Working with his hands—lifting, making, cleaning, or repairing things—was the only way he knew to lose himself, to shake off the leavings of the past, even temporarily. It occurred to him that was probably why Pop was always so restless. Pop also wanted to leave the past in the past. He kept to himself most of the time when he wasn't working or looking for work, and eventually he missed the farm and came back home.

When he got there, Pop had finished his new house. It was smaller than Mama's house, but the dogs stayed with him inside, keeping him company. Robert settled back into doing work right away, planting and pulling weeds, again working side by side with the men from Macedonia, their ramshackle settlement down the highway. He did not talk to them about Martin Luther King and Malcolm X, though he was curious what they thought about it. When one of the old ones sang his "Hey, oh," from the edge of the field, Robert joined in singing the response. And when the harvest was done, he followed them back to Macedonia and drank shine with them and listened when they played their banjos and guitars, but he did not bring his fiddle. In the spring, he started digging holes for a foundation for his own house. He built it in the shadow of the old place, with just a few yards of patchy grass between the low front porch and the road.

In the weeks and years that followed, Robert poured himself into farm work, kept to himself, and rarely left home. Edwina Hunter visited him, and eventually they married. They were married for thirty five years in relative peace and silence before she died. They often got news from Columbus, like when Dr. Stanhope finally passed away and when the women's college was forced by a lawsuit to start admitting men. There were continuing rumors about an entity that was half-wolf and half-woman who roamed the countryside after dark, particularly when the moon was full, but no proof of a Columbus werewolf ever materialized.

Pop lived on for a few years. By way of an unspoken agreement, he and Robert never talked about what had happened in that hospital room. Sometimes, though, Robert would catch Pop gazing at the night sky wistfully. Robert would leave him alone to his private remembrances. Nobody ever learned what happened to Eddie van Chukker, and he was presumed dead. Martha Jean sold her land and moved away.

Munford Coldwater married a librarian from Birmingham, but they divorced after a couple of years. He wrote a series of articles to follow up on the related cases of Eddie, Colonel Whitehouse, and Dr. Montalto, a series that became increasingly pessimistic and paranoid and which eventually led to his being ostracized by the journalistic community. By that time, he'd left Tupelo and moved in with his aging aunt in Aliceville. Robert would see him from time to time walking past on the road. On rare occasions, Coldwater would stop in at the house for a brief visit, and they'd exchange a few idle pleasantries. However, they too eventually fell out over Munford's obsessive ravings about the fireball, and Coldwater's visits became less frequent. When he did show up, Robert politely tolerated him for a cup of coffee or two and then asked him to leave.

A little community called Lyonesse had built up in the area. There was a school, a couple of churches, a grocery store, a post office, a drug store, a couple of fast food burger places, and a few other enclaves of new housing. Robert had seen the first of these developments sprout up in the mid-1980s. Every couple of years another one would spring out of the ground, turning the earth inside out like in a child's pop-up book. The pond was now dried up, and an Episcopal Church stood there—a stone building with stained glass windows that had been imported from Europe. Munford, now that he was retired from the newspaper business, worked there as the sexton.

The last time Robert saw Coldwater, if was over a strong cup of coffee at Robert's kitchen table. Coldwater said "How much do you know about what really happened that day?" It wasn't the first time the former reporter would ask about Wally, but Robert didn't want to talk about him or about that time, and he was not interested in hearing Coldwater's wild theories.

Normally, Robert would have argued with him for bringing it up yet again. But he remained calm. Perhaps he was weary. "It's been years. I've put it all behind me."

"Have you?"

Coldwater seemed old now, though it had only been a few years. He had put on a bit of belly and was no longer so bony. He'd grown out a gray beard, and his clothes seemed to fit him better. It was as if he was supposed to be this chubby old man all along. Robert thought about whether he really was finished seeking answers or clues in the mystery that had joined him together with Wally for those few months of his life.

"Think about it," Munford said. "When you're ready, if you retrace your steps, you might find something."

TWENTY-EIGHT

Robert, now sixty-eight years old, took in the view from his tenth-floor apartment on Highland Avenue in Birmingham. He surveyed the church steeples and retired steel mills below, impotent smoke stacks surrounded by green hills. Most of his few possessions were still packed in boxes, but he had unpacked the powder blue suit and it now was hanging, covered in plastic, from two hangers in the walk-in closet. The one-room apartment contained more closet space than he ever had in the old house. He'd never use it all. He placed his violin case on the shelf above the suit. A little shrine to the past.

The clothes he wore day to day were still in a suitcase on the closet floor. They would travel back and forth between the suitcase and a laundry bag until he got around to buying a dresser. When he sold the farm, he sold most of the furniture that came with it. The fewer things he could move the better, and Mama's antiques drew a nice price. He could do with something more practical. Maybe he didn't even need a dresser at all. He wasn't even sure he needed a bed. A mattress on the floor would do just fine for now, though his old bones might protest some nights.

As the heat of August dissipated into a cooler but humid early evening, he decided to take a walk. The avenue had been planned and built to be a pedestrian thoroughfare, and even though it was on the steep side of a craggy mountain, it had few crests and valleys, so it was easy for him to just keep walking without getting tired. Only a few of the hundred-year-old mansions that used to line this street remained, looming over the parks that sunk down below the sidewalks all along his path. Honeysuckle-choked hedgerows surrounded perfectly trim green lawns littered only with the occasional puddle of sundried azalea blooms. Among the stately old homes, the avenue held modern apartment buildings like the one where he lived, as well as some commercial spaces. But the history of the area seeped up from the ground and wouldn't be ignored. He walked all the way to Five Points, about a mile, an entertainment district full of bars, restaurants, and young people. He could use a drink, he thought, but he would wait until a little later, when he was on his way home. For now, he wanted to explore—while he still had the energy. This was nothing like the Birmingham he remembered from his youth.

He saw that businesses continued up the hill, so he walked that way. Eventually, he came to a shop that sold coffee, herbs, incense, and other esoteric items. A woman about his age sat alone at a large wooden table with a set of cards and asked if he'd like a reading. Her name was Esther Ruth.

Robert stopped talking and lay in the dark, still not touching her, unsure even if she was still awake and listening. He thought of all the times Edwina had asked him what he was thinking and he would say nothing. He had never even told her the entire narrative he had just laid out for Esther Ruth. Of course, Edwina knew the story more or less, though from a distance. He'd never talked to her about it. Now for the first time he could remember, he was desperate to know what someone else was thinking, but he wasn't sure how to ask.

Esther Ruth turned on the light. Without a word, she examined the white, hand-shaped scar on Robert's chest. She placed her hand inside that hand. It seemed to fit perfectly. They rested there for a little while, not moving.

"The girl you mentioned that went by the name Izzy. You liked her very much?" she said.

"I suppose so."

"Why didn't you come back to Birmingham to look for her? When you went wandering for those couple of years?"

"I don't know," he said. "I guess. I didn't think it would really be anything. She was just having some fun with me. And I guess I also knew I'd end up going back to the farm after a while, and I didn't think she'd be interested in that."

"You were a wise kid."

Esther Ruth removed her hand from his chest, stood and opened a dresser drawer. She brought over a black and white photo of two young girls, one in her late teens, the other adolescent. They were wearing fluffy dresses and standing in front of a blooming azalea bush. It was probably Easter.

"Izzy was my sister, my older sister. We called her Elizabeth. I don't know when she picked up that horrible nickname, but it did suit her in an odd sort of way. She ran away when I was twelve, when she was seventeen. I never saw her again."

"Your sister?" Robert was almost not surprised. Though it had been so many years, and he had only seen the girl twice, there was something similar about them. Especially now, looking at the photo of Izzy with the younger Esther Ruth, looking back at Esther Ruth now. It was the way things went with him. Nothing was a coincidence.

"She ran off with a black jazz musician. He didn't hang around long. You know how musicians are."

"Is that how musicians are?"

"I'm sure you're not like some of the musicians I've known. But some musicians, they don't like to stick around places. And after all that, my parents wouldn't take her back into the house. She was too proud to come home anyway. She died of a drug overdose. Heroin. It was about five years after she left, 1962. We found out when we read about it in the newspaper, a Jane Doe case over on the west side of town. We had an awful hunch, and we were right."

Robert gazed at the ceiling and thought about this sad end to one of the few people in the world he had genuinely liked. Maybe he had seen a resemblance with his mother, that vague yearning that only narcotics would calm. He could see Izzy trying to make it on her own, hopping from one jazz player's bed to the next one, taking only her poetry books and her little suitcase of clothes. That meant she had been nineteen when he knew her, on her own for two years, and with only three more to live.

"I'm sorry," he said. "I did hope she was still alive, even now. I almost hoped, in a romantic way that when I saw you in that store where you read my cards, that you were she. Of course, I knew you couldn't be old enough."

He winked at her.

"Not disappointed?" she said.

"Not disappointed at all."

She said, "I lost someone else too."

He almost admitted he was tired now, a little overwhelmed with all the information he had just dumped, and he didn't know whether or not he wanted to keep talking, but he felt reasonably sure that he could listen.

"When Elizabeth…ran away, it was more than just an affair. She was pregnant, and she had the baby. Her name was Kate. She was born sickly and died a few months later. Everyone in Birmingham knew about it, seemed like. I was damaged goods by association. Nobody wanted me either. I suppose that's why I learned to be independent. Elizabeth and I were a lot alike, it seems."

"Sure, now that you mention it," he said.

"By the time society changed it was the late sixties," she said, "I was set in my wild ways. I'm not making any big promises to you either, pumpkin. Though I do like you. Maybe I'll let you stick around for a while if you play your cards right."

"I'm glad you like me. I'll take my chances. At my age, I don't know how much time I have left anyway." Her fingers closed up, and she allowed her fingertips to drizzle through the gray hairs on his chest. "Kate," he said. "That's the name of your ghost."

"The very same. I never saw the baby alive. We got a letter from Elizabeth about it, and I just felt this strange connection immediately. It was years after that when I started to understand my…sensitivity…and was able to make contact."

"I'm relieved to know she likes me too," he said.

"I don't mean to take the spotlight off your story, sugar. You've just unloaded a truck-full. I'll tell you more of mine another time."

"I hope so," he said. He thought he could spend the rest of his days listening to her talk. About anything. Her voice made him forget himself.

"My point is, I recognized the hole in your heart that very first afternoon when we had coffee. It just took me by surprise that the hole was in the shape of a hand." She switched the bedside lamp off again and said, "Do you still play the fiddle?"

"I do," he said. "I'm still not very good at it though."

"Will you play for me sometime?"

"I will."

In the morning, while Esther Ruth was making coffee, Robert said, "I'm not saying I don't believe what you say about talking to Kate…I've just never experienced anything like that. But I have some questions."

"Like?" She was wearing a silvery-white kimono with pink and purple flowers, and she wore a chopstick in her hair. He had pulled on his wrinkled clothes from the night before, though he left his tie and jacket draped across the back of a chair.

"Like, can you talk to other spirits? Ghosts?"

"Can I try to talk to your brother? Is that what this is about?"

Robert considered for a moment if that was actually what it was about, and then he said yes, it was.

"That reporter you knew, Coldwater. He seemed to know something about your brother, but you never followed up with him."

"Are you changing the subject?" He poured himself another cup of coffee from the pot on the table.

"I'm just saying it's curious. You didn't want to know fifty years ago. Now you want to know? Would you want to retrace your steps?"

He considered this a moment. "I said at the time that I wanted to put it all behind me and only look forward. But also, I think I wasn't ready yet."

"But you're ready now?" she said. "What's different now, other than the fact that you no longer have access to Munford Coldwater and whatever he had found out about your brother?"

He said, "True. Coldwater is long dead, and his story died with him. Maybe you can contact him? Did you ever try to contact your own sister?"

"A spirit has to be open to being contacted," she said. "How far away is Pickens County?"

They drove with the top down in Esther Ruth's MGB Roadster down Highway 82 and turned left at the crossroads about three miles from the state line. A new housing development was being built off the highway, and they passed through it looking at the construction sites, all the build-up of the hamlet called Lyonesse. There was even more now than there had been when Robert moved to Birmingham a few months before. A taco place, another gas station, a newer and bigger grocery store.

They drove to the church that stood where the pond had once been. They parked the car in the lot outside and walked around.

There was a small playground to the side of the building, surrounded by rocks and trees, and Robert could still recognize the rock he dove off of that summer day in 1959 before the fireball fell from the sky and changed everything.

He walked over to it, turned, and took about twenty paces to where a swing set now stood, and then he sat down in one of the swings. The flexible blue rubber seat was still damp with morning dew. Esther Ruth walked over and said, "This is where you were when it happened?"

He nodded. It might have been his imagination, but it still seemed as if a mild rotten egg odor lingered over the area. She stood behind him rubbing his shoulders. When he looked up, he saw that her eyes were closed, and she was concentrating. "I sense a lot of energy here, but I'm not getting anything specific."

A person emerged from the nandina, seemingly from the ground itself. He was impossibly old, older than either of them, wearing coveralls and a cap from which he dusted leaves and twigs. Behind the mystic fog of his flowing white beard, Robert recognized the eyes of Eddie Van Chukker. It wasn't a spirit that Esther Ruth had called up from beyond. It was actually Eddie in the flesh.

"What the hell are you doing here, Eddie?" He must have been about ninety now.

Eddie said, "I come back here same reason you did, I reckon. 'Cause this is where it all happened."

Robert supposed he couldn't fault this reasoning. "But why now? Today of all days?"

"Oh, I come here 'bout every day lately. Waiting."

"For me?"

Eddie waved the question away like an odor. "I done already told that Coldwater feller all that. I mean to tell you what happened to your brother. That's what you wanted to know, ain't it? Who's this 'un?"

He was pointing to Esther Ruth. Robert made introductions.

"I was working with them NASA folks, trying to help them understand what was going on. 'Course, they couldn't let that get out, so they made like they had me in a secret prison somewhere. That much, you probably know from what Coldwater wrote."

Robert had paid only passing attention to the articles Coldwater had written at the end. The information had all been too overwhelming for him. Coldwater probably assumed he'd taken them seriously. But like the rest of the world, he thought Coldwater had cracked up. Meanwhile, Esther Ruth stood listening. She picked a flower and put it in her hair. She rubbed Robert's shoulders again, then wrapped her arm around his chest, just the way Wally had, placing her hand over the scar. He began to feel it heating up, a sensation he hadn't experienced in years, his insides becoming incandescent. If anyone could see through to the images in those flames, it would be her.

Eddie said, "Let's go get some coffee, so we can sit down and talk a little more."

They took Esther Ruth's car to a new Cajun diner called Nell's that had opened in the pre-fab shopping area that folks now called "town." Like Eddie, Nell herself seemed impossibly old, yet somehow ageless. She seated them at a large table in the corner, brought them café au lait, and then left them to their private conversation.

Eddie continued telling his story, "So I was there. We were all there, though nobody knew. We were hiding behind walls, watching and listening. We saw all of it. That's why when things... the operation...went wrong, Whitehouse was able to respond so quickly."

As Eddie spoke, Robert almost felt as if he could see it, as if he was watching it from the operation table, but now awake. Montalto had made just one cut, a long one at the seam above Wally's arm, along Robert's chest. It began to heal right away, just like when Robert had tried to cut it open himself that day in the barn. The doctor struggled with it, cutting again, holding it open, cutting on the other side while still prying open the first wound with his hands. A fireball filled the room with light and swallowed Wally whole, like the whale did to Jonah, and then it shot back out into space. It had not been a loss of blood that took Wally away. It had been whatever had been trapped inside them. Whatever it was had knocked the doctor out cold. Dozens of men in yellow hooded coveralls, Whitehouse's men, invaded the operating room and whisked Robert away. They had been watching all along, and Eddie had been there all along, watching them, watching the boys, reporting back to Munford Coldwater.

"But what was it? What was inside me, and how did it get there?"

Eddie had an answer for that too. "That Reverend Dollar and his ARC, the Alien Research Center. For a time, he was doing his research in the basement of his house in Mobile. Colonel Whitehouse was part of that too. Best we could figure, when your mama went to tell her parents she was gonna marry Dewey, she was pregnant with you. Somehow, she got infected by an alien life form, and the infection passed to you. You was born with it. Kind of like an egg, and the fireball that came down was like the sperm that activated the egg. See I told you all 'long they was hiding alien babies. The alien baby was in you, and Whitehouse got it out. What happened to your brother was, uh, what you might call a side effect."

Esther Ruth still gazed silently in Eddie's direction, even after Eddie finished talking, as if listening to the wind for the parts Eddie had left out. Hearing this account, however unbelievable, soothed the thing in Robert that he had not been sensitive enough to know was bothering him. If he could believe that Wally was not even perhaps dead but only transported, whether to another world or only another dimension of this one, somehow that actually made more sense to him.

Robert thanked Eddie for his time and offered to buy him another cup of coffee, but Eddie said, "No thanky. I done what I come here to do."

"Well," Robert turned to Esther Ruth. "What now?"

"Up to you. How do you feel?"

"I feel like I just woke from a dream and found myself in another dream…" He took her hand, and they walked back to the car. "This dream is much nicer." She had butterscotch candies in the glove box and offered him one, which he took and savored all the way back to Birmingham.

During his remaining years, which were not many, Robert sat with Esther Ruth on her front porch on warm nights and played his fiddle, only for her. And if he played "Stars Fell on Alabama," and the night was especially clear and especially warm, he was sure he could hear Wally singing along from somewhere high above.

APPENDIX A: SOUNDTRACK

"Angeline the Baker" – Stephen Foster, 1850
"Billy in the Lowground" – trad.
"Hey Good Looking" – Hank Williams, 1951
"Highland Balou" – Robert Burns, 1794
"Old Joe Clark" – trad.
"The Red Haired Girl from Tulloch" – trad.
"St. Louis Blues" – W.C. Handy, 1914
"Space is the Place" – Sun Ra, 1972 (deliberately anachronistic in the context of the story)
"Stars Fell on Alabama" – Frank Perkins and Mitchell Parish, 1934

From the author:
I wrote this novel to explore themes of Southern identity and space (inner, outer, and physical) using tropes of Southern Gothicism and 1950s American pop culture. In this story, I project traditional gothic elements—including unexplained supernatural events, mental illness, and the grotesque—onto the backdrop of this extremely volatile time period for politics, art, and entertainment. Even with all these lofty-sounding multi-faceted elements in play, my ultimate goal was simply to write a comic novel with some hopefully lasting value. What I struggled with the most was how to deal with race in the story. I hadn't planned to make any grand statements about race, but when I set my story in 1959 in Alabama, I couldn't avoid it. I did my best to have a balance between having a modern understanding of racism and portraying the characters in a way that was true to their nature and environment at that time. On the other hand, this is also a story that involves space aliens and werewolves.

Printed and bound by PG in the USA